GLENMORNAN

GLENMORNAN

BY
PATRICK
MACGILL

CALIBAN BOOKS

© PATRICK MACGILL

Published 1983 by Caliban Books,
25 Nassington Road, LONDON, N.W.3
Published in the United States by
Caliban Books, 51 Washington Street,
Dover, New Hampshire 03820, U.S.A.

ISBN 0 904573 81 8

Library of Congress Information:
Author: Patrick MacGill
Title: Glenmornan
Library of Congress No.: 837810
C.I.P. Data applied for

Printed and bound in Great Britain by A. Wheaton & Co. Ltd.

TO

MY OWN PEOPLE

CONTENTS

GLENMORNAN

CHAPTER I

MAURA THE ROSSES

I've learned the tale of the crooning waves
  And the lore of the honey-bee,
The Mermaid's Song in the lonely caves
  Of Rosses by the sea.
As I'm never let out to the dance or wake,
  Because I'm a gasair small,
I just stay in the house for my mother's sake
  And never get tired at all.

Ah! many a song she has sung to me
  And many a song she knew,
And many a story there used to be,
  And mother's tales are true;
So I know the tale of the crooning waves
  And the lore of the honey bee,
And the Mermaid's Song in the lonely caves
  Of Rosses by the sea.
                    —*The Faith Of A Child.*

I

MAURA The Rosses was a widow with ten
children. The oldest of her children
was twenty-three years of age, the
youngest five. She was the owner of a

9

farm of land, fifty acres hill and holm, in the townland of Stranameera, which is saying something, for Stranameera has in pasture and peat no land in the barony to equal it. The townland is situated in the big Glen of Glenmornan, its back against the hills and its toes stuck in the river Owenawadda. Glenmornan is in the parish of Greenanore, or, as it was once called, the Barony of Burrach. The oldest inhabitants of the Glen still call themselves the people of Burrach, the middle-aged speak of themselves, when abroad, as "the ones from Greenanore, it that used to be the Barony of Burrach in the old times," but the young generation of boys who smoke cigarettes and girls who wear hats, are content to call themselves the Greenanore people.

Maura The Rosses' maiden name was Sweeney, her marriage name Gallagher. She came from The Rosses. It was there that Connel Gallagher met her one night when he was coming home to his own Glen from the Fair of Reemora where he had been selling wool. It was the night of All Hallow's Eve and a big gathering of young people had assembled at Maura Sweeney's house, where all manner of games was in progress. This was one of the games :

A girl carrying a knife would go out to the cornstack in the field, thirty yards away from the house. When she arrived there she would stick the knife in the corn up to the hilt. Then, putting two fingers of one hand over both eyes and shutting them, she would walk round the stack seven times. On completing the seventh circle the knife had to be drawn out and waved seven times round the head. When this had been done the girl would open her eyes and they would rest on the face of her future husband.

Connel Gallagher, on his way home to Glenmornan, felt tired and hungry. On seeing a house near the roadway lit up and the door open, he went across the field towards it, with the intention of getting a bit and sup to help him on his journey. He left the road and made for the door, but on the way he passed a corn-stack with somebody walking round it. Connel stopped and looked at the figure. It was a girl with her hair down her back and wearing short petticoats that scarcely reached lower than her knees.

" What's she doin' at all?" Connel asked himself and at the same moment he recollected that the night was Hall' Eve, and he knew what the girl was doing. The same custom was kept in Glenmornan. With a quiet step he went over to the corn-stack, discovered where the knife was and waited there until the girl completed the seventh circuit. When, after waving the knife round her head, she opened her eyes, they rested on Connel Gallagher.

The girl uttered a stifled cry, recoiled a few paces, and coming to the stack leant against it. From there she fixed a pair of large frightened eyes on the spectre who had come from nowhere, out of the night. . . . Her man to be ! She had never seen him before . . . who was he ? Maybe the Devil himself. . . .

She sank down, but the stranger seized her in

his arms and pressed her tightly to him.   Glenmornan was never backward in making love.
. . . The girl felt very frightened; not an
idea remained in her head.   She could see as in
a dream the door of her home, the dark forms inside, the lighted lamp on the wall, the delft in
rows on the dresser. . . . The stranger seemed
to be crushing her; his hands were so big; his eyes
were looking through her; his moustache was resting on her lips and his knee was pressing against
hers.

"Gora! wasn't I in luck's way!" said the man
in a low voice.

"Giway widye and let me be," said the girl,
trying to escape.   Now that the man had spoken
just like an ordinary mortal she did not feel
afraid.   Indeed she became curious.

"Who widye be?" she asked.

"I'm from the Barony iv Burrach or Greenanore as they call it," said the man, tightening his
hold on the girl.   He might not have such a
chance again.   "But what does it matter?" he
said.   "I'm here anyway."

"What d'ye mane?" asked the girl.   "Don't
ye see that I'm beside me own house?"

The man released his hold.

"All right, golong with ye inside!" he said with
a contemptuous shake of his head.   "It's like
the girls down here to be like that.   Catch a
Glenmornan girl putting up her nose at a man
that she meets on a Hall' Eve night just when
she's out on the look to see who she's goin' to
marry. . . ."

"I wasn't on the look out for a man," said the girl, showing no haste to get away, now that she was free.

"Well, what did ye come out here for in the dark iv night if it wasn't on the look out for a man?" said Connel Gallagher.

"I only came out in fun," said the girl.

"What is yer name?" asked the man.

"It's Mary Sweeney. And yours will be?"

"Connel Gallagher. I have been down at the fair of Reemora sellin' wool, and now that I'm on the way home and tired and hungry I'm on the look for a bit to eat. I saw a light in the house beyont there and was just goin' over to it when I came across yeself."

"Then come in now with me," said the girl. "It's our house, mine and me own people's house and we'll make ye welcome."

II

Connel Gallagher went in with the girl and there in the house he met her father, Murtagh Sweeney, the Fighter. Connel had seen Murtagh, a great man for using his fists, once before. It was at the fair of Greenanore, and on that occasion Murtagh cleared out the fair with a stone in the foot of a woman's stocking. Sweeney was a tall, well-set man of great physical strength, with shoulders as broad as a half door and legs as sturdy as stakes in a byre. When he was drunk nearly everybody was afraid of him and the pick of men were loth to take him up single-handed in a fight. There was at that time a long-standing feud between the people of Rosses and the people of Greenanore and one parish was jealous of another. No harvest fair was worthy of note that had not settled a row between the Rosses people and the people of Greenanore. But no sooner was one dispute settled than another begun and the more blood shed the more complicated became the quarrel. Murtagh Sweeney always led the Rosses party and a Glenmornan man named Oiney Leahy always was at the head of the Burrach people. On one harvest fair Oiney fought Murtagh, both men using the ashplant in the quarrel, and Murtagh got beaten. After that the quarrels died down, but the hate still lingered. Murtagh Sweeney did not like the Greenanore people.

He had no great handshake for Connel Gallagher when he went in with Mary, but for all that he made him as welcome as occasion permitted and hospitality demanded. He gave Connel a bit and sup and a taste of duty-free whiskey and let him go in peace. Connel went home, but his heart was not as easy as it might be. Mary Sweeney was a comely girl and Connel thought that she would be a worthy wife for him. His mother had just died and he was all alone on his farm, a well-stocked holding that any girl might be glad to come into.

A month later he called at Murtagh Sweeney's house again, a bottle of whiskey in his pocket and

a next door neighbour on his right hand.   He
came to ask Mary to be his wife.   Murtagh would
not hear of the match.   A daughter of his marrying a man from Greenanore !   He would see her
cold dead at his feet before he would sanction
such a marriage !

But Mary thought otherwise and youth laughs
at age.   A fortnight afterwards Connel and Mary
were married, and Murtagh did not come to the
wedding.   The girl was cut off from the decent
people of Rosses for evermore.

Afterwards, despite the young people's assertion that they were getting far and away superior
to the old silly Hallowe'en customs, the growing
girls of the Rosses placed a knife in the corn-
stack every Hall' Eve night and walked round
the stack seven times with their eyes shut.

III

Married life had its troubles, even in Glenmornan.   Children came to Connel Gallagher and
Maura The Rosses.   As the children increased
in number,the live stock on the farm diminished
and naked poverty held control over the home.
Life became a hard struggle for the man and wife.
One year out of every three the crops went bad,
potatoes were stricken by the blight, and the corn
rotted in the swathes.   When the weather became
wet, the hay was carried away by the floods, and
the turf lay useless on the spread-fields.   There

was no fire in the house and no food on the table.
Connel would then look at his children and turn
to his wife. " It's a hard life the poor has," he
would say. " But wait till the weans grow up!"

" It will be a long time that, yet," his wife
would answer. " But this was how it was meant
to be and God is good!" she would add.

Connel was a good, hard-working man. He
got up from his bed at five every morning and
went up to the hill for a creel of turf, travelling
bare-footed to save shoe leather. When he came
back he had his breakfast. The meal consisted
of cold potatoes (if the potatoes were a good crop)
or Indian meal stirabout and buttermilk, followed
by a bowl of tea and a slice of Indian meal bread.
Dinner consisted of potatoes and milk and on
Sundays the fare was increased by a slice of
bacon. There was a drop of tea for the afternoon and supper consisted of Indian meal stirabout and milk. Connel worked from early
morning to late night and got poorer every day.
Eight pounds a year had to be paid in rent to
the landlord, a great gentleman who never set
foot in Glenmornan. He lived abroad, out in
the world somewhere and was very rich. Accord-
ing to the Glen people he had a great room in his
house and it was full of nothing but gold. Connel Gallagher kept adding eight pounds yearly
to the landlord's stock of gold and Connel got
very poor, which is the way of the world.

His eldest son was a boy named Doalty, a
scholar who was very fond of the learning. This
boy went to school and was a most intelligent lad.

When he left school, he worked on the farm, then went out into the world. At eighteen he found himself in London, labouring on the wharves. When there he wrote articles for the press and was eventually taken on the staff of a daily paper. He sent a great amount of money home and his parents were very pleased.

"I knew Doalty would be a good boy," said the mother. "But it's a pity that we couldn't make him a priest when he was here with ourselves. But we hadn't enough money to put him through."

When Doalty was twenty-three a number of his younger brothers and sisters were out pushing their way in the world. Columb, next to him in years, was away in America working in a saloon, Murtagh had a job on a Scottish railway, Grania and Eileen were on service away from home and money was pouring into the old home in Stranameera.

There were six cows on the farm now and the hill was white with sheep. Maura The Rosses, a thrifty and sparing soul, was very pleased and thanked God for the children which He had sent her.

"Them's the kind of weans to have," she often said. "Ones that never forget their own people."

IV

Connel Gallagher died from a very short sickness. One day when he was threshing corn for the mill he suddenly laid down the flail on the floor and turned to his wife.

"A sickness has come over me all at once," he said. "I'll go to bed."

Maura put him to bed in the kitchen, wrapped him up in the blankets and gave him a drink of hot milk. When he had drunk the milk he turned to his wife.

"Maura," he said, "where is Teague?"

Teague was a youngster of eighteen and the eldest boy now at home.

"He's building up the slap between us and Breed Dermod's," said Maura.

"Let him finish the work," said Connel. "Breed's cow is always comin' across and eatin' our grass. But find out where Eamon is and tell him to run for the priest."

"And the doctor, too?" asked Maura.

"The doctor's no good this tide," said Connel. "The priest is enough."

Maura went out to look for Eamon. On the street she saw Oiney Leahy's rooster and she had never seen it about there before. It was a bad sign. She crossed herself and said:

"It's the priest and only the priest that himself is needin'."

"Run for the priest and tell him to come at

once," she said to Eamon when she found him.
" Your father has taken to his bed."

The priest was a very old man with long white
hair and horned spectacles. He was not the
local priest, but a man from the next parish who
had taken up the job of the Greenanore priest
while the latter was away in hospital suffering
from some illness. The name of the old man to
whom Eamon went was McGee. Father McGee
was very fond of fishing and had no equal in the
barony for casting a fly.

" Me father has taken to his bed," said Eamon
when he met the priest leaving home with a fishing rod over his shoulder. " He wants you to
come and see him."

"Connel Gallagher isn't it, my boy?" said the
priest.

" It is, Father," said Eamon.

"God keep him!" said Father McGee, "and
it such a day for the fishing too. Now, my
boy," he continued, "you take this rod and go
back and put it against the wall of my house and
don't keep foolin' about with the hooks, and I'll
go and see your father, good man that he is."

Connel Gallagher was dead with the dawn of
the next day.

The offerings over him when buried were £13
10s. 6d., a fine lump sum which showed that Connel Gallagher, a good neighbourly man, friendly
to all and bounden to none, was well liked in the
Barony of Burrach. Murtagh Sweeney came to
the funeral. Everybody noticed this, for Murtagh had never set foot in Glenmornan since his

daughter got married. Another thing noticed by the people was the well-seasoned ash-plant which Murtagh carried with him. It was said that this ash-plant was the same that he used when fighting Oiney Leahy at the harvest fair of Greenanore.

Murtagh threw down a gold sovereign on the coffin when offerings were taken. None of the Glenmornan people ever paid as much as that and they did not like to see a Rosses man display such munificence.

" It's pride that made him do it," they said, for they knew that Murtagh Sweeney was a very poor man.

v

Maura The Rosses, a widow of forty-two and the mother of a boy of twenty-three, was a woman loved by her neighbours. A very hard worker and a good hand at driving a bargain all her life, she now set herself to run the farm.

To her children she was a very wise woman, knowing everything. What stories she could tell ! Sitting by the turf-fire at night she told tales of Fin McCool, Deirdree of The Sorrows, The Red Headed Man and Kitty the Ashy Pet. Kitty, who was once very poor, became a princess and when married she always combed her hair with a golden comb and washed her face in a golden basin. Maura spoke of these people as if she had known them personally and one had to believe her because her words were so simple and full of conviction.

When the children went to school and learned poetry they would recite it in a sing-song voice over the fire at night. The mother would listen and after a while she would say, "It's nice to know poetry be heart, but it's better to know yer prayers."

She made a point of not favouring any one particular child, which was very sensible, seeing that she was the mother of ten. Besides, she knew that it was a sin to love one child more than another.

Sometimes when a neighbour died her children would ask her if he had gone to heaven. If she liked the man she would answer, "Of course he's gone to heaven, being such a good man." But if she did not like him she would modify her answer and say, "He may have gone there for God is good!" If she spoke of a dead man in that way the children knew that his soul had gone to hell.

The good woman had no time to exert any continuous care over the children. At a certain age they were sent to school, their books in a satchel and two turf under their arms. There they learned their Catechism and could answer any question in the book, but seldom knew what the answers meant. Mere parrots, they could reel off the Three Theological Virtues, the Seven Deadly Sins, The Nine Ways In Which One Could Be Guilty Of Another Person's Sins, in a high pitched sing-song voice. The girls at the school preferred to answer their Catechism in unison, the whole class swaying from side to side as they chanted. Now and again when stopped in their swing they would forget every word of the answer and find themselves in a fix similar to that of dancers in a six hand reel when the fiddle strings break.

VI

The children of Maura The Rosses learned their Catechism without understanding it.   One fact could not be gainsaid, however. They could answer any question in the book.   When this stage was reached they were confirmed in their faith.   They knew all about it then, its tenets were made manifest to their little souls and they had found them worthy.   Their belief in the faith being strong, they were confirmed and ordered to take an oath, promising to abstain from intoxicating liquors until they reached the age of twenty-one.   And in this way the children of Maura The Rosses were brought up in the love and fear of God.   If they went wrong after leaving their home it was surely due to no fault of the good woman.

Maura was very devout and not in the least emotional; but she believed in fortune-telling, charms, omens, ghosts and fairies.   To her there were no kind fairies, though she always spoke of them as good people or gentle folk, styling them "gentle" or "good" merely to placate them. When cows calved before their season or went dry before their time, when they fell sick with shot or staggers, the mooril or the lifting, Maura ascribed all these ailments and ills to the fairies. Was it not evident that the good people were tormenting the cattle when the beasts ran wild from the pastures in the hot noon of summer and galloped into the river and stood belly deep in the stream? The woman knew that all this madness was due to the fairies. The brute beasts were aware of this as well, and also knew that fairies cannot touch running water. That was their reason for rushing into the Owenawadda. After churning milk the good woman placed a pat of butter over the door for the good people. When this was melted by the sun, or washed down by the rain, she knew that the fairies had found it to their liking and taken it away.

Maura did not like red-haired women and knew that if she met a red-haired woman on the way to market the day would be bad for a bargain. She would not go outside the door of her house on All Souls' Eve, for she did not want to see the dead passing by. She knew that Eamon the Drover's people, next door neighbours but one to her they were, always drank seven drops of blood from a black cat on the day they were born. This made them very fierce and ill-tempered for the rest of their lives. This family had the evil eye, so also had two other families in Glenmornan. If they looked on your stock it would never thrive.

She also knew that Hudy Heilagh had read Harry Stattle* and was full of black magic and legerdemain tricks. One word from you that did not please him and in the shake of an eyelash he could bring the sea up to your house and drown every living soul inside. Hudy was sib to the Gallaghers and in his young days he was a wild fellow for the girls.

Maura was very kindly and never let a beggar go past her door without a bite and sup. When the cattle of the people near her went dry she gave them part from her own churning, but if she lacked milk herself she would not take any from a soul. "Our people never took charity," she would say, "and thank God they never will."

She seldom left her own house, but now and again with a stocking and knit-needles in her hand, she would go out, look over the hedge that circled the house and take stock of all that was happening in the Glen. As she watched she would pass a running commentary on the doings of her neighbours. She knew that the town land was divided amongst thirteen families and her family could marry into three of these who had acres and cows' grass equal to her own.

VII

On the June of 1913 Maura The Rosses got a letter from Doalty. She was standing out by

* Aristotle.

the hedge when she received it. She put down her knitting on a stone and read the letter. Then she called to Norah, to Teague and to little Hughie, a boy of five, her youngest child. " Go down to Greenanore," she said to Norah. " Get a poke iv flour, a bag iv meal, a stone iv currants and raisins, a side iv bacon and a bottle iv whisky."

She said to Teague :

" Get the floor scrubbed clean, whitewash the house and pull that grass off that's growin' on the thatch."

" And you, Hughie," she said, " don't go about dirtyin' yer bits iv rags, for ye'll need them all next week, when Doalty's comin' home here to his own people."

That night the Gallaghers sat up very late preparing the house for the returning boy. In the morning a stocking, a clue of yarn and knit-needles were discovered lying in the gutter outside the door.

" To think that I forgot to put that by yesterday !" said Maura The Rosses as she looked at her ruined knitting.

CHAPTER II

The Gombeen Man, scraggy and thin,
Is always getting the money in,
Round his throat is a red cravat,
Sixpence at most he paid for that;
Boots in which Decency wouldn't stand,
He must have got them second hand;
Face as dry as a seasoned fish,
Head as bald as a wooden dish—
Silent and sleekit as a trout,
With the hair on his chin all sprouting out.
Boast of belly and bare of back,
A fellow that never paid his whack,
He has rolls of notes and bags of gold,
As much as a wooden chest can hold—
This he has and nobody knows
What will be done with it when he goes—
But where will he go when he leaves it? Where?
Nobody knows, or seems to care.
                              —*The Gombeen Man.*

I

GLENMORNAN is a grand glen. The natives say its one of the finest in all Ireland. The glen is ringed with a line of hills, some of which rise to a height of two thousand feet, and none of which are less than seven hundred. The oldest rocks in Ireland are to be found here—granite, quartzite, mica slate and limestone. Looking from the glen to the west Sliav-a-Tuagh can be seen, a sharp-edged peak with its feet in the sea and its head in the stars. Eastwards Croagh-an-Airgead stands aloof, a solitary peak brooding over its own isolation. Carnaween to southwards looks down in immense scorn on the valleys and moors at its feet.

A river and road run through the centre of the valley, the road, dry and crooked, a good one for travel, and the river, unruly in flood time, a bad one for the hay in the bottom lands. Sometimes in wet weather, a great amount of low-lying hay in the glen is carried away by the floods when the river rises over its banks and covers the fields. In addition to this the streams, coming from the hills, sweep the upper lands, carrying the corn and potatoes down with them. The peasantry fear the floods.

The streams falling from the hills have cut deep gullies in the braes, and these gullies— "awlths" they are called—are thick with birch, holly and hazel bushes. Trees are very scarce; the country is now almost denuded of them. This has been due to wet seasons when few turf were saved and when wood had to be used for firing.

On the eastern corner of the glen where the hill rises with a gradual incline, the floods do very little harm. Up there dwell the mountainy people, big limbed, hairy men and strong swarthy women who seldom wear boots. The mountainy man can be picked out at any fair or market. He is a sullen and suspicious creature who walks with a hop on the most level path and has his eyes always fixed on the ground under his feet. This is due to his life on the high levels of the glen, where in his daily work he has to hop from stone to stone over the marshy lands. He lives in a wretched house, keeps his cattle under his own roof, is miserably fed, and instead of boots wears thick woollen socks, called *mairteens*.

The people further down the glen are better set up, the young men are tall and bold, the young girls good-humoured and handsome. They never have any intercourse with the mountainy people, whom they do not consider fit society and whom they will not allow right of entry to their dances and airnalls (gatherings). With the people down the glen "mountainy" is a term of reproach : an awkward and ignorant person is termed mountainy. "You're a mountainy man and as thick as mud," is a saying of theirs.

Up the glen the people seldom read anything, having neither the time, inclination or education. Down the glen they like to hear the news of the world outside the range of the hills and read whenever they have the opportunity. They are very curious and their nature hankers after knowledge. Superstition gives an imperious explanation to everything which general ignorance cannot solve, and religion is ever at hand to supply the why and wherefore of things. To them any newspaper is always "the paper," and they are indifferent to the edition or date of printing. Little boys going to the neighbouring shops with three eggs in a handkerchief are generally told to get the goods purchased, wrapped in "the paper." In this manner Glenmornan keeps in touch with the news of the world.

The distance in time and space from the events described does in no way diminish the readers' interest in the stories. That they are so far removed from the world in which such things occur, gives the people a certain amount of comfort. "Strange things are always takin' place in foreign parts," they say to one another. "It's good to be here where things like that never take place."

But more intelligent and more progressive than any of the glen folk are the residents of the village of Greenanore. These people have got the quality toss with them and have the most genteel manners. The latest English music-hall songs are all the rage in the village. Little Gwendoline Quigley (what a quality name Gwendoline!), daughter of the biggest publican, can sing two songs in French, which is more than any girl in the lower end of the glen can do. Gwendoline, of course, will not associate with any of the glen people, who in her eyes are the lowest of the low and just the merest fraction removed from the mountainy people. Neither will Gwendoline sing an old Cumallye song like "Nell Flaherty's Drake" or "Pat O'Donnell." But this is quite right from a quality standpoint, for the village cannot descend to the vulgar level of the glen.

Gwendoline's father, old Pat Quigley, is a gombeen man full of money and land. He has a club foot and turns on his heel when walking. His nickname is "Heel-ball."

II

There are many families in the glen and each family has its own little farm, which rises in a narrow strip from the river to the top of the hill. The arable land is small in proportion to the extent of the glen and is not in all places of the best quality. The meadow land which fringes the river is seldom dug. The ground of the braes is full of stones, both upon and under the surface, and it also abounds in whin bushes, which have to be taken up by the roots before the land can be cultivated. Some of the glen farms stand practically on end, and these have to be dug uphill, a most difficult job. It is of course easier to dig downhill, but if this is done the clay at top will be gradually carried to the bottom. But despite the husbandman's care, the clay, continually borne down by the rains, collects in heaps at the bottom of the braes. When this rises to a certain height it has to be carried up again. Therefore cultivation is arduous and expensive in Glenmornan and requires no end of energy and labour. But the people never lose heart at the tilling of the soil. On it, the noblest labour of all, depends their daily bread.

The people live frugally and are for the most part very poor. Most families have sufficient land to keep two cows and some can keep more. A household is judged by its stock, and a family with four cows' grass to its name, will not marry into a family which can only boast of three cattle.

There are three Protestant families in the glen, but religious rancour is not known. , The class differences are more pronounced than the religious differences. The Quigleys, with one of their family a priest and another a nun, hold themselves as much aloof from the poor Catholics as from the poor Protestants.

A Glenmornan house is generally a one-storeyed building with a flagged floor and a thatched roof. Only three or four houses in the place are slated. The roof beams of a house are generally of black oak which has been dug from the bogs. The principal room of a house is the kitchen, a large and spacious apartment where the household assemble for meals and where all the family foregather when the hours of outdoor work come to an end. There is seldom more than two rooms in a house and both serve as sleeping chambers. The byre is attached to the house, but ducks and pigs are kept in a separate building.

The food of the people, for the most part, consists of tea, bread, butter, potatoes and porridge. This latter dish is always called " porridge " by the quality of Greenanore; those who dwell in the butt-end of Glenmornan generally call it "stirabout," but the mountainy people always call it "brahun-ray." The various degrees of refinement in the barony can be traced by the names given to this simple dish.

Eating is a very casual matter with the glen people. The women generally eat standing, breaking off at intervals to do some job or another. The children squat on the floor when eating, but the men for the most part sit round a table. There is no fixed hour for meals. The glen people eat when they are hungry if there is food to go round.

There are very few amusements and very few holidays in Glenmornan. Work is always carried on, Sunday and Saturday. Cows have to be milked, fed and tended, children have to be cared for, dishes have to be washed on every day of the week. The labour of a farm never comes to an end. None but the very rich can observe a strict Sabbath in Greenanore. It is just the same in many other parts of the world.

III

It was Bonfire Night, the Eve of the Feast of the Nativity of Saint John the Baptist, and Stranameera, never behind hand in its observance of the night, had its bonfire flaring on the hill. For weeks before the townland people had spent all their spare time gathering in bundles of heather, sticks and brambles to the pile of fuel, heaped high on the brae behind the house of Maura The Rosses, which was now ablaze. The whole townland was gathered round the fire that roared redly over a deep, sloping awlth filled with ash, birch and holly. Through the awlth ran a brook, gobbling like a clutch of young turkeys.

The night was wonderfully clear and not a cloud hid the glory of the stars. On the other side of the glen, Garnaween could be seen, a calm silent peak, clear cut and dark against the sky, A slight breeze rippled up the brae and set the birches a-quiver. The awlth was full of strange whispers, and no wonder, for the place was the home of the gentle people. If a cow strayed in there the animal was sure to be elf-shot; sickness came to the children who went to gather hazel nuts in the gentle locality, and in the awlth was stored the butter which the fairies had stole from the townland of Stranameera. Whenever Maura The Rosses looked on the place she crossed herself three times, once on the forehead, once on the lips and once on the breast.

But now that it was Bonfire Night, Maura The Rosses, who seldom left her house, was one of the first to come to the fire. She could be seen a little distance away from the blaze, sitting on a ditch, a white cloud over her head and dressed in a striped blouse, a red woollen petticoat and a pair of heavy boots. She was speaking to one of her neighbours, a crook-backed, barefooted old woman, whose yellow, wrinkled face peeped furtively out from the folds of a gosling-grey, woollen handkerchief.

The woman was named Grania Coolin. Grania was a poor widow, skilled in the art of midwifery and the knowledge of the medicinal properties of various herbs. She knew that bog-bine (marsh trefoil) was a remedy for heartburn; that onions would give a person a decent sleep; that tansy could destroy worms and that houseleek was a specific for sore eyes. She also knew several other herbs which were certain remedies for toothache, warts, gravel, headache and various other ills. Grania believed in fairies, but what woman in Glenmornan does not believe in the gentle people? In addition to believing in them, Grania knew where they were hidden, and she generally placed the first butter from a churning, the first meal from a milling and the first glass of whisky from a keg of potheen on the ground outside the haunted raths. The fairies always accepted Grania's gifts, for on the day following that on which the woman tendered butter, meal or whisky to them, not one trace of the gifts could be found on the ground where she had placed them.

The old woman believed in dreams. One night she dreamt that there was a crock of gold hidden in Hohn-a-Thiel (The Rump of the World), a hob of hill which rose behind her house. Next morning she went out with a spade at dawn and started to dig for the gold. When she had dug for a while a great pain came on her wrist and a wild animal called a *dorcha* (it had seven legs and an iron nose on it) came and attacked her. Grania had a red woollen petticoat and she took it off of her and put it on a rock beside her. The *dorcha* does not like red petticoats and it came forward with one roar and hit the petticoat with its nose. And it was killed. Then Grania Coolin came home. Grania believed that this had happened to her and she often told the story to her neighbours. The old people believed the story, but the young of the glen made fun of the old woman. "Poor old Grania!" the youngsters would say with a wink. "She's a plaisham (fool), God help her!"

On the brink of the awlth, beside Grania and Maura The Rosses, a number of ragged children were rolling over on the ground and tormenting a little puppy. One of the little children was Hughie Gallagher, Maura's youngest child, a brave little rascal of five, who was gripping hold of the puppie's tail and striving to drag it into the ravine. When the little dog whimpered Maura would raise her head and shake her finger at the youngster.

"Now, Hughie Beag," she would say, "don't ye be pullin' the wee dog about. If ye do it again I'll take ye in and skelp yer wee bottom."

On hearing this Hughie would let go the puppy, stick his finger in his mouth and fix a pair of big eyes on his mother. Standing thus he would wait until the woman took up her conversation with Grania Coolin, then he would turn to the dog again. . . .

IV

The young boys and girls of the townland, who had come out in crowds, were assembled round the fire, flinging banter to one another and grinning broadly, showing their white teeth. A little distance apart from the fire a boy and girl were seated on the ground, the boy with his arms around the maiden's waist and placing wild flowers plucked from the ground in her hair. The girl was trying to push him away, but even when she succeeded in freeing herself from his embrace she did not get to her feet and run off. This showed that she did not object to his attentions. But what girl could? for the boy was Dennys Darroch, or Dennys the Drover as he was popularly called, one of the handsomest youngsters in the glen. All the girls round about the place were wild after him. Even Sheila Dermod, with whom he was sitting, was said to be in love with him, and Sheila had had the privilege of refusing three wealthy suitors, full of money and land. She was a girl of eighteen, living with her widow mother, a woman who had hard work to do to make both ends meet.

Dennys suddenly got up to his feet, looked round at the assembled crowd and then bent down over the girl who was still seated on the grass.

"Well, and if ye won't, ye won't," he said with a laugh, apparently referring to some subject under discussion, and made his way towards the fire. He walked with a great swagger, swinging his shoulders. He was a fine rung of a fellow, sinewy as a seasoned ash-plant, with a handsome face, grey shrewd eyes and a voice like an echo on the Donegal hills. He spoke quickly and as quick speakers do, loudly. Words rushed from his lips like a torrent, just as they would when calling from one hill to another as he was on the look-out for sheep. He possessed a dauntless view of life, had a careless, defiant manner and upright courage. The sharp, steady glance of a face from which a certain expression of scorn was never wholly absent, marked him as a man who was afraid of nothing. He lived with his mother and sister on a little farm which boasted two cows' grass and hill enough for twenty sheep. But Dennys did very little labour on the farm. He preferred to deal in cattle at the fairs and made a tidy penny in that manner. He seldom bent over a spade. "Cuttin' worms is not for me," he often said with an oath and nobody was offended, for strength gets its due respect in Glenmornan.

Having left Sheila Dermod, Dennys went to the fire, raised a heavy lump of wood which was lying on the ground and flung it with one great heave into the centre of the flames. The young girls uttered a startled shriek as a shower of sparks flew into the air and careered away on the breeze.

"Finished skiftin'* now, Dennys?" asked an old man who was standing near, his hat well back over his white hairs and a fiddle under his arm. Dennys the Drover laughed.

"Wouldn't ye like to be in my place, Oiney?" he asked the old man.

"Years ago when I was yer height I wouldn't leave a girl to sit be her own self," said the old man. "I would sit be a girl till she got up! But nowadays young men are not worth their boxty.† Sheila Dermod would rather have meself sittin' be her side than any young man in all the four corners in the glen. Wouldn't ye now, Sheila?"

"I would indeed, Oiney," Sheila answered, coming up to the fire. As she spoke she looked at Dennys and laughed, her teeth sparkling as the firelight caught them.

"Is it Oiney Leahy that I hear speakin'?" someone called at that moment.

"It's me that's in it, Maura The Rosses," Oiney replied. I've come with the fiddle. But tell me before I begin if it's true?" he asked, going across to the ditch on which the woman was seated. "It must be true, for everyone is talkin' about it up and down the glen."

"Oh! it's true," Maura The Rosses replied. "I got the letther there-yisterday‡ and he says that he's comin' back to his own people."

"For good?" Oiney asked.

"For good as far as I can see," said Maura The Rosses.

* Flirting.
† Potato-bread.   ‡ Ere yesterday. The day before yesterday.

"He'll have made his fortune, I suppose," said Oiney, as he put a short black clay pipe in his mouth. "There's fortunes to be made over there if all accounts bees true. Some people are lucky when they go out into the world. There was Wee Micky Eamon from Meenaroo, second cousin to me wife, God rest her! he was, and he went away beyont the water and stayed there for short on five years and came back and bought old Columb Beag's farm. A hundred and thirty-five pounds, money down, he gave for it. I was there meself when the luck's-money was handed over. Think iv that! And all made in less than five years! And how long would it be now since Doalty went away? Seven years, come the end of next month, isn't it? I mind the time, for there was a big flood in the glen the day he went away, and the mountainy sheep came down be the river."

"It's just short on six years since he went away," said Maura The Rosses. "He's been a good boy since he left us, too, and he's never backwards in sendin' some money home to his own people."

"And he had the learnin' too," said Oiney. "There's nothin' like the learnin'. D'ye mind the song about it?"

"Sing it, Oiney," a voice called from the fire.

"That's Sheila Dermod that's speakin'" said Oiney, putting his pipe back in his pocket. "She's the one to be skiftin' about with the boys and it looks as if it was only yisterday that she was playin' tig and Jackstones on the road to

school. . . . I'll sing the song for ye, Sheila,"
and without another word Oiney began the song :

"Labour for learnin' afore ye grow old,
For learnin' is better nor silver and gold !
Silver and gold it will vanish away,
But learnin' itself it will never decay,
And a man without learnin' wearin' good clothes
Is like a gold ring in a pig's nose."

"That's the song and a very true one it is,"
said Oiney, cuttin' a caper with his legs and
jumpin' up in the air. "Not bad, that, for a
old shanachie!" he laughed, looking at the party
round the fire. "There's many a good honest
soul that has gone down the road, carried on big
shoulders, since first I stood on a dancin' floor,
and there's life and to spare in the old dog yet."

"Come on, Oiney," and play the fiddle,"
Dennys the Drover shouted. "It's time for us to
be shakin' our legs if we want to make a night
iv it. Meenawarawor and Meenawarabeag have
their fires all lit up and the dancin' is goin' on
over there."

Oiney went over to the fire, sat down on the
grass, tuned up his fiddle and lit his pipe. The
dancing started.

V

Midnight passed by and the fire was dying
down. Old women like Maura The Rosses and

Grania Coolin had gone down to their homes long since, taking the young children with them. Meenawarawor was still aflare and the shouting from there was echoing across the glen. Meenawarabeag was silent and lights showed in the houses of that townland. The people there were going to bed. But the dancing was yet going on at Stranameera and old Oiney Leahy was still playing the fiddle, a happy look in his eyes and a good-humoured smile all over his wrinkled face. The old man had reached his eightieth year and in his young days he had been a great man for fighting, drink and the women. Even now his day's work was not to be laughed at, and as a fiddler he knew no equal in the barony. As long as boys and girls were able to dance Oiney was willing to play.

A dance came to an end and the young were slow in starting another.

"Shake yer legs, me buckos!" Oiney shouted, as he took his pipe from his mouth. "There's life in me, an old dog, yet. The hand is ready if the feet are willin'. Get to yer feet again, ye rascals. Show Meenawarawor what ye can do."

Dennys the Drover and Sheila Dermod got to their feet.

"The six-hand reel, Oiney," Dennys shouted, looking round at the other couples who were waiting to start.

"I wonder what Doalty Connel will be like when he comes back," Sheila remarked to her partner. "He was a nice quiet gassair when he left here."

"He'll just be like any tea-man or shop-boy when he comes back," said Dennys in a disparaging voice. "A big, high, white collar he'll have round his neck and he'll be looking over it like a donkey over a whitewashed wall. They're all the same when they come home. One wouldn't think that they were brought up on scaddan and sgiddings.* And they won't talk to a soul that they knew. I can't stand them."

"He'll have plenty of money, no doubt," said Sheila.

"Maybe he will and maybe not," said Dennys, "but he'll try and look as if he had it, anyway. . . . . But Sheila, am I to lave ye at home the night?" Dennys asked, bending down and almost touching the girl's hair with his lips.

"I haven't asked ye to come home with me, have I now?" said Sheila.

"That means that ye're not goin' to let me, then?"

"Take it that way if ye like."

"Then I'm goin' with ye."

"I didn't ask ye to come, did I?" the girl enquired, with a chuckle.

"All right then, Sheila Dermod," said Dennys in an impatient voice. "Go home be yerself if ye want to."

"The first time that I ever seen Dennys The Drover not able to stick a dance out!" Oiney Leahy shouted through the flying figures in the

* Scaddan and sgiddins—sprat and small potatoes.

maze of the six-hand reel. Dennys and Sheila edged in and took their places.

When the dance came to an end Sheila went over to her girl chum, Eileen Kelly, and caught her arm. "I think it's time to be goin' home," she said. "My mother won't know what's keepin' me."

"But isn't Dennys goin' home with ye?" asked Eileen. "He hasn't left ye all the night. . . . . And it's not time yet to go home."

Eileen was a pretty little girl, with a three-cornered mouth and dark eyes that darted to and fro elusively. She was mischievous, merry and fond of fun.

"Time!" said Sheila. "It's time to be home and past time. I don't want to be beholdin' to Dennys for to take me home. He's so full of pride and thinks that everybody is dyin' after him. . . . Well, I'm not." She spoke emphatically.

"That's like ye, Sheila," said Eileen. "All the men are mad after ye and ye won't take no notice iv them."

"But I don't want them to be after me."

"Ye would then if they took no notice at all iv ye," said Eileen Kelly.

"That might be," said Sheila quietly. "But I don't want any iv them."

"It's because ye're so good lookin'," Eileen, who was more than a little envious of her beautiful friend, remarked. "Well, we'll go home together the both iv us. Come, we'll run down the brae as quick as we can. Tig on ye!" she laughed, and hitting Sheila on the shoulder she scampered off, to be followed by her friend down the hillside. The pair of them came to the bottom of the hill together and Eileen sat down on the dew-wet grass.

"Do you know who was wanting to come home with me the night?" asked Eileen.

"Not Dennys, was it?" asked Sheila, catching her breath a little as she spoke.

"No, not Dennys," said Eileen. "He has never eyes for anybody when ye're there, Sheila Dermod. But who asked me but Owen Briney! He's forty if a day and as near-goin' as an eye-lid."

"But he has money and a good bit of land," said Sheila with a little laugh of mockery.

"If he had the whole parish and beholdin' to nobody I wouldn't be seen comin' home the same road from a dance as him," said Eileen, puckering up her three-cornered lips and allowing a thoughtful smile to steal over her face.

"Tig on yerself then!" Sheila cried, touching her friend on the arm with her fingers. Then running away, she skipped across the ditch and made for her home.

VI

Eileen walked down to her own house, her head sunk down over her breast, apparently deep in thought. She went to the door of her home to find it open.   Inside all was dark, for her father and mother, who had been up at the bonfire, were now in bed and fast asleep.   She went back along the road she had come and was in time to meet Dennys The Drover returning from the fun of the night.

"Ah! ye're not in bed then, Eileen Kelly?" said Dennys on seeing her.   "If the priest hears about this he'll not like it at all."

"But what'll he know about it?" said Eileen. "Nobody'll tell him."

Dennys laughed quietly as if he did not want to be heard.

"But ye must tell him the next time ye go to confession," he said in a whisper.   "And then there will be such a penance.   Ye'll have to go to Lough Derg on yer two knees."

Both of them were silent for a moment. Dennys kept his eyes fixed on the girl's face and thought her wonderfully beautiful. . . . . Surely no girl in the glen . . . . Even Sheila was not as fair to look at. . . .

"Why do ye keep yer eyes on me, Dennys The Drover?" she asked.

"A cat can look at a nice print iv butter if it likes," said Dennys in a husky voice.   "Can't it now?"

"There's somebody comin'!" said Eileen in a whisper as a man could be heard approaching, humming a tune as he walked.   "It must be old Oiney gettin' home."

"Then we'll run down the lane and hide," said Dennys, catching the girl's hand in his own.

The two of them ran off together, keeping on the grass to deaden the sound of their footsteps.

"We'll stand here," said Dennys when they came to the gable-end of Eileen's home. "We've got to be as quiet as two wee mice." As he spoke he pressed her hand with a firm grip.

"What are ye doin' with me hand, Dennys The Drover?" asked the girl. "Let it be, won't ye?"

"Why should I?" Dennys asked in a low whisper. "Do ye think that I'm goin' to run away with yer hand?"

As he spoke he bent down, caught both the girl's hands and kissed her red three-cornered lips. She tried to break away from him, but her efforts were useless. Instead of breaking free from his arms she felt herself getting pressed closer and closer to his breast. A sense of grandeur and desolation swept over her and she no longer resisted him. She felt as if dropping into a swoon. . . . Dennys spoke and released her from his arms.

"Ye almost made a fool iv me and iv yerself, too, Eileen Kelly," was what he said. "Away into the house and get ye to bed. Ye should have been in bed an hour ago!"

He walked away towards his home swinging his shoulders and humming a tune under his breath. Once or twice he came to a sudden halt and looked at the mountains. "I was near making a fool iv meself," he muttered each time he stopped. "If it isn't one woman it's another, and I suppose they'll get hold iv us in the long run." By "us" he merely meant himself.

When he entered his home he took a meal of stirabout and milk; then he went to bed and slept soundly till morning. Eileen Kelly did not close her eyes in sleep that night.

CHAPTER III

DOALTY GALLAGHER

I will go back to my father's house and live
on my father's land,
For my father's house is by Rosses' shore that
slips to Dooran strand,
And the wild mountains of Donegal rise up on
either hand.

—Going Home.

I

"SO you're going back to Ireland again?
Back to your own people and leaving
London! Boys will be boys I suppose
and will rove about all over the world
before they settle themselves to the ordinary
routine of daily life. . . . But sit down while
I pour out a cup of tea and tell me all about yourself."

The time was late June of 1913, the place a
drawing-room in " Ermara," a large house on the
banks of the Thames near London. Lady Ronan, the owner of " Ermara," was speaking to a
visitor, young Doalty Gallagher, son of Maura

48

The Rosses, who was now employed on the editorial staff of a large London daily paper. He had come down that day from London and was going to spend the week-end with the Ronans. Young George, Lady Ronan's only boy, was working on the paper with Doalty and both men were great friends.

Lady Ronan poured out the tea, handed Doalty a cup and sat down on a sofa facing him. She was a well-preserved woman of forty-five, who had once been beautiful, and was now graceful.

"Now, tell me everything, Doalty," she said, speaking in a voice so low and coaxing that Doalty felt that she hoped to hear some wonderful secret. She always called him by his Christian name.

"There's nothing to tell," said Doalty, "I'm going home. I'm tired of London. That's all."

"I know you want to go home," said Lady Ronan. "Who doesn't, especially to Ireland, where the people are *so* charming. But to stay there!"

There was protest in the woman's voice. She spread her fingers out on her knee and fixed her eyes on her daintily manicured nails.

"You have been there," said Doalty. "But you never told me how you liked it."

"I loved it," said Lady Ronan, nodding her head with the decision of a verdict beyond repeal. "Everything was *so* nice, and the Irish I met *so* kind and good-humoured. But it was always raining."

" It generally is," said Doalty.   " What part of the country were you in?"

" The South.   Killarney and about there."

" Saw the old monastery of Ballyruden?" asked Doalty.

" I was there," said Lady Ronan, tapping a long, tapering forefinger on her knee as she spoke.   " And the old man who told me the history of the place !   He was *so* delightful."

" Told you how St. Patrick fought the serpent in the adjoining lake and how the serpent got killed?"

" Yes."

" And called the serpent ' the worm?' "

" That's so."

" And how the story was a true one because the lake is there still as proof of the incident."

" Yes, that was what he said," said Lady Ronan.   " And *so* charmingly Irish !"

" One could not wish—I mean an English person could not wish—for anything more Irish," said Doalty Gallagher.   " That old scoundrel knows it too.   A few stupid remarks like those are his professional jokes.   His little townland is his stage and the English tourists are his audience and his prey.   They find him there, looking into the lake as if he had been sitting on its banks since the beginning of time and would remain there until the crack of doom.   That is how they expect to find him and he knows it.   To them, that lazy creature with a faked fund of so-called humour, is Ireland.   They put a whole race in the same category as that professional entertainer

who has borrowed his jokes from the stage Irishman. Judgment is passed on the Irish race by
professional tourists who have come into contact
only with Killarney guides and Dublin Jarveys."

Lady Ronan shrugged her shoulders in a helpless fashion.

"You young men are *so* clever," she said.
" George is just like you. He can prove black
is white and vice versa. But he is not in earnest
about it."

" But I am in earnest," said Doalty," placing
his cup on the floor. " I'm not saying clever
things just to drive a point home. I mean what
I say. It's the truth. The English don't know
the Irish."

" The poor English!" said Lady Ronan, lifting Doalty's cup from the carpet and pouring
the cold tea into the slop-basin. " So you think
that they're not as intelligent as your countrymen?" she asked.

"No, I don't mean that," said Doalty. " Far
from it. What I mean is this : the English don't
know us and never will. They think we are
lazy, for example."

" But if that's true about Irish at home it's not
true about them when they get out of their own
country," said Lady Ronan. " When they're
over here they soon get to the top."

"One or two may get to the top," said Doalty.
"You hear about it when they do, but one never
hears about the thousands who remain weltering
at the bottom. Now take my glen for example.
Dozens of young people leave it yearly. They

go away to Scotland, to England, to America.
The boys become masons' labourers, navvies and
railway porters, the girls become drudges in the
kitchens of big houses. One may get on well.
I might, for example, if I stuck to journalism."

"Of course you would," said Lady Ronan.
"Your editor who came down here the other day
was loud in his praises of you. Said that in a
couple of years you would have made a great
name for yourself."

"I might even get to the top of the tree,"
Doalty assented, sarcasm in his voice, "that dear,
delightful tree under which the poor grovel as
they bring sap to its roots. One day people
might notice me and then they would say: 'How
the Irish people get on abroad!' One man out
of every ten thousand might get on as well at
home if there was such an opportunity. But
there isn't. . . . The people talk about the
laziness of the Irish peasantry. Listen."

Lady Ronan lay back on the sofa, one eye on
her finger-nails, one on the window, which looked
out on the avenue leading to the road. Her son,
when he returned from town, would come in that
way.

"In my glen at home there is an old man,"
said Doalty. "His name is Oiney Leahy. He
has a farm of land, a mile in length and about the
width of this floor across. The farm runs from
the river to the top of the hill and the public road
runs through it. From the river to the road the
bottom land is a level strip. From the road to
the top of the hill the farm stands on end, and

half way up this precipice, which the poor man calls (real Irish humour this time) his farm, the farmhouse is situated. Oiney's house, a mere hovel, could not be built from east to west, for the farm is too narrow. It had to be built from north to south, one gable-end looking on the road, the other looking up hill. From the upper gable wall to the top of the hill the brae was one mass of rocks thirty years ago. Oiney took it into his head that this tract of land was going to loss, so he decided to turn the rocky brae into a pleasant field. I don't think he ever heard that remark about the man who could make two blades of grass grow where only one had grown before. But whether he heard it or not he set himself out to do it. When he had any time to spare he put a creel on his back and went down to the bottom land by the river, filled the creel full of clay, carried it up the precipice and emptied it on the rocks. It took him three quarters of an hour to carry the burden up and he did the job barefooted, for the stoney path up hill was too severe on shoe-leather. And so he worked day after day using every spare moment to make a little field amidst the rocks of Glenmornan. Old Oiney was a man who out-rivalled Columbus the explorer. The latter discovered new land, Oiney made it. And then when this poor peasant had a field laid out on the precipice the landlord saw it and raised the rent of the farm."

II

At this moment a young man and a girl entered, Lady Ronan's two children, George and Myra. George had a certain talent for writing and was gifted with a ready pen. He was a handsome, graceful fellow, a dandy in dress, a master of smart conversation and as much at home in a drawing-room as in an editor's sanctum.

Amusing and easy mannered, with complete confidence in himself, he was received cordially everywhere. Now and again he was a little violent, but his friends liked him none the less for that, for he looked as if he never meant his words to be taken seriously. He appeared to regard everything trifling as serious and everything serious as trifling. In his stories, for example, he would write in a joking fashion about a workman's strike and take up a serious standpoint when dealing with a dog-show. From his utterance one might gather that the former was a holiday amusement and the latter a matter of national importance. Despite this he was very serious about his newspaper work and as a matter of course he spoke lightly about it as befitted a man of the world who tries to act as if he did not attach any particular value to his toil.

Myra Ronan sat down on the sofa near the window, giving a careless nod to Doalty Galla-

gher as she did so.   She was a girl just past her
twentieth year, wilful and passionate, with an im-
pulsive spirit and a great love for out-door life.
In her whole bearing, the lines of her perfectly-
formed body, the contour of her full bosom, the
curve of her neck, the sweep of her eyebrows,
the bold look in her eyes, there was something
attractive to all men and dangerous to herself as
well as others.   Doalty Gallagher had known her
for eighteen months, but he had never been on
very intimate terms with her.   She held herself
aloof, treated him with an almost wilful careless-
ness, and even her manner to him had a shade
of something like hostility.   She was a strange
girl, one whom he could not understand.

Young Ronan looked at Doalty.

"So you are really here," he said, and went
across to his mother and kissed her on the cheek.
Then he sat down.

"Now a cup of tea, mater," he said.   "I'm
famished.   I promised to meet Doalty at Pad-
dington, but couldn't get off in time.   I had to
scrap one story and work up another.   The old
man is the deuce of a temper to-day."

"I never hear about him being other than in
a bad temper," said Lady Ronan.   "But when
he comes down here he is as gentle as a lamb."

"He is a lion in Fleet Street," said George.
"A lion with a thorn in his paw.   But putting
him to one side, has Doalty been telling you?"

"He has," said Lady Ronan.   "Going home.
. . . Going to remain in Ireland and work on
his wee farm just the same as his neighbour . . .

what was that man's name, Doalty? I've forgotten."

"Oiney Leahy."

"Yes, that's it," said Lady Ronan, nodding her head. "Poor old man. He was. . . . But does not George know the story?"

"I suppose I do," said George with a careless shrug of his shoulders. "I hear these tales about Glenmornan so often. . . . It's a funny thing though. When Doalty came to the office two years ago it was impossible to get a word from him. He sat at his desk every evening biting the tip of his pen and brooding, as it seemed, over the destiny of the universe. But one day, he had been a year with us then, he spoke about Ireland and he seldom talks about anything else now. It's strange the way Irishmen learn to love their country more, the longer they are out of it. The greatest Irish patriots are American born, I believe. . . . Wait till Doalty is three months in his own country and then he'll be glad to come back here. . . ."

"Never," said Doalty. "I'm never going to come back. I would prefer———"

"A wee Greenanore girl in an ould plaid shawl," said Myra Ronan with a malicious shrug of her shoulders.

"Now children, no argument on such a fine evening," said Lady Ronan, rising to her feet and looking at her nails. They seemed to be a source of perpetual interest to her. "Run out and take the boat on the river. I'll come with you, if you behave yourselves and leave the

Irish questions to Redmond and Carson."

Ten minutes later the four of them were on the river.

III

Doalty Gallagher and George Ronan were sitting in the library, George on the sofa swinging his legs aimlessly and Doalty on a chair, his hands under his thighs, his head erect and his eyes staring through the window into unfathomable distances.   A butler with an official smile on his red, fat face, came in, bearing a tray of coffee.   Doalty looked at the butler, took in, with one swift glance, the man, his red face and his smile.   This smile seemed to be always there on duty, now and again asleep, of course, like a sentry on guard, but ready to wake up at the sound of a foot or the rustle of a skirt.   When Lady Ronan's guests asked him to do them a service he did it so hastily that one would think the man was more interested in the guest's welfare than in his own.   He placed the coffee on the table, retired a few steps, walking backwards, bowed and went out.

"Now why are you going back to Ireland?" young Ronan enquired, lighting a cigarette and lying back on the sofa.   Are you in love with some dainty Irish coleen, like Biddy Cassidy, with a little pig and a brogue and an old mother that sits all day at a spinning wheel? And Biddy,

God bless her, will have a wolf hound and a harp."

"The former's extinct and I've never seen the latter until I left Ireland," said Doalty. "It's a funny country," he went on. "It's people are difficult to understand. In the first place they hate this country with a traditional hatred, the hatred of a vendetta. And no wonder, for English laws have ground them down to the very dirt. The gombeen man is just as bad, nay! he is worse than the landlord, and the poor respect him after a fashion. Why should they not, for is not the priest and the gombeen man the greatest friends in the world? Is not one half of the Irish priests the sons of gombeen men? You should hear the priest make a sermon on the torments that await men who are damned because they have not paid the debts due to a gombeen man. Good God! If I had my way with priests like those I'd hang every man of them from the crosses of their own altars."

"Easy, Doalty my boy, easy," said young Ronan smiling lazily. He looked round to see if an ash-tray were near, but not seeing one he flicked the ash from his cigarette on the carpet. He was always a good listener, and Doalty, when the mood was on him, was a great talker.

"It's enough to drive one mad at times to find the way things are done," said Doalty. "Now in my own place, for example, who is left there? The young men and the young girls grow up and when they reach a certain age they clear out of the country. Nine go away out of a family of ten. The tenth remains and he is generally the weakling. Not much good in him going away, so he stays at home and marries a weakling like himself. Soon there will be none in the country but the inefficient."

"All that is very evident," said Ronan with a smile, flicking some more ash to the carpet. But I can't follow your meaning. Why are you going home? Have you made a fortune and are eager to spend it?"

IV

"My worldly wealth is some thirty pounds," said Doalty. "I'll spend that easily. No place like Ireland for spending money. I'll have to give some of it to my mother. She is always putting a little by. That is her one ambition, to put some money in the bank. If I gave her ten thousand pounds she would put every penny of it in the bank and continue living just as she is living now. She might, of course, buy another bit of land and get so superior that she would not speak to a neighbour. In her own townland she is a great swell; she looks down on her neighbours as it is, because she has six cows' grass and most of the people about her have only feeding for two or three cattle."

"But still you have not told me yet why you want to get back there," said Ronan, again flicking the ash to the carpet.

"I want to get back to my own people," said Doalty. "I am going to work as they work and toil in the fields and mow the hay and dig the potatoes. I am going to do some real work, not such as I do here. What do we, the moulders of public opinion, really do? For myself, I get out of bed in the morning at nine o'clock. In Glenmornan half a day's work is finished by then. I go down to the office and hang about there, chewing the top of a pen until lunch. After lunch I come back to the office to find that the news editor has found a story for me. I have got to call on old Mr. Plodder, who has made a fortune as head of Plodder's Grocery Stores. He will be in the next honours list, for he has given piles of money to charity. He has risen from the gutters and now he is at the top of the business world. I have to get his photograph (an easy matter) and interview him, get the story of his wonderful career, how he got rich, etc. Two things I know before I see the man. One is that he has read Smiles' Self-Help and the other is that he does not know how he amassed so much money. He will say that he became rich by steady toil and honest endeavour. But that means nothing. Oiney Leahy, of Glenmornan, is as steady a worker as Plodder, and Oiney hasn't got a penny. So I see him, write him up in the most glowing manner. I do it to make my living, the newspaper does it because Plodder advertises in its columns. I'm not in earnest about the job; it gives me no pleasure. In short, I'm sick of it. I'll be much happier in Glenmornan."

"And you'll be glad to get back here again, I bet," said Ronan.   "Six months will be quite enough for you there.   Let me know when you're coming back, Doalty.   I'll see that you're taken on the paper again."

Lady Ronan was part proprietor of the daily on which Doalty was employed.   She was a very wealthy woman.   Her husband who had died recently left a large fortune.

"And if you get any good stuff send it on," said Ronan.   " The old man will give it a place, I know.   He likes your work."

There was a tap at the door and Myra Ronan entered.

"Are you two coming with me for a walk?" she asked.   "Down by the river.   It's such a fine night for a stroll."

Doalty had got to his feet and stood looking at the girl.   George stretched himself out on the sofa and puffed rings of smoke into the air.

"I'm not going for a walk at this hour," he said.   " I've got to go on some job or another (I forget what it is) to-morrow morning.   Take Doalty with you, Myra.   He's leaving here on Monday and maybe he'll never come back again."

"Will you come, Doalty?" Myra enquired. Like her mother and brother she always called the young Irishman by his Christian name.

"I'll be happy if you allow me," said Doalty eagerly.

Five minutes later they were both on the bank of the river.   There was a breath of freshness

from the quiet water and a soft breeze rustled
through the tall grass that was not yet tramped
down by the feet of holiday makers. The night
was very clear, with a sky studded with stars.
The horizon on the east across the fields glowed
a pale white and heralded the moon which would
presently rise

"To think of remaining indoors on a night like
this!" said Myra in a voice of feeling. "If nobody came with me I would have come out alone.
Shall we have a long walk, ever such a long walk?
You don't mind, Doalty?"

"Mind! Certainly not. Where shall we go?"

"Oh! anywhere," she said, as if abandoning
herself to Doalty's guidance, then paused as if
considering the question. "I know," she exclaimed, after a moment's silence. "We'll go
along the river till we pass the church in the
fields. Then we'll go across through the meadows
to Pyford. . . . You've never been to the village of Pyford, Doalty?"

"Never," he replied.

"Then you'll like it, especially by moonlight,
when all the people are asleep," she said, stepping out briskly, as if on the point of breaking
into a run. "It's a little village with a crooked
street and such old houses. I have often gone
out there on moonlight nights. . . ."

"Alone?" asked Doalty.

"Why not?" queried the girl, casting a cursory
glance at Doalty. "I'm able to take care of myself."

"But one never knows what might happen."

"So mother says," Myra replied. "But I did not think that you would have ideas like that. They are so old-fashioned. A girl is as well able to protect herself as a man."

"From whom, and from what?"

"From anybody and anything, from a tramp or a mad dog," said Myra. "From—oh!"

Doalty bent to lift her almost as soon as she reached the ground.

"What happened?" he enquired as he helped her to her feet.

"My foot caught in a root and I tripped," she said. "It's so dark, and going through this grass you don't know what you are going to step on."

"Have you hurt yourself?"

"No."

"Well, let me take your arm, and I'll try and save you from falling when you meet the next root."

He took her arm as he spoke and both proceeded on their way along the river. The moon withered at one of its corners, rose over the fields and lit up the whole country with a strange misty light. The air was full of the perfume of recently cut hay and from the distance came the sound of a train on its journey to London.

"What a wonderful night!" Myra exclaimed. "If I had the choice of dying when I pleased I would choose a night like this. And this wonderful walk, Doalty! Do you like it?"

"Yes, it's wonderful," Doalty replied, then spoke again, as if he had not already concluded his sentence. "Very wonderful, Miss Ronan," he said.

She drew her arm away from his, stood still and looked at him. Doalty knew that she was going to ask a question and he guessed what that question would be.

"Why do you always call me Miss Ronan?" she asked. "I always call you Doalty. I hope it does not annoy you."

"I would have called you Myra long ago, but I was afraid to do so," said the Irishman in a voice which had suddenly become strangely husky. "It somehow seems that I have no right to do so."

"You have as much right as I have."

"Have I?"

"Have I—what?"

"Myra."

"Now you may take my arm again, Doalty," said the girl, with a smile. "There are roots all through this grass. And here is the church."

It showed through the elms near the river, an old building with its spire standing clear cut against the sky. The base of the church was steeped in coal-black shadows, through which wisps of mist were wandering aimlessly.

"It's hundreds of years old," said Myra, "and there's no road near it. Do you know why that is?"

"I'm afraid I don't know, Myra." He dwelt on the name lovingly and his hand touched hers.

"The church was built at a time when the country was covered with trees and when people

travelled more by water than land," said the girl.
" They came to church by boats. Services were
held here hundreds and hundreds of years ago.
Probably the ghosts of the old worshippers are
about the place yet. Suppose we saw one of
them come out now. Oh! I would be so frightened!"

As she spoke a slight shudder ran through her
and she clutched Doalty's hand.

" So you are really afraid of something?" he
asked, pressing her fingers tightly. " But there
are no ghosts, you know," he assured her. "At
least not in England."

" But there are some in Ireland," she said.

" Oh, yes. Behind every hedge and under
all the holly trees."

" And you want to go back to see all these
ghosts again," said the girl.

" It's not altogether for that purpose, Myra,"
said Doalty. " I'm homesick and I'm tired of
living here."

" Tired of us all?" she asked, but by her tones
it was evident that "us all" meant herself alone.

" Oh! I'm not tired of you, but still————"

" Then I suppose you really are," she said diffidently, then as if some work had been accom-
plished to her satisfaction, she remarked : " It's
about time that we went back. Mother will be
anxious."

They turned round and retraced their steps arm
in arm, their hands clasped and the little village
of Pyford quite forgotten. Doalty's mind was
filled with the thoughts which can never be absent

from a young man's mind on such an occasion.
What Myra was thinking of it was impossible to
say. Anyway, she did not withdraw her hand.
They walked along the river in silence, passed
through the gate and up the carriage drive. The
hall-door of Ermara was left half open and a lamp
was still alight in the hall. Not a soul was to
be seen there. Myra withdrew her hand from
Doalty's as they crossed the threshold.

"I must go up and tell mother that we have
come in," she said, and without bidding her com-
panion Good-night she tripped upstairs.

v

Doalty followed her and went to his bedroom.
It opened out on a long narrow passage in the
second floor. Opposite it was the bedroom in
which Myra slept.

Doalty sat down on a chair, lit a cigarette and
left the door half-open. The passage outside
was in darkness save where the light from Doalty's room showed across the floor and lit up the
door of Myra Ronan's bedroom. He would see
her go into her room when she came along the
passage. Why did he want to see her? He did
not love her and he was certain that she did not
love him. But he did not think of this. All he
could think of was the pressure of her hand when
she clasped his by the old church, her white
throat, her soft delicate cheeks, her charming

eyes, the poise of her chin. . . . A feeling passionate and primitive, which is never wholly absent at twenty-one, welled up in Doalty's breast, almost choking him with its exquisite pain.

Myra came along the passage, stopped opposite her bedroom door and looked in at Doalty in his room.

"You're not in bed yet, Doalty," she said in a whisper, as if afraid that somebody, other than Doalty, was listening to her.

"Neither are you in bed," he replied, getting to his feet. He spoke as if the fact of Myra not yet being in bed was sufficient excuse for him to be up.

"Oh! neither of us could be as yet, for we have only just come in," said Myra, placing her fingers on the handle of her door and drawing them away again. "You did like that church in the moonlight?" she asked in a whisper.

"Yes, it interested me very much," he whispered in reply. It almost seemed that the sight of the old building by moonlight was a secret known only to the two of them and which had to be kept hidden from all other mortals.

Myra came to the door of Doalty's bedroom, stepping very softly on the carpet and trembling a little as she reached him.

"There's a picture of the church hanging on your wall near the window," she said nervously, blushing as she spoke.

"A painting?"

"Yes."

"Which of these pictures is it?"

He went across to the window and looked at one picture in a gilt frame. It was certainly not the painting of a church, but he looked at it as attentively as if his very gaze would transform an etching of two children playing with a dog into an ancient home of religious worship.

When he looked round again he found Myra behind him, looking at the same picture.

" That's not it,'' she said, " I don't think it is really here. It was, some time ago, but I think mother has taken it away for her own room. She is always changing things.''

" And this picture of the boy and girl playing with a dog,'' Doalty said. " You are the girl, I suppose.''

" She's not like me, is she?''

" I don't know. It's so dark here that I cannot see it very well.''

"Well, I'll get up on a chair and have a look,'' said Myra, drawing forward the chair on which Doalty had been sitting a few minutes earlier. She sprang up on it with a bound, active as a kitten, and her head became level with the etching.

" It is very dark,'' she said, " and this chair is so woggeldy. Just don't let me fall on the floor, Doalty. If I come down I'll waken the whole house.''

He held her arm and steadied her while she examined the picture. As he did so his heart was filled with a strange, joyful emotion and a great feeling of tenderness towards the girl.

"Well, I hope I never looked like that,'' she

whispered. " She's an ugly little creature. . . .
Whisht! there's somebody coming up the stairs.
One of the servants maybe, putting out the
lights."

Doalty rushed to the door of the room and
looked out. Nobody was to be seen, but the soft
thud of heavy feet in slippers could be heard
coming up. Doalty shoved the door to and shut
it. Then he turned round to see Myra standing
in the middle of the room near the bed, her head
thrust a little forward and one hand over the ear
in a listening attitude.

Outside the steps sounded along the passage,
halted for a moment at the door, then went back
again and died away.

" It's the butler, I think," said Myra in a hoarse
whisper. " He's always prowling about like a
fox."

" If he had come in !" Doalty hazarded.

" If he had," said the girl with a deep intake
of breath, and a horrified expression showed in
her eyes. Never before had Doalty seen the girl
look so beautiful. Her look, her eyes, her round
chin magnetised Doalty. Something fierce and
ungovernable, a mad wild passion took posses-
sion of him, and the next moment he found himself sitting on the bed by her side, his arm round
her shoulders, his lips resting on hers, pressing
them in against her white teeth with wild undisci-
plined violence. And the girl yielded to his
embrace, returning his kisses and caresses. . . .
Ah, the glorious passion of twenty-one.

" Suppose somebody saw us in here," she

asked shyly, when several minutes had passed, apparently conscious for the first time of the position in which she had placed herself.

" It doesn't matter," Doalty said with a superior masculine smile, resting her head in the crook of his arm and kissing one eye, then another. " You are not afraid, are you?"

" No, Doalty, but still, it doesn't seem right, somehow," said Myra.

"If anybody knew."

She sat up, drew a deep breath and ran on tiptoes towards the door.   She stood there for a moment, listening, then waved Doalty, who was approaching her, away.

" I'm going to my own room," she whispered, looking at him and then averting her eyes.   " It was wrong of me to come in. . . . Good-night, Doalty."

With these words she opened the door, rushed out into the passage and disappeared.   Doalty could hear the door of her room open and close. Then silence followed.

He drew his chair up to the door and sat down on it, with his eyes fixed on the closed bedroom, and imagined many things for a full hour afterwards.

"She'll be asleep now," he said at last, and getting up he undressed, put on his pyjamas and lit a cigarette.   Then he went up to the mirror which stood over the washstand and looked at his face in it, while a wild sensual feeling surged through his blood.   The novelty of an hour ago had died away, only the desires remained, leaving Doalty dissatisfied and despondent. He should not have allowed her to run away. If he had been firm she would have remained—she would be in the room now. He rubbed his handkerchief over the mirror where his breath had dimmed it and looked at his reflection again. His heart beat violently, the veins on his temples throbbed, and his arms shook as if with cold. He threw his cigarette into the empty fireplace, put another in his mouth but did not light it. Instead he went out of his room, stepped softly up to Myra's door and listened with his ear to the keyhole. No sound was to be heard, no movement, no breathing. He went back to his room again, turned out the light and got into bed.

VI

On the following morning he was late in getting out of bed. When he went down to the dining-room he found nobody there. Lady Ronan had gone off to church and George had departed for London. He would return to his home that night. But Myra was also absent. She generally had breakfast with Doalty when he had visited the house before. Breakfast was laid for him and he sat down and poured himself out a cup of tea. It was then that he noticed a letter addressed to him lying on a plate by his side. The writing on the envelope was Myra

Ronan's. He opened it and read the hastily scrawled letter. This was what it contained:

Dear Doalty,

I am sorry that I have to go away without bidding you good-bye. I intended to tell you about my intended departure last night when we were out for the walk along the river. I am going to stay with a girl friend at her home the other side of London and I shall be there for several days. You shall be in Ireland by the time I'm back home again. I hope you'll enjoy life over there. Let us know how you are getting on when you have time to write a line. We'll, all of us, be delighted to hear from you. Excuse this hurried scrawl.

Yours sincerely,

Myra Ronan.

"Well, I'm damned!" said Gallagher in a puzzled voice as he placed the letter back in the envelope. "'Let *us* know how you are getting on!'"

He took out the letter again, read it twice before replacing it in the envelope. Then leaning over the table he looked in the cup as if the tea had suddenly possessed some great attraction for him.

"All this had to be," he muttered to himself. What was I expecting? I did not love her, I could not love her. She does not love me, and I knew it. . . . I amused her I suppose." He smiled bitterly and lifted the tea-cup from the saucer, placing it on the table. Then he sat upright, placed both hands in his pockets, lay back on the chair and fixed a vacant look on the window opposite.

Doalty was a well-built young man with light brown eyes and very dark hair. He left school, the mountain school of Glenmornan, when he was fourteen. At fifteen he came to London with a crowd of Irish labourers and got a job as nipper in the employ of a jobbing contractor. He was a voracious reader and tried his hand at writing when he was seventeen. At nineteen, when working at the London Docks, he sent some contributions to a daily paper, stories of labourers, sailors, tramps and doss-house residents. All the stories were published and paid for. He sent more stuff to the paper and this was also taken, then he himself was taken as reporter on the staff. He had now been on the paper for two years.

Now as he sat there alone in the Ermara breakfast room, thinking of Myra Ronan, he recalled women he had known and a little typist in the newpaper office came to his mind. The journalists called her Fluffie amongst themselves. She was a pretty, fair-haired girl of nineteen when Doalty first saw her. She attracted him and he fell madly in love with her. She was in his thoughts all day and in his dreams all night. But he never disclosed his passion to the girl. In her presence he felt tongue-tied, impotent. Even once when he had a chance . . . But no . . . It was in the office, in a dark passage on the ground floor that he met her. . . . She was coming along with a sheaf of papers, and as he passed her she gave a little shriek and clutched his arm.

"What's wrong?" Doalty stammered as if the sweet shiver which ran through his body, had communicated itself to his tongue.

"I thought I saw a mouse running along there!" said the girl, with a slight catch in her voice.

"No. . . . nothing! said Doalty with a little laugh.

"I'm so sorry, but I'm terrified of mice," said Fluffie, and a little smile hovered on her eye-lashes. Then she scuttled away.

That night Doalty sat in his room, lighting cigarette after cigarette and throwing them in the grate when they burned to his fingers. At four in the morning he went to bed. When he fell asleep he dreamt of Fluffie, and in the dream she was asking him to save her from a dreadful monster that was attacking her. He tried to help her, but his efforts were futile. The monster was dragging her down, down along with him into a dark pit. Doalty tried to drag the girl back but could not. Instead of helping her he fell with her down, down . . . He woke up.

Next day the editor called him to his office. Fluffie was there, bending over the typewriter. As Doalty went in the girl left, first fixing a knowing look on him, as if some secret of his had been revealed to her.

"Well, how do you like this work?" asked the editor when the room was left to the two men.

"I like it well," said Doalty. "But it needs getting used to a bit."

"It does," said the editor, smiling slightly and fashioning letters with his forefinger in the air. This was a habit of his when immersed in thought.

"Life is not the same here as in the East End where you have been working," he said. "There a man can do his job with a cap on; here a man needs to wear a hat. There a man can wear trousers patched and baggy, but here————. For my own part, I don't care what a man wears; it's the man that counts and not his rags. But when reporters go out on a story they have a better chance of getting there in a top-hat than in a cap. It's funny, but still————. Well, I've got a story for you," said the editor without changing his tone of voice. "It's about," etc.

As Doalty went out Fluffie came in again. It almost seemed as if she had been waiting behind the door. Probably she had been listening to the conversation.

Next morning Doalty came to his work in a velour hat, a new lounge suit and trousers that were carefully creased. Hitherto he had worn a cap and trousers that were both a little the worse for wear. A week later Fluffie left the office. He never saw her again.

Then there was a girl at the tea-shop where he and his mates used to have tea in the afternoons. All the young journalists, with the exception of Doalty, vowed that they were in love with the girl, whom they called Pussie. They made collections amongst themselves and bought the girl boxes of chocolate. The boxes were always bound in pink ribbons with pink bows. Pink was Pussie's favourite colour. After a time she went from Fleet Street to a job in a Piccadilly tea-shop. All the young men, with the exception of Doalty, made love to the girl who came to replace her. Doalty, however, went to tea in Piccadilly afterwards and continued going there until Pussie got married to a taxi driver.

He read Myra's letter again, crumpled it up and put it in his pocket.

"It doesn't matter and I don't care," he said, gazing ruefully at the cup in which the tea had become quite cold.

CHAPTER IV

IN HIS MOTHER'S HOUSE

I have been gone from Donegal for seven years and
    a day,
And true enough it's a long, long time for a
    wanderer to stay,
But the hills of home are aye in my heart and
    never are far away.

—I Will Go Back.

I

THE soft Summer night was falling and a few stars already showed over Carnaween, though the colours of the sunset still lingered behind Sliav-a-Tuagh, where that hill rose over Meena-warawor to look out on the sea. The evening twilight settled on boreen and brae and showed densely dark in the awlth behind the house of Maura The Rosses. The brooks reeling down to the river looked white and ghostly as they fell over the rocks. A young girl was driving the cows home from the hills and the cattle could be seen, coming down carefully, picking their way over hillock and hobeen. The girl could be heard shouting in a shrill, clear voice : " Come home with ye now, ye silly crathur ! Have sense and get on with ye, ye wee divil ye !"

The peasantry were coming in from the fields, the men walking with a slow, decided step, their pipes in their mouths and their spades over their shoulders. The women, more in a hurry, were coming into their homes well ahead of their men folk, singing as they made their way through the long grass of the meadows. They had much work to do still, for the cows had to be milked, the stirabout had to be made ready. The men had been working hard all day and it would not do to keep them waiting for their suppers. Many of the cows were already in the byres tied to the stakes, their full udders yearning for the hands of the milkers.

Doalty Gallagher, home from foreign parts, was sitting on the ground outside the door of his mother's house, his soul drinking in all the glory of the Irish nightfall. A bat, whirring in the air over his head, now and again swooped down and round him, almost touching his ear. He had come home that day at noon, and up till a few moments ago, he had been inside the house speaking to the neighbours who had come to see him. He felt very happy. Everything in the glen and around him seemed beautiful and full of meaning. His soul was filled with peace and goodwill towards all men and he wished to everyone the same happiness as that which filled his own heart. He was looking on everything with a fresh mind in which there was no bitterness.

The smell of the midden, the turf fire and the rich grass was in his nostrils and all this woke pleasant remembrance in the young man. It recalled to him his childhood and the days that had gone. "Ah! how very good it is to be back again," he said. "Everybody is so happy and they are all so glad to see me! And the little boy, Hughie! What a ripping little rascal. He's not in the least afraid of me. But why should he be?"

He got to his feet and walked along the field for a couple of hundred yards, then sat down again in the grass that was already getting wet with the dew. He bent his lips to the ground, kissed it and looked round to see if anyone had observed him. Nobody was nigh. "If they saw me they would think that I was a fool!" he laughed. "Wonder what mother would do if she saw me kiss Ireland? She would shake the holy water over me, I'm sure. And I saw the bottle of holy water to-day. Under the roof beam, just where it used to be seven years ago. And the bottle was once used for whisky. The label is on it yet."

The air was pure and fresh, making him feel a little drowsy. He looked down the dip of the meadow and he could see the white streak of the glen road losing itself in the gloom. Lights appeared in the houses and more stars were creeping timidly out in the heavens.

"Just as it used to be," he said. "Just the same as I mind it. In London I used to have pleasure in looking forward; here somehow the pleasure is in looking back."

"Go on little cow, now! Do ye not want to be milked the night?"

The girl up on the hill was still calling to the cattle.

II

"Doalty! Where are ye? Come in and have yer supper!"

It was his sister Norah who was calling. She had just milked the cows, two of which were giving milk. Three were springing and it was expected that one of these, a white faced animal with a belly taut as a drum, would calve twins. So Maura The Rosses told her son.

"I'm here," said Doalty in answer to his sister. He had got to his feet and lit a cigarette.

"Come in then, afore yer supper gets cold," she said.

He went across to her.

"How many cigarettes d'ye smoke in a day?" she asked.

"About—I don't know how many—twenty maybe."

"And what d'ye pay for them?" she asked.

"About a shilling for twenty," he said.

"A shilling," said Norah. What a lot iv money. Can I have one?"

"Of course you can," said Doalty and handed her a cigarette.

"D'ye know who's comin' to see ye?" Norah said. She was a very handsome girl, well proportioned and light on her feet.

"Who?"

"Old Oiney," said Norah. "I met him on the hill a minute ago when I was up for the cows and he said that he was comin' in to see ye when he got his cattle in. He is very fond iv ye."

"I like old Oiney," said Doalty. "Is he as lively as ever?"

"He's an old omadhaun," said Norah. "He's always talkin' about the old times and we are all sick iv listenin' to him."

"Go on, wee cow, now! I'm tired iv ye, ye wee divil ye!"

"Who's that on the hill?" asked Doalty, as he heard the voice of the girl again. "She seems to have trouble enough with the cows."

"It's Sheila Dermod," said Norah. "The Dermods have only two cows on their bit iv land, and to hear her speak one would think that she has whole drove iv them."

"You're not friendly with her, are you?" asked Doalty.

"Our ma and her ma fell out two years back, and we have never passed a word with her since then," said Norah. "Breed and Sheila live together and they are as proud and distant as the hills. And Sheila thinks that every boy in the glen is mad after her."

"So you're jealous of her," said Doalty with a laugh.

"Me jealous iv her!" Norah exclaimed. "Jealous iv Sheila Dermod and her one iv the lowest iv the low. God forbid me that I would!"

III

Doalty and Norah went in home together. A good red turf fire glowed on the hearth and beside the fire Maura The Rosses was seated, on a wooden stool, a stocking in her hand, and her bare toes peeping out from under her red woollen petticoat. Wee Hughie was rolling on the floor, a puppy dog frollicking around his bare legs and barking merrily. Doalty's youngest sister, Kitty, a girl who was getting her education at the convent school of Greenanore, was seated at the stirabout pot which stood on the floor, eating her supper. A lamp hanging by a nail from the wall, lit the smoky atmosphere of the room with a soft, mellow light. The walls were turf brown, a tint which harmonised with the dun colourings of the floor. A long beam of bog-oak stretched across the rigging of the house, under the scraughs, and from this beam and the rafters, raying fanwise out from it, all manner of utensils were hanging, trahooks,* scythes, spades and shovels.

* Trahook. A twister used in making ropes.

"So here ye are, Doalty," said the mother, rising from her seat and pouring out a bowl of milk which she placed on the table in front of a dish of stirabout.   "There's yer brahun-ray, so made a good meal iv it."

"I'll make a good meal, never fear," said Doalty.   "When is Oiney coming in to see me?"

"He'll be in at any minit now," said the mother, sitting down again by the fire and resuming her knitting.   "There he's comin', I think. I hear his steps."

At that moment Oiney Leahy entered without rapping.   They never rap on the door in Glenmornan.   With his hat on, for the people never remove their hats when entering a house, Oiney went up to Doalty and caught both the young man's hands.

"And is it yerself that is back to the barony iv Burrach again, Doalty Connel?" he said, his eyes gleaming with emotion.   "I'm so glad to see ye again after all the time that ye were away from yer own home . . . . And ye've got to be a fine hearty man too.   And a Gallagher, a Gallagher, every inch iv ye!"

"So he hasn't changed so much that ye wouldn't know him?" asked Maura The Rosses, touched by the old man's hearty welcome for her son.

"And d'ye think that I wouldn't be knowin' Doalty, the oldest son iv Connel Gallagher, God rest him!" said Oiney in a voice of protest.

"Know him! Be Goigah! I'd know his skin on a bush."

The old man released Doalty's hands and stepped back a few paces and surveyed him minutely from head to heel.

" Just as I expected him to look," he said, when the inspection came to an end. " He might just be the same as he is now, if he had never left home. Just sittin' down to his brahun-ray and butthermilk like anyone in the glen. . . . And how long will ye be stayin' with us now?" he enquired.

By "us" Oiney meant the people of Glenmornan.

" I'll stay for quite a long time," said Doalty.

" Iv course ye will," said Oiney, again clasping the young man's hands and shaking them. " There's maybe no place like yer own bit iv the world when all's said and done. . . . It must be an awful thing to live away in the big town where ye're seein' hundreds iv people day after day and never the same face two times over. And I'll bet ye now, that there's no place like Glenmornan after all! Isn't that so, Doalty me boyo?"

" That is so," said Doalty. " And you're looking quite well on it, Oiney."

" Then I'm as well as can be expected," said Oiney with an air of decision. " But all the same I'm a worn-out old fellow," he continued, not without a certain complacency, and paused, as if waiting to hear his remark contradicted.

"Mary and Joseph! but ye're not old lookin', Oiney," said Maura The Rosses, working her knit-needles violently, as if to emphasize her assertion. "Ye look as young this very day as ye did ten years ago. Now what age are ye?" she enquired.

"Well, I'll tell ye," said the old man. "And this is how I know. 'Twas on the day that I was married and Condy Mor iv Meenawarawor, since dead, God rest him! said to me, 'Oiney,' says he, 'If ye're alive and well, come Candlemas next, ye'll be such and such an age on that day.' So ever since then I know me years. Eighty years, Candlemas past, is my age."

"Well, ye look a young man yet," said Maura The Rosses, pandering to Oiney's coquetry---the coquetry of years.

"Do ye think so, Maura?"

"Think it, Oiney!" said the woman. "I don't think it. I'm sure iv it."

"Well, ye may be right, thank God," said Oiney, seating himself on the chair which Norah Gallagher had pushed up towards him, and drawing his old, weather-worn hat down over his eyes. "There's life and to spare in the old dog yet. And happy! Be Jarra! I never was as happy in all me life. An old dog for the hard road and a pup for the level, as the sayin' is! I was always on the hard road and I've never had a doctor to me in the whole iv me life."

"Is that true?" asked Doalty, sitting down again to his interrupted meal.

"May I die where I sit if there's one word iv a lie in it," said Oiney. "Look at me! Eighty years if an hour I am, and I've never had a doctor to me in all me life. No, nor a taste iv physic either. . . . But what's the good iv it anyway? It won't keep a man alive for iver. If sickness comes me way it's just what would come to anyone, and if it came I would hold me peace and not give it the nose to let it draw one yelp from me. But look at the people in the barony nowadays! If they're goin' to die their first thought is on the doctor and not on the Last Sacrament. It was different when yer father, God rest him, was taken with the sickness, Doalty. He said, 'Send for the priest and don't trouble about the doctor.' . . . Ah! the old times————"

"There were no times like them," said Doalty Gallagher.

"There were no times like them and niver will be again," said Oiney, as he pulled out a little black clay pipe from his pocket and put it in his mouth. Oiney was an adept in the art of colouring clays.

"Don't light up yet for a wee minit," said Maura The Rosses, as she rose from the stool and made her way to the big room. When she came back she had a large bottle of whisky in her hand. Filling a glass she handed it to Oiney. The old man raised it to his nose, smelled it, then put it down again. He reached out his hand and clasped Doalty's.

"Ah! It's glad to see ye back here again

that I am," he said, and a new warmth had crept
into his voice. "I often have been thinking
iv ye, Doalty, me boy. And it's glad that I am
to know that ye made any amount iv money beyont the water. Nobody deserves to make it
more than a son iv Connel Gallagher."

He raised the glass to his lips and emptied it
at one gulp.

IV

"It's good stuff," he said. "And d'ye know,"
he went on, launching into a fresh subject, as if
the drink had given him the inspiration. "I
used to make a lot iv money meself at one time.
But that was years back. . . . Now it's everybody for himself. But in the times that wor
there wor good men in this arm iv the glen. That
was thirty years ago, when yer father, God rest
him, was a young man, Doalty. He was a splendid gasair and would give ye the very sugar from
his tay."

"And you could make money then?" said
Doalty.

"Lashin's and lavin's iv it, me boy," said Oiney, thrusting his hat back and running his
fingers through his white hair. "'How did I
make it?' ye'll ask. Well, I'll tell ye, but never
a word, mind. I don't want the people iv the
barony to know how I made it. In the old times

I was able to help them when their rent was due,
but nowadays they look at me and laugh behind
me back.   They helped me to spend the money
and gave me nothin' in exchange for it but the
bad name. . . . And God knows why! I was
never stingy, for what is the good of being near-
going and close-fisted?   Greed puts wrinkles in
the soul as well as on the forehead. I have seen
this though people may be laughin' at me and
callin' me a droll ould card.   But mind ye, I
can talk sense though I never put money by.   I
take life easy, have a drink when I can get one,
am merry and say me prayers.   Take everything
as it comes from God is me way and if one job
isn't finished at night I can take it up again in the
mornin'.   But look at some of the people about
here," said the old man with a sly grin as he put
a live coal to his little black clay.

"They're workin' late at night and up again
in the mornin' before the blackbird shakes itself.
Not to go further away than next door but one,
look at Owen Briney. . . . He's always workin' and lavin' by and what will be the end iv it
all for him and men like him? They have days
to make money but never an hour to spend it.
Accordin' to their way iv lookin' at things they
have nothin' done as long as there's anything to
do.   They'll begrudge the hour to die in.

"When they go there'll be somebody to spend
the money for them," Oiney went on.   "I know
many a man who has gone and left a fortune behind him.   Then his sons drank the money or

his daughters spent it on hats and dresses.   I
don't know what's comin' over the glen girls
nowadays," said the old man, fixing his eyes on
Norah Gallagher as if the remark was meant for
her.   "It's all flounces and hats and fine boots
and shoes, and paper pads over their breasts and
over their bottoms.   They puff out their bodies
in a way that God never intended them, and they
think that they are queens.   But in the ould days
yer hand could feel what the eye saw and ye
were never disappointed.   Now it's hoodwinkin'
us that they be all the time.   They can't go outside the door without puttin' their boots on.

"But look at me," continued Oiney, running
the   pipe-shank   through   his   chin-whiskers.
"Eighty years if a day and I can go out and do
a night's cuttin' iv green rushes on Meenawarawor
without a boot to me feet.   Once—ye wouldn't
think it now, widye?—I had as much money as
any man in Glenmornan and ye know what that
means."

"What does that mean?" asked Doalty.

"Mean!" said Oiney.   "It means everything
me boy.   I could at that time go into the fair iv
Greenanore and put every man in shoe-leather
as drunk as a king.   I was a man then and could
carry a bag of Indian-buck, two hundredweight
that, home on me back after drinking glass for
glass with every man I met.   That, too, at the
heel iv the day, and never put me bottom down
for a rest on the whole journey, and all the way
up-hill.   But look at the men nowadays!   Not
one in the whole barony, bar young Dennys The

Drover maybe, can do the same. I would be ashamed to be like that, wouldn't I now, Maura The Rosses?"

"Ye would, indeed, Oiney," said the old woman, placing her stocking on the floor and bringing out her snuff-box from her breast. She handed it to Oiney Leahy. He got hold of the snuff between finger and thumb and drew it through one nostril. Then he tried the other, the right, but finding it stopped, he drew it a little apart and inhaled violently.

"It never gives me the sneeze iv late," he said and looked round. . . . Nobody was up now except Doalty and his mother. Little Hughie was lying in the kitchen bed, his two big blue eyes staring out at the old man.

"Oo don't see me, Oiney," he called.

"I see ye, ye vagabone," Oiney said. "Ye're there in the bed and yer two eyes lookin' out."

"Not my two eyes," said Hughie.

"Who's eyes, then, tell me?"

"Eyes iv the Wee Red Head Man," Hughie answered. His mother often told Hughie the story of the Wee Red Headed Man who went to Tirnanoge, The Land of Eternal Youth, to marry the Queen of The Fairies.

"Ye get to sleep, Hughie," said Oiney as he got to his feet. "I've got to go home now and have me sleep meself."

"Another drop of this before you go," said Doalty as he filled a glass and handed it to Oiney.

"Fuxey very nice," Hughie called from the bed, but Oiney did not hear him. Raising his glass the old man gripped Doalty's hand once more and tears started to his eyes.

" I'm glad to see ye here again," he said. "Ah ! Doalty Connel ! it's grand to see ye back again, a big man. And I can mind when ye were a wee gasair not the height iv me leg. I can mind it well, Doalty Connel, and yerself not the height iv me knee !"

So saying, he old man drank the glass at one gulp and walked out sideways through the door without another word.

V

Maura The Rosses looked at her son, and her half-drowsy, half-watchful eyes had in them a look of tenderness, not unmixed with curiosity.

" Well, and how d'ye like him ?" she enquired.

" He's a grand old man," said Doalty.

" He'll be at the turf now," said Maura The Rosses.

" What ?" Doalty questioned.

" He'll be at turf now and taking a creel home with him," said Maura The Rosses. " He hasn't got one turf on his bit iv a hill, for he didn't cut them in time last year, and so he did not save a clod. But all the same he must get his bit of a fire, poor man. And he's so proud that he'll not ask anyone about the place for the len iv a creel. He comes round at night and steals them. It's

us one night, and then it's Owen Briney the next
night, and round and round he goes, stealin' them,
the old fool, when he could get them for the
askin'."

"Oiney's a feef," said Hughie from the bed.

"Ye get to sleep, ye rogue," said the mother.
"If ye don't get a sleep on ye this very minit I'll
give ye no breakfast in the mornin'."

"Come into bed, maw," the little boy called
after a moment's silence. "Want oo tell me a
story."

"That's like the wee vagabone," said Maura
The Rosses, looking at her son Doalty. "It's a
story every night before he goes to sleep for him,
and he won't sleep one wink without it."

"Me want story, maw," the little boy called
again from the bed.

"And what's that Oiney was saying about the
time when he could make plenty of money?"
Doalty asked. "Was it when he belonged to
the Schol Gaelig (Irish School)?"

"That was the time he was talkin' about," said
Maura The Rosses. "He was making good
money as a Cath Breac* then. Twelve pounds
a year it was, I think."

"And he was trying to turn everybody Protestant, wasn't he?" Doalty enquired.

"I think that was what it was for, the Schol
Gaelig," said Maura The Rosses. "Oiney had
a wee school in his house, and the glen boys

---

* Speckled cat.

used to go there just to help poor Oiney to make a decent penny. There used to come a man twice a year and put out the Catechis on the boys, but the Catechis was different to that put out in the schools. One question used to be: "How many Apostles were in it?' And the answer to that was: 'There was twelve Apostles and one iv them was the divil.' . . . The man who used to come and put out the questions was always dressed in black, and one night when this man was seen going away from Oiney's house the glen boys that lay out be the road to have a look at him, saw that he had two horns stickin' out iv the top iv his head. Think iv that! and the man used to say that he was teachin' the Gospel. His money was good anyway, and Oiney at the time that he was gettin' the money was one iv the best dressed men that went to Mass iv a Sunday.

"Yer father, God rest him in peace! used to go to Oiney's and was a scholar in the Schol Gaelig school," said Maura The Rosses. "Oiney in addition to his pay, used to get two shillin's for every scholar he had in the school, and one shillin' he used to give to the scholar and one Oiney kept himself. . . . And sometimes on a dark night the young gasairs used to go before the Man in Black three times, dressed different each time. . . . . Oiney had no light in the house barrin' the turf fire and it was hard to say whether a man had been in before or not. Sometimes a scholar used to pass three times and that would be six shillin's to the good iv the glen. Often, too, after an examination, when the strange man left, the boys used to get hold iv him as he was crossin' the bogs on his way to the town in Donegal and pitch him into a hole. But it has all stopped now because the priest came to hear about it and he said, from the steps iv the altar, that he would make every Cath Breac in the parish go to Lough Derg on their knees as penance for their sins. After that was read out the people did not like Oiney because they thought that he was half a Prodesan."

" Isn't oo comin' bed the night?" Hughie called.

Doalty got to his feet and went outside, to smoke a cigarette. When he returned his mother was in bed and telling a story to Hughie Beag.

VI

" Once upon a time when the cows were kine and the eagles iv the air used to build their nests in the chin-whiskers iv giants," Maura was saying, in a low monotone, " there lived a funny people in a funny wee wood. There was the cow and the sow, and the ox and the fox, and the cat and the bat, and the wren and the hen, but one day there came a big famine and all died iv the hunger, all bar the cat and the bat and the wee red hen."

" Maw!" said a little voice from the blankets.

" What's wrong widye, now, Hughie Beag?"

"Don't like that story, maw. Tell me nuvver story."

"Ye get a sleep on ye and close yer eyes, Hughie Beag," said the mother, and went on with her tale.

"Well, when it was Spring the cat and the bat and the wee red hen went out to dig the ground for the corn. They had a wee crooked spade——"

"Oiney has a cookit spade, maw," said Hughie.

"True for ye," said the mother. "Well, they went out to the field and looked at one another. 'Who's goin' to dig the ground?' they asked. 'I'll not,' said the bat. 'I'll not,' said the cat. 'But I will,' said the wee red hen.''

"Me never heard cats or hens say anyfing," said Hughie from the blankets. The mother took no heed of the remark of the youngster but continued the story.

It told how the cat and the bat would do no work at all and the wee red hen did everything, dug the ground, planted the grains of corn, one for the mouse and one for the crow, one to rot and one to grow. When the corn grew up the hen cut it with a wee crooked scythe in the harvest season. Then when it was winnowed the hen carried the corn to the mill in her beak and it took her seven days to do the job. The miller was a wee hedgehog who had a wee mill, in a wee hole, in under the holly bush, beside the holy well. He milled the corn and the hen carried the meal back to her little home in the funny little wood.

Her neighbours never did a hand's turn to help her, for the cat was always washing its whiskers and the bat was always blind. But for all that, they were, both of them, ready to eat the bannock of bread, made from the meal, when it was baked by the wee red hen. The brown bannock was placed on the floor when ready and the hen went out to the well to get some water for the tea, and when she came back the bat and the cat had eaten the whole loaf.

"And that is the way iv the world, Hughie Beag," said Maura The Rosses, in the same low monotone. "Its the hardest workers who go most often without their bit iv bread. Isn't that the way iv the world, Hughie Beag?" she asked in a whisper. There was no answer. The little boy was asleep.

Doalty went into the big room, and began to undress. How grand and great this day had been, he thought to himself. How dull and useless London seemed compared to this. The hills, the meadows, the turf smoke, the girl calling the cows in from the braes, old Oiney. . . . "I love them all," said the young man. "To-morrow I'll go out to the bog and gather the turf. . . . I'm so happy. . . . 'It must be awful not to see the same people one day after another.' . . . It is, Oiney. Here everything stands still. The table, the stool by the fire, the holy water bottle. . . . All the same as when I left years ago. If I was away fifty years and came back there would be no change. The hills, the glen, the river, the thatched houses, the lamps getting lit in the evening, all, all the same. . . . And old Oiney. . . . What a fine story I could make about him. . . . But that would be a sin."

Doalty went into bed and was presently asleep.

CHAPTER V

OINEY LEAHY

If there's no woman in the house,
　　To milk the cow, or wash the delf,
The poor, old man, who's left his lone,
　　Is always talking to himself.
He makes the fire and rakes it out,
　　He leaves the ashes by the hob,
And all the time his heart is sore
　　For there's no woman on the job.
It's funny when a man gets old
　　And no one heeding what he'll say,
He'll sit beside the fire his lone
　　And speaking to himself all day.
　　　　　　　　　—A Peasant Song.

I

OINEY Leahy lived all alone, in his little house on the brae. He had married when he was a young man of twenty, and two sons were born to him. These went out into the world, and as he never heard from them afterwards, he did not know what had become of them. Probably both were now dead. His wife, a good upright woman, died when Oiney was fifty years of age. Since then he had lived by himself and worked hard, tilling his little bit of land.

Strange stories were going the rounds of the barony about him. His neighbours knew that he had been a Cath Breac in his young days, and gossip had it, that he had often stuck a red-hot dagger through the statue of the Virgin Mother. For this he was supposed to receive the sum of twelve pounds. The fact of the matter was that Oiney belonged to the Hibernian Bible Society, a body which had for its aim the propagation of the Gospels through the medium of the Irish language. Oiney became a teacher of the Gospels and as a teacher he received a certain wage from the Society. The Glenmornan peasantry were not loth in aiding and abetting Oiney to get as much money as possible from the "dirty straps that were trying to make everybody a Protestant," and the young of the glen came to the old man's school for examination once a year, when a mysterious Man In Black attended Oiney's house to ask questions on the Gospel. These scholars got a shilling apiece when the examination was over, and for each scholar who appeared Oiney got another shilling in addition to his regular pay. When the Man In Black left Oiney's, the master and his scholars had a night of feasting and drinking. Duty-free whisky was plentiful in Glenmornan then and the stills were always at work on the hills.

Being a Cath-Breac gave Oiney a bad reputation however, and the more educated people of the glen did not like it. Old Heel-Ball, of the

village of Greenanore, who had a son a priest and
a daughter a nun, disliked Oiney, not so much
owing to the fact that Oiney was a Cath-Breac,
but because he was one of the most clever makers
of potheen in the parish. The publican did not
like the potheen makers, for their illicit stills
interfered with his legitimate business. He com-
plained to the village priest, old Father Devaney.
The priest put a curse on Cath-Breacs from the
steps of the altar and Oiney gave up teaching the
Gospel from that day forward.

Oiney, handy man with his fists, was also very
strong, and as a young man he had no equal at
cudgel-play, wrestling or fighting, in the whole
barony. He also had a reputation as a poacher,
and no policeman had ever caught him at the job.
Once, after his marriage, a process-server came
to his house to serve him with a process for the
rent. The neighbours went into the house an
hour afterwards to see how Oiney was dealing with
the man and they found the process-server, sitting
in front of the fire, eating the process while Oiney
stood over him with an ash-plant in one hand and a
bottle of potheen in the other. The ash-plant
was needed to give the man an appetite; the
potheen would help to wash the meal down. So
Oiney explained to the neighbours.

His little house was not a very clean one. The
outer wall had once been whitewashed, but the
lime, having grown dim, now formed a back-
ground for various layers of dirt which had settled
on it. These layers, drying up, grouped themselves into strange and fantastic patterns. Near

the ground the wall was slimy black and plastered with dung, but further up towards the thatched roof, on which the corn was sprouting, the dirt lay in solitary little dots that stood out in strong relief against the white lime.

Inside, Oiney had a dresser for crocks and delf, a bed, with a straw mattress, a fireplace flush with the flagged floor, a fiddle, generally out of tune, a dog, always busy hunting fleas, and a cat with a taste for eggs. When alone and not busy, Oiney was either speaking to the animals, or playing the fiddle.

But the old man was seldom idle. He had a ready hand for any job. He could gueld young cattle, kill a pig, apply a leech to a sick neighbour, treat a cow for disease, build a creel, let ropes for the thatching of a haystack, cut scollops for a house, mediate between neighbours who had a quarrel about trespassing cattle or march boundaries, wash a corpse and dress it for burial. Oiney was a handy man and very willing to oblige a friend when called upon to do so. Despite the fact that he was read from the altar, the neighbours liked the old man.

II

Doalty Gallagher left his home the next morning and made his road over the braes to see Oiney Leahy. On his way he had to go through Breed Dermod's bit of land, and there he saw Sheila, the girl whom he had heard driving the cattle in from the hill on the previous evening. She was herding a cow on a green verge of grass which ran round the cornfield. Now and again when the cow reached out and plucked a mouthful of corn Sheila ran up with a switch and hit the animal's flanks with it. "Get away from here, ye wee divil ye," she would shout. "Can't ye behave yerself?" Suddenly the girl looked round and saw Doalty gazing at her. The blood rose to her cheeks, she laughed shyly and began beating the green corn with her switch. The cow which had just run off, came across the field to the corn again.

"Away with ye, ye rogue," the girl shouted, and ran after the cow.

Without speaking a word to her, Doalty went across to Oiney's house. He had only a very dim remembrance of Sheila, but he recollected that she was a girl going to school with two turf under her arm when he left Ireland seven years ago.

Oiney was in his home as Doalty went in. He found the old man feeding the dog and cat with milk from a hole in the earthen floor.

"Ah! it's a stranger ye are, me boyo," he said, looking up and seeing the young man. "It's a long while since ye've crossed this door-step now, isn't it?"

"A long while indeed, Oiney," said Doalty.

"Lie down widye, won't ye!" said the old man, catching the dog by the tail and drawing it away from the milk. " Let the wee cat have her's. It's wantin' it all, ye are, yerself."

He gripped the dog by the tail, raised it in air and let it hang head downwards.

" Not a yelp," he said, turning to Doalty. " That's what shows ye what it's like. A good dog and no mistake. " And the cat," he continued, "it's a wise wee divil. Washin' itself behind the ears it was this mornin'. That's a sign iv rain."

" How does it know that the rain is comin'?" Doalty enquired.

" Oh! he knows," said the old man. " An animal is as cute as anything. Look at the hare! He can see out iv the back iv his head. And he has two holes to his den, one at the back and one to the front. He never sleeps and he can always see what's comin' at the front or back and he always rests with his tail to the storm. And the weasel! If ye annoy him he'll spit poison into yer milk. I saw him do it. 'Twas in a bowl iv milk that I left outside the door that he spit. I would be a dead man this good day if it was not that old Micky Thady of Meenawarawor came over here to help me at a day's work; and Micky, he's dead now, God rest him! never did any harm to a weasel. So when the little animal saw him comin' it came up again and turned the bowl of milk over on the street. It did not want Micky to be killed because it's spite was only against me. Wasn't that a strange thing now?"

" It was indeed, Oiney," said Doalty.

" The animals have more sense than people

allow them," said Oiney. "There's the grana-
ghay (hedgehog), a cute fellow. He'll climb an
apple tree, stick his pins into an apple and carry
it down on his back. Then there's the cat that
can come home even if ye lose him at the other
end iv the barony, and the bee that can find his
nest in a ten-acre meadow. Then there's the
trout that ye put in the well to keep it clean and
eat the worms. I have two meself in the well
under the rock behind the house. When one of
these will die he'll turn, belly up, to let ye
know. They have more sense than a man has.
Don't ye think so, yerself?"

"I think so, Oiney," said Doalty. "Where
are these two trout?"

"I'll show them to ye in a minit," said Oiney,
"Just a minit. But wait now."

The old man went across to the bed which
stood in the corner of the room, groped under the
straw mattress and brought out a big bottle.

"Not a word, Doalty Gallagher!" he said,
placing his left eyelid flush on his cheek. "Just
have a drink iv this, and tell me what ye think iv
it." He poured part of the contents into a bowl
and handed it to the young man.

"Drink it," he said.

Doalty drank.

"It's good stuff, Oiney," he said. "Where
did it come from?"

"Not a word, me boyo, not a word," said the
old man, and he winked as he spoke. "Seven
years old, if a day, and duty free. But they never
make a drop like it in the hills now. It's potheen,

and ye'll go far before ye'll get a better sup. . .
Come out with me now and see the well."

The two men went out to the well, which was
hidden under a rock. Oiney bent over it, shoved
a twig under a stone, which lay at the bottom.
Two trout came out, circled round and round the
stone for a moment, then disappeared.

"They know me," said the old man proudly.
"They're not in the least afeeard!"

"And that's me wee pratee patch," he said,
getting to his feet and pointing at a plot of potatoes which lay behind the well.

"Oh, yes," said Doalty. "That was the little
field that it took you years to make. Had to
carry it up from the holm?"

"That's right," said the old man. There's
some blood and sweat in that wee patch, I'm tellin' ye. And then the foreign lady that came to
Glenmornan some years back!" The old man
shook his head, and a curl of superior disdain
showed at the corner of his lips.

"Who was she?" asked Doalty.

III

"Oh! a grand lady intirely," said Oiney.
"She came here, and her goin' to cure the decline.
'Ye are to be much cleaner than ye are,' she says,
'and ye're not to have yer duhals (dung-heaps)
so near yer houses.' She came up here one day
and pointed out where the duhal was to be.

' Well back there,' she says, and points to that wee
gubben iv pratees. ' Dig down there,' she says,
' and make a hole, and it will do well for a midden. It'll be a good distance away from the
house and then ye'll be free from disaise,' she
says. I looks at her. ' Lady,' I says, ' that gubben iv land was at one time nothin' but a bare
rock and I set about to improve it. I began to
carry up creels iv clay from the holm, and every
creel took me the best part iv an hour to carry. I
did it all barefut too and I'm tellin' ye I left some
blood and sweat on the wee caisin (path). It took
me hours and hours, and days and days, and
years and years to make a little patch iv land fit
to bear a crop. ' Now,' says I, ' if I make a duhal
in the middle iv that spadeland, it will take away
the ground-space iv four pratee ridges. Besides
that,' I says, ' it's not the place for a midden at
all, for the soft iv the byre will ceep out between
clay and stone and get lost. Also, how am I to
get the soft iv the byre up here?' I asks. ' I can't
carry it in a creel, and to take it in a bucket will
take the whole day, every day, at the job.'

" ' But what about yer health?' outs me lady.

" I looks at her. ' There's not much bad health
about here, lady,' I says. ' In this, a townland iv
twelve families, there are fourteen old people gettin' the old age pensions. And people have to
die anyway, when God sees fit to call them. If
a man has decline he'll go, it doesn't matter how
far away from the midden he is.' . . . But sorrow take the woman away, the foreigner! Her
people sucked the marrow out iv our bones in the

old days and now they come over here and teach
us how to keep in good health. . . . I'm gettin'
the old age pension," said the old man, looking
at Doalty, "and it's more than some iv them will
ever get, though they maybe haven't seen a midden in all their life."

Doalty Gallagher laughed, but it was not at
Oiney's remark.

"That drop of potheen you gave me, Oiney,
was very strong I think," he said. "It has gone
to my head."

"Iv course it has," said Oiney, and a good-
humoured twinkle stole into his eyes. "It's the
best stuff goin'."

"Where was it made?" Doalty asked.

"Ah!" said Oiney, winking and laughing.
"Where was it made? Ah, me boyo, that can't
be said! Ears and tongues are too long in Glenmornan nowadays, to say where anything is made.
Where was it made?" the old man repeated, with
a chuckle. "I don't know," he replied, as if
in answer to his own question. "And if I knew,
wild horses wouldn't draw it from me."

Doalty lit a cigarette.

"Will you have one, Oiney?" he asked.

"I'll keep to the pipe," said the old man, pulling his little black dudheen from his pocket and
putting it in his mouth. "There's nothin' like
a clay," he went on. "Look up there, in that
pratee field, and see the white rocks."

Doalty looked and saw a number of white
stones placed here and there amidst the potato
tops.

"What are they for, Oiney?" he asked.

" They're markin' me pipes," said the old man.
" I put the pipes under the ground there and let
them lie for a while.   Then I dig them up again,
and to smoke them then, it's somethin' not to be
forgot for many a season.   It's like havin' a
woman's arms round ye and ye behind a holly
bush and nobody about."

" So you like the women, Oiney?" Doalty enquired.

" Once on a time I would go far to spend a
night with one," said the old man.   " That was
when I was yer size, Doalty.   And yerself," he
enquired.   " Don't ye like to speak to them at
all?   There's many a nice girl in this glen now,
and mad after the boys.   There's Ellen Kelly
and Sheila Dermod, both iv them laughey cutties
and wild for the gasairs.   Did ye not see Sheila
this mornin' when ye were comin' across here?"

" I saw her, but I didn't speak to her," said
Doalty.

" Young Dennys The Drover is mad after her,"
said the old man.   " But she'll not have anything
to do with him, for she is so proud.   She'll have
to have a man shortly, for only herself and her
mother are workin' the farm and it's too much
for two women to do.   But Sheila!" he added.
" As nice a make iv a girl as ever put white feet
on green grass!"

" Her father died shortly after I went away,
didnt' he?" Doalty enquired.

" That was the time he died, God rest him,"

said Oiney. "He was a thran man, as busy as a pismire and hasty as a brier. . . . Speak a man fair he would not, for he was full iv malice, which is not a good thing, for malice kills itself with its own poison. He was always tellin' lies about everybody, and though the way to truth is but one and simple, he never found the way there. God forgive me for sayin' the hard thing about the dead, but old Shan Dermod was a hard man to put up with. And ye've never heard how he died I suppose? Well, this was how it was. He was lyin' on his death-bed and it was a harvest day, and the hay was lyin' on the holms, ready for the tramp-cocks. All at once he got up and goes to the door. 'Breed,' he says, turning to his wife, 'there's a big black cloud over Carna-ween, so it's better for yerself and Sheila to go out and gather the hay in at once.' He goes back to his bed, and just as he lay down, he heard the rain rattlin' on the window panes. Then he dies, God rest his soul! He'd have died happier if he went away an hour earlier. . . . I hope it won't be rainin' the morrow," said Oiney, as if the memory of Shan Dermod's death had turned his mind to the weather. "I'm goin' to get some iv me turf rikkled the morrow and young Dennys The Drover is comin' to give me a hand."

"I'll come too and help you if you'll let me," said Doalty.

"Come if ye can and I'll be glad iv yer help," said the old man. "I'll be needin' the new turf in a wee while, for I haven't many left over from last year now. So ye'll come, will ye Doalty?"

"Of course I'll come," said the young man.

"Well, a dhrop to sweeten our partin'," said Oiney. "Come in with me to the house and have a drink afore ye go back across the brae."

IV

Doalty went up to the hill with Oiney Leahy and Dennys The Drover the next morning. They had their breakfast at Oiney's house and Oiney brought out the black bottle again. The bottle was filled with potheen to the neck.

"So you've got some more," said Doalty.

"Ah! a wee drop," said the old man. "It was the fairies that gave it to me."

"If the polis sees them fairies it'll be a black day for them," said Dennys The Drover, lying back on his chair and lighting his pipe.

"Isn't it a good thing that the rain didn't come this mornin'," said the old man, as if to change the conversation. "I thought that it would be rain after the cat was washin' himself behind the ears yesterday."

Dennys The Drover winked at Doalty, as if to show that he thought old Oiney was a fool.

Doalty liked Dennys, liked his hearty laugh, his frank, open countenance and alert and supple figure. Dennys had a quiet look of assurance in his eyes and a proud bearing; in fact, he had the carriage of a young man who had a very high estimation of his own worth. When Doalty

asked him a question, he closed his eyes and pon-
dered for a minute before answering.   No doubt
he was endeavouring to discover why the young
man back from beyond the water was anxious to
know so many things.   But The Drover liked
Doalty.   "He doesn't dress up like a shop-boy
or a teaman," Dennys said to Oiney that morning
when he saw the young journalist coming across
the fields to the day's work.   "But ye never can
tell what the like of him is up to," he added, with
the air of a man who was not as yet certain of his
own judgment.

When speaking to Oiney, Dennys was never
at a loss for words.   He spoke rapidly and without the awkwardness which he showed when con-
versing with young Gallagher.

"We'll get up to the hill now, me boys," said
Oiney, when breakfast was at an end.   "It's a
long step from here to the top iv the hill.   So,
God with us! and we'll get away."

The journey from the house to the bog was a
long, trying one, and Doalty was glad when he
got there.   The turf lay all over the spread-field,
bundled together into little heaps.   A fair amount
of the turf, not yet ready for stacking, but dry
enough for a slow fire, had to be built in clamps.
A clamp is a narrow little heap in which the turf
could dry a little more before the stacking season
came round.   In the event of wet weather coming, the clamps would hold through the winter,
though the turf in them might not be the best
quality for the fire.   Still it was better to have
turf half-dry than to have none at all.

From the spread-field Doalty could see the whole of Glenmornan below him, the white road running through the meadows from the mountain down to the village of Greenanore, and the river, a sliver of silver, that sparkled brilliantly under the rays of the sun. A light haze rose from the meadows and cornfields, but Carnaween and Sliav-a-Tuagh stood aloof, clear cut against the blue sky, looking at one another. The little thatched houses rested snug and warm under the cliffs, the cows were out on the pastures, eating the green grass, and the young children were herding them. Sounds of laughter and singing could be heard, rising shrill and clear over the roar of the waters falling from the rocks. . . . Everything down there was in amity and repose. Never had Doalty beheld such peace. A great happiness, not unmixed with sorrow, filled his soul. Conscious life, at that moment, seemed a very meagre interval to him, a mere moment, giving so little time to enjoy the great glory and wonder of created things.

"That's Sheila Dermod that I'm seein' down there, isn't it?" asked Oiney, fixing his eyes on a green field in which a young barefooted girl with a shawl over her head was herding her cow.

"Sheila it is," said Dennys The Drover.

"A fine girl she is, isn't she?" asked the old man, fixing a pair of roguish eyes on the young man.

"Not so bad," said Dennys.

"She's wild after ye," said Oiney.

"He thinks that every girl in the parish is mad

after me," said Dennys, looking at Doalty and alluding to Oiney. "I do find them willing to
dance with me," he continued, not without a certain pride, "but that is nothin'. They must have
their bit iv fun, just the same as ourselves."

"I know the kind iv fun ye want," said Oiney
with a laugh, winking at Dennys, and poking him
on the chest with a miry thumb. "Ye're just
the same as I was when I was yer own age. And
the girls I used to have hangin' about me. Ah!"
—he shook his white head mournfully—" I don't
think they ever told the truth about their doin's
at confession after I spent a while with them," he
added.

"Why not?" asked Doalty with a laugh, which
could not hide his interest in the old man's avowal.

"Why? Ah! me boy, why?" said Oiney, drawing himself up and pulling his chin in. "If they
told everything that took place between themselves and me ye would see all the girls in Glenmornan goin' to Lough Derg on their two knees.
I was a funny bucko then. . . . And Dennys
The Drover! He's just the same now as I was
then. I was just the same cut iv a boy. And
ye do have yer bit iv fun with the girls, don't ye
now, Dennys?"

"I do iv course, Oiney," said the young man.
"I try and have any fun that's goin'."

"And what sort of fun is that?" Doalty asked,
looking at the young man.

Dennys closed his eyes for a moment, then
opened them again.

"Oh, just any kind iv fun at all," he said in a

non-committal voice, nodding his head as he spoke.

"That's the way to hide it," said Oiney in a bantering voice. "Yer fun can't bear the light iv the world on it, Dennys. I mind once, a good many years back it was, and it was at a hay-stack that old Shan Dermod—God rest him!—was building. I had a drop too much in me when night came on, and if my legs were stiddy my head was in a maze. That's always the way with me in the drink. Well, I got up to me feet in Shan Dermod's house when all the townland were there and I says,—I was told of what I said afterwards, for I didn't mind a word iv it meself,—I says, 'Hide it as much as ye like, but one person is as bad as another in this glen. There's a down-drop in every thatch,' says I, 'and I'm goin' to tell everything that bad report has about everybody in the townland. Aye,' says I, 'if the priest iv the parish was here himself I could tell him things about his own doin's that ud make him redden to the butts iv his ears. Now I'll tell ye,' I goes on, 'tell ye all yer sins that ye think are hidden, for ye are all sinners in the eyes iv God and man.' I was as wild as a March hare then, and there was no stoppin' me when I made up me mind to go on. Well, widye believe me! but not a soul stopped in the house to hear what I had to say barrin' Sheila Dermod, and she couldn't leave the house, for she was then a child in the cradle. But the others went out and I often wonder what it was that took Anna Gorth first out iv the house, and her holdin' up to be the holiest woman in the barony."

"But who told you about it afterwards, seein' that ye didn't remember it yerself?" asked Dennys The Drover.

"Who, guess, but Owen Briney, the sly cadger!" said Oiney. "He told me all about it the next mornin'. 'And ye went out too?' I says to him. 'I didn't want to stay in when all went out,' says Owen, and be the way he spoke ye would think that butter wouldn't melt in his mouth." 'So ye stayed outside iv the door,' says I, 'and listened to hear what I said?'

"'I did not, for I didn't want to hear any bad about meself,' he says, laughin' as if to put it by.

"'Ye would endure that,' says I, 'to hear bad about yer neighbours.' And if ye, yerself, Dennys The Drover, were there that night, ye'd have gone out too," said the old man.

"I'd have been one iv the first," said Dennys, laughing as if a compliment had been paid him.

v

"Well, we've done very well for the mornin'," said Oiney Leahy, as the three men sat down for their dinner at noon. A peat fire was ablaze in the heather and on it a can of tea was bubbling merrily. Oiney had brought up the food for dinner in the morning. The meal consisted of home-made bread, baked by Oiney, butter, eggs and tea.   There were three eggs for each man.   All were hungry and they left a very poor decency bite for the birds when the meal was at an end.

"Yes, ye've worked very well the two iv ye," said Oiney as he lay back in the heather and lit his pipe.   "And Doalty, boy, ye've made a good fist iv the work, which is more than some who come back from foreign parts can do.   Now the shop-boys, the scrape-the-pots, look at them! When they come back, it's a collar and tie they have on, all the time they are here.   Indeed, it's not much iv their time they spend here at all. Glenmornan is not quality enough for them and it's all the while down in Greenanore that they are 'tryin' to get on the skift with Heel-Ball's daughter or somebody like that.   But yerself, Doalty," said the old man, and a note of deep feeling crept into his voice, "yerself is just like one iv ourselves."

"And damn it, Oiney, why shouldn't I?" asked Doalty.   "Could I have any better company than you now?"

The old man fixed a startled look on Doalty. Oiney had spent so much of his time defending himself against censure, imaginary and otherwise, that he was utterly at a loss when confronted with words of praise.   Now, he sought security by changing the conversation.

"Ye can carry a good creel iv turf, and swing it on yer shoulder almost as good as Dennys himself," Oiney remarked.

"He's every bit as good as me," said Dennys.

"You are far and away too modest, Dennys," said Doalty. "If I had shoulders and arms like you I would become a boxer or a wrestler or something like that. You are wasting yourself here."

"Do ye think that I'd make much iv a wrestler?" asked Dennys, and a look of interest lit up his face. "I never tried it much, but when I did, I was fit to hold my own."

"Ha! ye limb iv evil, ye!" laughed Oiney. "Almost fit to hold yer own! Listen t'ye! The night the four polismen tried to collar ye, ye almost held yer own! Ye couldn't tell a Greenanore polisman from a bundle iv bandages for six weeks after ye had finished with them. Ah! no, ye're not able to hold yer own, Dennys The Drover, me boy," said Oiney, and an ironical smile showed in his eyes. He was amused at the modesty of Dennys The Drover.

"Can ye wrestle at all, Doalty?" asked the young man.

"I used to—a little—at one time," said Doalty.

"Will ye show me something about it—the way ye have of doin' it and that?"

"I don't mind, in the least," said Doalty, getting to his feet. "I'll show you some of the throws that I learned. . . . If I fling you over my shoulders you are not to be annoyed, mind. I'll show you how it's done afterwards, and you'll find that you'll be much better at it than me when you have a little practice."

The two young men, their sleeves thrust up, their breasts bare, faced one another on the heather.

"We'll try catch-as-catch-can at first," said Doalty. "It's the kind done away from here. . . . In this way. . . . You catch me wherever you can and try and throw me down to the heather. When you get my shoulders square with the ground it will be a fall in your favour. Now, try and grip me."

Oiney, sitting down and smoking, put the pipe in his pocket and fixed himself in a contemplative attitude. The one-time master cudgel-player of the Barony of Burrach was eager to see every move in the game. The first move mystified the old man. He saw Doalty and Dennys come to grips and the next instant Drover Dennys was lying flat on the ground.

"Well, how is it done?" asked the old man, getting to his feet and looking at Doalty with eyes that were full of new interest.

"I'll show you," said Doalty, whose face was flushed and red with excitement. "You put your arm round my neck, turn your back on me, shove your buttocks under my stomach and bend down as sharp as you can and pull me with you. Then you'll do the same to me as I've just done to Drover Dennys."

Oiney did as he was directed and bent down, pulling Doalty with him. In some mysterious manner the young man left his arm and when Oiney looked round he saw Doalty lying in the heather.

"Ye went over me back just like a feather," said the old man, in a pleased voice. "Ah! I wished I knew that trick in the old times. I would have let them see. . . ."

Two hours afterward Oiney looked at the sun, then at his own bleeding arm, at Dennys' torn shirt and Doalty's peat-covered face. Wrestling practice on the Glenmornan hills on a hot July day is a weary pastime.

"It's past three be the sun now, and it's time to be clampin' some more iv the turf," said Oiney, his voice betraying his reluctance to leave a sport into which he had entered with an enthusiasm as great as that of the younger men.

VI

Having taken a few sups from the bottle of potheen which Oiney Leahy handed him, Doalty bade the old man good-night and left for home, feeling weary after the hard day's work. Dennys The Drover remained behind and Doalty guessed that part of their conversation would be about him when he left them, and also about the fairies who, now and again, supplied potheen to the inhabitants of Glenmornan.

The sun was setting behind Sliav-a-Tuagh and behind that giant crest the sky was flushed and glowing. Red rays slanted down the braes of Glenmornan, colouring the waving grasses in the holms and gleaming on the ripples of the river Owenawadda. Overhead, in the clear, blue sky a flight of crows was winging its way homewards to the rookery in Meenawarawor. The sparrows were chirping in the bushes and a dog was barking somewhere on the hills where the young girls of Stranameera were bringing their cattle home for the milking. The streams were reeling over the rocks and Doalty could see the foam flying in air as the torrents bounded down to the river. The sound of the waterfalls made the young man's eyes and ears quiver as he heard it. His nostrils were filled with the scent of the glen, of the growing grass, the peatfires and the generous earth, and his heart was deeply moved by it all.

His life was mapped out clearly now, his future career defined. It almost seemed that whatever would come to him now, it would be the work of his own hands. He was living simply, a peasant, beset with the cares and worries of a peasant's life and he was very happy. He had forsaken everything that would make for fame and advancement in the field of life; he had put all that London held for him aside, and his mood of self-abnegation pleased him. "Will this happiness last?" he asked himself and answered in an audible voice, "Of course it will, for I am doing the right thing."

Deep in thoughts like these he strode across Owen Briney's land and entered a hazel clump on Breed Dermod's farm and it was here he met Sheila.

The girl was sitting on the ground under a hazel bush, her bare feet tucked up under her skirt, her head wrapped in a shawl, her hands busy knitting a stocking. As Doalty entered the glade, she sprang to her feet and fixed a pair of big, blue, startled eyes on the young man. He looked at her and felt that a thing more beautiful he had never seen or imagined in all his life. The young girl gazed at him, a blush mantling her cheeks; her mouth a little open, the hand which held the stocking hanging by her side. The bold sweep of her high eyebrows, the straight nose, the nostrils, dilating slightly, as if to the promptings of some hidden passion, the eyes glowing and darkening at the same moment, the splendid shoulders and full throat caused a strange yearning to rise in Doalty's heart. But he felt more courageous now than on the previous morning. When he saw her then, he could not summon confidence enough to enter into conversation with the girl. But now—Oiney Leahy's potheen was very strong and gave a man heart.

The girl was still looking at him, apparently debating as to whether she should run away or remain where she was.

" Good evening, Sheila Dermod," said Doalty Gallagher.

" Good evening," said the girl in a shy whisper, letting one of her knit-needles drop to the ground. Neither herself or Doalty saw it fall.

" You've got so big since I saw you last," said Doalty, " I hardly know you."

" And I hardly would know yerself," said Sheila Dermod, making this remark, because it was the only thing she could think of saying.

Doalty was at a loss for a moment.   He looked
diffidently at Sheila's bare feet as if to find a topic
for conversation.   Then he turned his glance to
her face again.   The girl was blushing crimson,
ashamed no doubt at being seen barefooted.

"You are such a beautiful girl," said Doalty
boldly, a little amazed at his own coolness.

"Am I?" asked Sheila in an almost indifferent
voice, which might mean that the compliment
would be gratefully received from a man more to
her liking.   She laughed and her nose puckered
up slightly.

"Ye've been drinkin' some of Oiney Leahy's
potheen I suppose," she added.

"No, I've not," Doalty replied, colouring a
little.

"Oiney would not be pleased if ye went out iv
his house without a drink," said Sheila, as if she
knew that Doalty was not telling her the truth.

"What have you been doing here?" Doalty
enquired.   "Knitting your stocking?"

"That's what I was doin'," said the girl, pulling her shawl tighter about her shoulders and
turning half round as if with the intention of going into her home.

"Sheila," said Doalty in a low voice and
coughed awkwardly as he spoke.

"What is it?" she enquired, turning round and
gazing, as it seemed to him, over his shoulder at
the setting sun which was reflected in little points
of fire in her eyes.   Her beautiful hair straggled
out in little curls from under her shawl; one hand

held the stocking and the fingers of the other were fumbling with her petticoat.

"What is it that ye're goin' to say to me?" asked Sheila again, when she had looked in silence at Doalty for a moment.

"Nothing, only that you are very beautiful," said Doalty, hardly recognising his own voice.

"Then ye must be drunk," said the girl, with a laugh, and she ran away through the hazel bushes, leaving the young man staring after her. In a moment she was out of sight, but presently she stuck her head through the branches again, fixed a mischievous glance at Doalty and a confused smile showed on her face.

"Good-night, Doalty Gallagher," she called in a loud whisper, peeping slyly out from under her eyelids.

"Good-night, Sheila Dermod," Doalty replied, and Sheila disappeared.

"She thinks that I am drunk," he repeated to himself, as he bent down and lifted a shiny needle from the ground. Then he made his way homewards, pondering over the girl's remarks.

"Maybe I am drunk," he said with an air of decision after a while. "I wouldn't behave as I've done if I was sober. . . . and Drover Dennys is going to marry her one of these days," he mused as he was entering his mother's house. "I hope he does, for she is a good girl and he couldn't do better. . . . But such a throat and chin and such eyes. . . . That's the reason. . . . I'm drunk."

He kept continually repeating this latter remark

during the evening, repeating it with the peculiar insistence of a man who wishes to believe it.

VII

The days passed quietly for Doalty Gallagher and he felt very happy and contented in Glenmornan. London, its rush, worry and excitement, seemed to belong to an age beyond recall; when people whom he had known, Lady Ronan, George and Myra recurred in Doalty's memory, they seemed to be shapeless impressions of a troubled dream. Soon these impressions would be dulled beyond restoring.

He got out of bed in the early morning, sprinted down to the river Owenawadda, and plunged in for a dip. Now and then Drover Dennys accompanied him and both went into the stream together. By the time Doalty got back to his house, his breakfast was laid out and all the family was afoot, Maura The Rosses and Norah busy with the housework, Teague at work in the fields, Hughie Beag playing with the puppy, his favourite pastime, and Kitty getting ready to go to the convent school of Greenanore. Amongst other branches of education, the young girl was learning cookery, and it was said that she was one of the most skilful cooks at the school and she could make dishes fit for the table of a queen. But she never made those dishes at home because suitable ingredients could not be purchased in the village. Even if they could be obtained, there was not an oven in the whole glen. . . .

Oiney Leahy heard of the young girl's tuition in the culinary art, and what he said, when he heard it, was common gossip in Glenmornan for many weeks.

"I don't know what the learnin' is comin' to," said Oiney. "The young girsas go down to Greenanore and they learn to make the grandest meals in the world, and when they come back home at night they have to feed on scaddan and sgiddins. If they were learned to cook just like their mothers, it would be all right; but here they go down to the town and learn how to cook what God doesn't send us. It's a sin and a shame the kind iv learnin' that's in it nowadays. . . . The other day I went over to Phelim Biddy Wor to get the len iv a garra madagh* and Phelim's wee gasair was sittin' on the stool be the fire and his head sunk in a book. 'What is it that ye're readin', Gasair Phelim?' I put to him.

"'I'm readin' about the many miles that this world is away from the sun,' he tells me.

"'And how many will it be now?' I asks him.

"'So and so,' he answers me.

"'And how many miles is it from the head-end iv the Barony iv Burrach to the butt end iv the Rosses?' I asks him.

"'Then I don't know, Oiney Leahy,' he says.

"So I don't know what kind iv learnin' it is

* A creel-rest.

that's comin' to the people now," said Oiney. "They learn how to cook things that they never see and to measure distances that are no good to man or beast. The lady that came to make me move the duhal away from the front iv me house must have learnin' just the same as that. Destroyin' me bit iv a farm just to cure me from the decline that I never had. I would, if it was left to me, rather die with the decline than with starvation. . . ."

During the day Doalty Gallagher used to see the old man at his work, delving the jealous earth, his old back crooked over his spade, his face streaming with sweat and his mind full of vague thoughts, reveries and dreams of old times. The old man worked slowly, silently and without any apparent waste of effort. But with a judicious expenditure of strength and a steadiness that brooked no distraction, old Oiney on the spade-land, was a worker second to none in Glenmornan.

Oiney spoke about his house one day when Doalty Gallagher went across to see him.

"It's not much to look at now, is it, Doalty?" he asked. "But one time ye could travel far before ye could set two eyes on a neater house," he continued. "Ah! Doalty, if ye saw it when I took in me wife, God rest her, to it. It was then as clean as the white stone at the bottom iv a spring well, with a floor hand-smooth, and not a trace iv dirt on it, with thatch that threw the water off, just like the wing iv a wild-duck, and walls that were as white as the shell iv an egg. It would do a man's heart good to look on it.

"And the way the two iv us were gettin' on and puttin' a bit by. There was milk and to spare from the cows in the byre, and the corn was sproutin' on the brae-face, and Breed used to do good work at the spinnin' iv the wool. That was enough to make any man glad, for what did they say of old? What, but this :—Three slender things support the world best : the thin blade iv corn on the holm, the thin stream iv milk into the pail and the thin thread runnin' through the fingers iv a woman. And the cloth that used to be made then, Doalty! It sat well on man and woman; elegant and comfortable it was and it was fit to wear out the years of a hearty life. . . . But now, look at the times that's in it! . . .

"But maybe things will change a bit some day," he added, after a short silence. "Maybe I'll be well-to-do yet. For ye know, Doalty, that I can work as well as any man in the glen yet and I can go up and down that hill for turf, just as easy as I was able to do it thirty years ago when I was a youngster. . . . And ye did see me at the rassle the other day on the bog. I was fit to get me hand in at it very quick and I made a good fist iv it afore we stopped, didn't I now?"

"You did indeed, Oiney," Doalty replied.

"Iv course I did," said the old man with a complacent smile. "If I practice it a bit, I'll be able in another couple iv years to make some iv the young ones sit up."

"Or fall down, Oiney," said Doalty with a laugh.

"That's it," said Oiney. "Fall down

They'll go down if I get me arms roun' them. Ye know who I would like to show some iv the tips to."

"Owen Briney," said Doalty, who was by this time aware that there was no love lost between the cattle dealer and Oiney Leahy.

"Yes, Owen Briney, since ye say so," said Oiney, in a voice which tried to suggest that he was thinking, not of Owen, but of some other person. "Yes, I would like to put Owen Briney flat on his back, the dirty toe-rag."

VIII

The fresh life of the glen and mountain was a tonic to young Doalty Gallagher. He lived content and was happy. After breakfast he went out to his work on the fields or hills, gathered in the turf and helped to build them in big stacks on the high hillocks of the spread-fields. His brother Teague worked with him and this youngster was a bit surprised at Doalty's readiness to take part in the labour of the farm. Maura The Rosses was a little bit annoyed.

"I don't know why Doalty just goes about the same as if he had never been away from here," she said once. "He goes out and works, just as if he had only been away at the harvest in Scotland or England. The Greenanore people (Maura meant the Greenanore people of the

Quigley class) will think he has been nothin' at all, when he was abroad in other parts."

But she never showed her annoyance to Doalty, though one day she asked him why he never put a white collar round his neck.

" I'm more comfortable without a collar," said Doalty.

But Maura, who did not like seeing her son descend to the ordinary occupations of the farm, was herself a great worker and she never had an idle moment. One job followed fast on the heels of another, and Doalty, who often watched her toil, marvelled at her energy. He often saw her go out to the well for a bucket of water to make the stirabout. On her way out she would stop for a moment to lift a stray peat or a thorn from the street. On the way back she would place her bucket on the ground, tie a stray strapper in the byre, or chase the pigs or ducks into their croaghs. On bringing the water in, she would place it in the pot that hung by a crook over the fire, sit down and knit a sock while she waited for the water to boil. Not a moment was lost, and even at night, when she knelt to say her prayers, she would place her knitting on the chair near her, so that no time would be lost in resuming her work when she got up from her knees. Maura The Rosses had never had a day's illness in her life.

Doalty went to mass every Sunday. On the first occasion he knelt when all the others knelt, but it was rumoured in the barony afterwards that he failed to bless himself when others did so. On the second Sunday he did not kneel during the whole service and this was noticed by the congregation.

"It's the faith that he has lost abroad," they said, and shook their heads. "It's bad for the young to leave their own country."

The priest of the parish was an old fellow named Devaney, a man belonging to a bad type, the peasant-born extortionist. Doalty knew him of old, when a barefooted boy at the national school. He feared him then, now he detested him. Devaney was a gombeen priest, who played on the fears and dreads of the poor and drained the needy of their last penny. For collecting stipends, offerings and plate-money, Devaney had no equal. Nothing escaped him and it was said by the people of the parish that the priest could make a corpse blush in its coffin if the offerings were small.

Devaney had built himself a large residence near the village, making the peasantry pay the money for the building, taxing them to the extent of eight pounds per family. In addition to this the men folk had to go and work, wage free, at the building of the house, the quarrying and carting of stone, the draining of the garden and the upkeep of paths leading to the residence.

One day Maura The Rosses spoke to her son. The woman had been down at the village market selling a butt of butter, and as she got a good price for it she was in a high humour. It was in the evening after her return that she spoke.

"On me way back I met the priest," she said,

and a pleased look appeared on her face. "He just came up to me and spoke so kindly."

"And why not?" Doalty asked with bitterness in his voice. "Are you not ten times better than he is?"

"Better than the holy priest?" asked Maura in a shocked voice. "To think iv ye sayin' that, Doalty!"

"But surely, mother, you don't think that he is a more worthy creature than old Oiney, for example."

"Oiney's an old plaisham, and ye know that yerself, Doalty," said Maura The Rosses. "Why ye mention him in the same voice with the priest I don't know. And he's comin' up to see ye too."

"Devaney?" Doalty asked.

"Father Devaney is comin' up to see ye," said the mother.

"But I haven't asked him."

"I don't know what's come over ye at all, to speak in that way, Doalty," said the woman. "It's not to every house that he would come, even if he was asked."

Doalty grew angry and tried to prove to his mother that the priest was a most unworthy man, that he was a tyrant and a rogue. But his words seemed to make no impression on his mother. She listened, her hands resting on her lap, but Doalty felt that his words redounded from her as from a stone wall. She heard them, but she had her own convictions which nothing could shake or drive away.

"If he comes here to see me without being invited I'll pitch him into the midden," Doalty cried.

"And for doin' that the house and yerself will never have any luck," said Maura The Rosses.

"And you believe that?" Doalty enquired.

"Nobody with any faith would doubt it," said Maura The Rosses in a dogmatic tone. "Nobody in the whole wide world."

Doalty was a puzzle to the neighbours. That he did not behave like a shop-boy pleased them at first, but after a while they became a little suspicious. The peasantry are always suspicious of that which they do not understand. That a young fellow, with money and learning, behaved as Doalty behaved was something they could not understand. "He's curious," they said, when speaking amongst themselves, a world of meaning in their voices. "Well, if he is, he must have taken it from his mother's ones, for there's no understanding the Rosses people," they added. Even Dennys The Drover did not know what to make of Doalty. One day he said to him :

"Are ye never for leavin' here again, Doalty?"

"I'm not, if I can help it," said Doalty. "I'm better here than anywhere else."

"Well if ye look at it in that way!" said Dennys The Drover, but down in his heart he thought that Doalty had left London because he had got into trouble there.

The two young men often went out fishing together. They would sit by the river throwing their flies on the stream. Now and again, when they saw the water-keeper coming along the bank, Dennys would turn to Doalty and say, "We'll run in and hide in the wood," alluding to one of the spinneys near the banks. Then the two of them would hide there until the water-keeper had gone out of sight. When danger was past they would come out again and resume their fishing.

One day Doalty saw the water-keeper coming down the glen.

"We'll get into the wood," he said, turning to his friend.

"What for?" Dennys enquired.

"I see the water-keeper coming," said Doalty.

"Let him come then," Dennys replied, a gleam of anger lighting up his eyes. "To think that we cannot get fishin' under our own houses! Didn't God make the water for us to fish in, just as much, and more, than for them that comes from abroad!"

He sat there with Doalty until the water-keeper, who had observed them, came down to the bank of the river.

"Have you permission to fish here?" asked the water-keeper, looking at the two men.

"What the hell is that to ye?" asked Dennys The Drover, and gripping hold of the man he flung him with one mighty heave into the river. Then he pulled him out.

When he stood on the bank, wet and shivering, Dennys looked at him.

"Hook it!" he yelled, catching the man by the

collar of the coat and shaking him. "Get about yer business, and if ye say anything about this I'll kill ye, be God I will!"

The water-keeper went away and Dennys heard no more about the matter.

Next time the water-keeper came along the glen road both men hid in the wood.

"There's some things that can be done once," said Dennys The Drover. "But there's danger in doing them too often."

The two young men often wrestled with one another and Dennys, who was much stronger physically than Doalty, was making great progress in the art. He was willing to attempt anything and when he scored a point, his face would light up with delight and he would say, "I'm gettin' me hand in, Doalty. I'll soon be almost as good as yerself."

Now and again Doalty met Sheila Dermod and Eileen Kelly going down the road to the village. The two girls were great chums and always went to mass and market together. Eileen was a winning slip of a girl, charming but capricious, good-hearted but coquettish, fond of her parents but fonder of the boys. She would be a good match for some young man when her parents died, for she was the only child and the farm coming to her was a good one, with grass for three cows and twenty sheep. She lived next door, but one, to Sheila Dermod, and Owen Briney's land divided the two farms. If Owen was a younger man he might have married one of the girls, but as it was,

he was no match for either of them.   Owen was
a stingy, near-going creature, one of those who
asks a pipe of tobacco in return for a light.   Glenmornan girls were loth to have their knitting spoilt,
as they say, by a man like Owen Briney.   Sheila
or Eileen never spoke to Owen.   " As if we would
give him the nose," they often said   " We
wouldn't be seen on the same side of the road with
him."

Sheila Dermod was of a very retiring disposi-
tion, but despite that everyone was aware that she
was very proud and conscious of her own beauty.
Eileen' Kelly was good looking, but whenever
Doalty Gallagher met the two together and his
eyes rested on Sheila, he would forget all about
her friend.   Sheila, gracefully built, hardly
seemed to have reached her full development yet.
Meeting Doalty on the roadway, her big, blue eyes
would look at him direct and bold for a moment,
then her eyelids would faintly droop and the expression on her face would become very deep and
tender.   On these occasions a strange thrill of
excitement would pass through Doalty's whole
body; his heart, stirred by a vague, endless antici-
pation, would fill with a happiness which he could
neither analyze or explain.

On Sundays Sheila wore a hat when going to
the village, but on week-days she wore a shawl.
Doalty thought that she looked better in the latter
garb, but he never noticed what apparel became
Eileen Kelly best.

" Well, I hope that she gets married to Dennys

The Drover," he often remarked. " The two are made for one another. And he's such a fine fellow. . . . I've never met a man whom I liked so much."

CHAPTER VI

THE FAIR OF GREENANORE

At night when the old ones
  Have finished their jobs,
And trading is over,
  They sit by their hobs,
Counting their money,
  For that is their way,
When they're back from the fair
  At the shut of the day.

At night, when the young ones
  Are doing a lot
Of kissing and courting,
  And paying their shot;
They spend all their money,
  For that is their way,
When they're down in the fair
  At the shut of the day.

—The Fair.

I

IT was early morning of Lammas Day, the day
on which the fair of Greenanore was held,
and Doalty Gallagher stood on the glen road,
where it ran through Stranameera, watching
the people go by on their way to the village.   The

road was black with men and women, cattle and
carts, with mountainy men, straggling by, driving
their sheep and cows, accompanied by barefooted
women, carrying their big hanks of yarn on their
backs and their boots slung over their shoulders.
These women would put their boots on, when they
came near the village, for though their own per-
sonal comforts vetoed boots, convention and
mountainy pride demanded that they should be
worn at the fair. The mountainy people had been
on the road all night, for the journey from the
head-end of the barony to the village of Greenanore was a distance of twelve or fourteen miles.

Every townland in the parish was passing by;
Croagh An-Airagead and Croagh Gorm, with their
carts of wool and droves of sheep; Knock Letter-
ha and Greenans, with their helfted cows from the
pastures and their butter from the churning;
Cornagrilla, a townland of looms, with its webs of
homespun heaped on the weavers' backs, and
Granaroodagh, the townland of sally bushes, with
its bundles of home-made creels and baskets.
Parties of drovers, dark-skinned men, with vigor-
ous eyes, who swore with every breath and pre-
faced every remark they made, by spitting through
their teeth, hurried along, driving their wild bullocks before them. In the midst of the crowd
came a cart, heaped with butts of butter, the results
of a month's churning in the upper arm of the glen.
On one of the white butts sat the driver, his head
bent forward and a short black clay pipe in his
mouth. Behind him sat two women, their shawls
wrapped tightly round their heads, one, sitting

very still, her eyes fixed on the ground and her thoughts on the price which she would get for her butt of butter, the other woman, telling her beads, praying, no doubt, for a good market.

Immediately behind, came an old, bearded man, in a white, woollen wrapper, leading a little lame nag, which was drawing a cart of apples. Whenever the wheel of the cart creaked as it ran in a rut, the old withered man, who was chewing a plug of black tobacco, turned to the nag, shouted, "Whoa eep, now! ye limb iv the divil, ye!" and spat on the dusty road.

"It's a nice morning," said Doalty.

"'Tis, thank God," said the man. Then the wheel creaked. "Whoa eep now, ye limb iv the divil, ye!" said the old fellow, spitting in the dust and continuing his journey.

Following the apple cart came Dennys The Drover, driving a dozen short-horned bullocks, a cigarette between his lips, an ash-plant in his hand, and his cap thrust well back from his forehead. From his swinging gait and the careless look on his bold, open face it was easily seen that he was in a high, good humour.

"Good mornin' to ye, Doalty!" he called in a ringing voice and his face lit up with a smile. "Are ye ready to come in with me now?"

"I'm ready," said Doalty. On the preceding day the two young fellows had arranged to go to the fair together.

"There'll be some fun the day, I'm tellin' ye," said Dennys, catching his ash-plant by knob and ferule with both hands and curling it round his shoulders.

"I hope so."

"And the girls that'll be there!" said Drover Dennys, giving one of the bullocks, which stopped to eat some grass from the roadside, a skelp on the rump with his ash-plant. "I have two or three in me mind for the night, so I'll try and get rid iv all the stock the day, for I don't want to take them home again and miss the fun. . . . Ah! the girls that'll be there!" he repeated with a laugh. "No man need go empty the night."

"But *you* can have any girl that you want," said Doalty. By this he really meant that Dennys could have Sheila Dermod if he so desired.

"Sometimes I'm in luck's way," said Dennys carelessly. "But then, ye never know what to make iv them. But if yerself comes with me the night we'll be sure to get two. I'll see that ye don't go without a girsa."

He spoke in an off-hand manner, as if he had control of the whole female element at the fair of Greenanore; then he hit a bullock near him with his ash-plant and the two young men made their way together to the fair.

Dennys had a worthy reputation amongst the cattle dealers. He never exaggerated the number of brilliant bargains which he had made, a rare trait in a drover. But despite his successes, things did not prosper with him and hard work was not at all to his liking. "What he makes in the fair he loses in the field," the neighbours said, when speaking of him, and this was in a great

measure true.   His mother and sister did most
of the work of the little farm, carried in the peat
from the hills and planted the potatoes and corn.
Bending over a spade was not to the liking of
Drover Dennys.   But he was very generous and
straightforward.   He haggled over shillings and
pence in a bargain, of course, but that is as it
should be.   That a drover must never have the
worst of a bargain is a tradition, which men, who
deal in cattle, must live up to.   But after a bargain was concluded, Drover Dennys was ready to
spend the money that he made, not on himself, but
on his boy and girl friends.   Even when he had
not a penny to spend, he was still popular, and
this is good testimony to the worth of a man.

II

The market place was crowded when the two
young men got there.   A great amount of hand-
shaking, shouting and bargaining was going on.
Owen Briney was there and Doalty stopped for a
moment to watch him bargaining for a cow, with
an old barefooted woman whose thin weasened
face was almost hidden in a gosling-grey handkerchief.   The woman was Grania Coolin of Stranameera, next door neighbour but two to Maura The
Rosses.   But, although living so near Doalty's
home, she had never come to see him since his return.   The reason for the old woman's unfriendly
attitude was this.

When Doalty was a little boy of eight, Grania had a white duck which used to lay out. At night Grania would try this duck and find that it had an egg. Putting the duck under a creel, she would wait for it to lay   But the duck was generally obstinate and refused to part with its egg when in confinement. Morning and noon would pass, but still no egg would be seen. By that time Grania's husband (he died one day with a great pain in his side) required the creel to carry in turf from the hill. Then the duck had to be released, but Grania, before allowing the bird its freedom, used to tie a string to its leg, and for the rest of that afternoon she would follow the string through the meadows and woods near the house. But for all that, she never could find the white duck's nest. She found out something else, however, and this cleared up the mystery of the duck in her eyes. She discovered Doalty Gallagher fishing for gillets* in the Owenawadda, and his fishing line was made from the strings which Grania had tied to the leg of the white duck. Afterwards she never spoke a civil word to Doalty Gallagher and never broke discourse with his people until he left the country.

Doalty looked at Grania, then turned his eyes to Owen Briney. Owen was an ungainly man of medium height, with yellow wrinkled skin, furtive, cunning eyes, high cheekbones and an exceptionally heavy jaw, which, when he smiled, he drew in, until it rested on his Adam's apple. He had a

* Minnows.

discreet forehead that hid most of itself under his
hair, leaving hardly the breadth of a forefinger ex-
posed.   Owen did a little bit of cattle jobbing
and it was said that nobody had ever got the better
of him in a deal.   Although not having much land
to speak of, it was common talk that he had money
and to spare.   His farm, all hill, lay between
Breed Dermod's land and Kelly's land.   Joined
to either of those farms it would make a place
worth talking about. . . . However, no young
girl would be expected to marry a man like Owen
Briney. . . . So the Stranameera people said
when their conversation turned on march ditches.
Owen had a nickname, for very few people in
Glenmornan are without nicknames.   His was
" Yellow Behind The Lugs."

" Well, I'll tell ye what I'll do," Owen Briney
was saying to Grania Coolin when Doalty came
up.   " I'll give ye five pounds, good money, every
penny iv it, for the baste.   And the luck's-money
a half-crown."

" Seven pounds is what I want," said the old
woman, pressing the handkerchief back from her
wrinkled forehead with thin gnarled fingers.

" Seven pounds!" said Owen Briney, placing
emphasis on the word "pounds."   He drew his
chin in and rested his tobacco-stained teeth on his
lower lip.   " Seven pounds!" he repeated, em-
phasising " seven " this time and fixing a look of
pity and commiseration on the woman.

" That's me price," said Grania Coolin.

" Well, I'll tell ye what I'll do," said Owen,
pressing his elbow against his hip and unclosing

his fist.   He spread out his fingers to their full extent and gazed at the leaf of his hand, as if he hoped to find something there.   " I'll give ye five pound, half-a-crown, and with the luck's-money that'll lave ye five pound clear to yer own pocket.   And it's much more than the baste is worth.

" I'll not sell, a penny less than seven pounds," said the woman.

" Ye'll not see the colour iv that money this good day," said Owen in a gruff voice.

" The market's young as yet," said Grania Coolin.

" Well, seven pounds is more than I'll give for that ranny," said Owen, walking away. He would come back presently and start the bargaining over again.

Doalty looked at the old woman, at her bowed head and her hacked feet that were covered with the dust and dung of the market place. One of her heels was bleeding, showing that she had stepped either on a thorn or a piece of glass. And she was very poor. If she got six pounds for the old cow she would be very happy. She did not really expect to make more than five-pounds-ten, and probably, before the fair came to an end, she would sell the animal for the money that Owen Briney had already offered her.

Doalty, seized with a desire to regain the good graces of Grania, went across to her. He had, in fact, forgotten all about Grania's antipathy towards him, until one day, shortly after his return, he was reminded of it by Maura The Rosses.

"How much are you wanting for the cow, Grania?" he enquired as he stood by the woman.

Grania looked at him.

"It's Doalty Gallagher I'm seein', isn't it?" she asked, and dropping the switch which she carried, she caught his hand with her own two. "Ah! it's glad I am to see ye, Doalty," she said, with warmth in her voice. "I heard tell that ye were at home and I was just goin' over to see ye every day, but one thing had to be done one day and then another another day, and I couldn't get away from me own place at all. . . . And ye're wantin' to buy the cow?" she asked.

"I am, Grania Coolin,"' said Doalty. What's the price of it?"

"Seven pounds," said the old woman.

"All right, I'll give you that," said Doalty.

The old woman looked at Doalty; a startled and suspicious expression showed in her eyes. To find a man agreeing so readily to her price surprised her. No doubt he was trying to make a fool of her.

"Money down?" she enquired.

"I'll give it now."

"And the luck's-money?"

"You needn't trouble about that," said Doalty.

"Ye don't want any luck's-money?" she asked in a dubious voice.

"No, you needn't trouble about that," Doalty assured her, with an awkward laugh, as if trying to placate the old woman. He paid her the money and sent the cow up to Stranameera with a young bare-legged boy, a servant in Eileen Kelly's house, who was going back to his work on the farm.

Doalty sauntered round the market and came across Dennys The Drover speaking to Oiney Leahy. Dennys, whose stock was good, had got rid of all the bullocks and his pockets were bulging with money. Oiney, who had brought in an old white-backed cow to sell, was not so successful. " It's not a market at all, this," he said to Doalty. " Racharies iv cattle and nobody to look at them. And no wonder, for if ye hefted some iv the cows that's here for a moon, ye'd be bate to give them a showy elder.* I wish," he added, with a helpless gesture of his shoulders, " that I could get rid iv this bit iv a baste iv mine. If it was off me hands I could get down the street to see the girls."

" Are ye comin' down the street with me ?" asked Dennys, turning to Doalty. " We'll see what's goin' on there. I'll see ye after a while when ye come down yerself, Oiney," he said, turning to the old man. " Ye'll find me in Heel-Ball's."

" I'll be lookin' for ye there, then, Dennys, me boy," said Oiney. " But I don't want ye to be runnin' away with the girsas and lavin' me when I see ye," he added.

" No fear iv me doin' that," said Dennys The Drover. " I'm not goin' to have anything to do with them this night. I'm goin' to be a good boy."

" Well, be careful anyway, and ye'll be all right," said Oiney Leahy.

*Udder.

III

Although the Glenmornan girls had not yet come in, there was a big crowd of people in the village, and great business was being done. The white butts of butter stood in rows on the pavements, and beside them were the big hanks of mountainy yarn which Doalty had seen coming down the road that morning. The old appleseller, with the woollen wrapper, had his standing laid out and the golden apples were gleaming amidst the brown straw of the cart in which they were lying. Near the apple cart was a secondhand clothier, canting clothes from a van on which he stood, knee-deep in a huddle of old coats, trousers, blouses and skirts. He was shouting at the top of his voice and giving vent to a sharp whistle now and again. His shirt sleeves were thrust up to his shoulders, and his face, puffed and florid, was beaded with sweat.

" A snug wee frock for Paddy Beag to go to school in," he shouted, holding a boy's coat out in front of him. " He'll be as snug as a bug in a rug in this ! Phew ! A pair of breeches with it, too, and the whole lot goin' for six shillin's—five shillin's—four shillin's—three and six. Nobody wants them ! Did ye not sell the wee brannat cows the day ? What are ye goin' to do with Paddy Beag to-morrow then ? Phew ! If ye want him to go to school I suppose ye'll have to blacken his backside and send him out bare-naked.

Phew! I never had any schoolin', but I would, if a bargain like this was goin' when I was young. I never was at school, but I met the scholars. Buy up! Buy up! and we'll not leave a rag for the Rosses! Ah! what have we here now? Phew! A dress for wee Biddy and in the latest fashion. Put her in this and the Yankees won't be able to hold a candle to her when they come home. . . . Seven and six for the wee dress for wee Biddy— six and six—five and six—five. I'll make a present iv it to ye for four shillin's! Who'll make an offer? Nobody? Phew! Poor, unhappy Ireland!"

Further along was a cart on which stood a sallow man, nimble of finger and wrist, selling watches. A watch cost a pound and with each watch a leather purse was presented, gratis, to the buyer. The man made the pretence of filling the purse with silver before giving it to purchasers of a watch.

"A pound for this watch and cheap at the money," he said, piling the silver into a purse. "A pound for a watch, and worth double the money. And you get the purse with it. I don't promise a fortune in the purse," he said, and his voice was free from deceit. "But there'll be something in it. A little certainly, and a lot maybe. It's a pastime of mine, this, and—who says a pound, a pound for the watch and I'll fling the purse, and all that's in the purse, into the bargain."

Doalty and Dennys were watching the man when Oiney Leahy came up.

"Did you sell the cow?" asked Doalty.

" I got red iv it," said Oiney. "At a good price too considerin' the nature iv the market."

IV

Oiney looked at the gentleman on the cart, then he turned to Doalty.

" I've seen the like iv him afore and here in this very town too," said the old man, pointing his thumb towards the cart. " He was just doin' the same things, legerdemain, thimble-riggin', black magic, Harry Stattle, or whatever ye like to call it. Anyway, he got his tricks from the divil and we didn't know that, at that time.

" He came here—I mind the day well, for it was a harvest fair in the year iv the big floods— and I brought in three young animals to the market. Sold them all, and sold them well, too, for between me and yourself, Doalty, and before Dennys The Drover, who can bear me out, no man ever got the better iv me in a bargain. It happened in the evenin', after we had eaten a bit and had a drink, or two, or three, for the old times were the times for drinkin'. We used to have one to wet our whistle when makin' a bargain, one when the bargain was done, and one to wash that one down, and another one when we got into the nearest aisy, then another for the luck's-money, and would ye believe it, the spendin' iv the luck's-money never went beyond the counter where it was handed over. Well, as I was sayin', one iv

these legerdemain fellows came into the town, and
he gets up on a cart, almost like a priest—God forgive me for saying it—at the altar on a Sunday,
and he had a little bag with him and lots iv wares,
and as he ups, upon that cart, he says : ' I am not
here to sell anything.'   Then he takes out a hand-
ful iv pocket-knives, lead pencils, pens and watch-
chains, and hundreds iv other things, and he
throws them right down into the middle iv us, and
ye should have seen the scramblin' !

"I got only a watch-chain and me not havin' a
watch.   But I also got a black eye from some man
—from the Rosses he came—who said he had
more right to the watch-chain than I had.

"Well, so far, so good.   We were in a maze,
seein' a man like that, that was throwin' things
away !   But one wonder followed another.   He
takes out a purse and he puts a watch into it, and
then he puts money into it, throwin' it in as hard as
he could wallop—five-shilling pieces, sovereigns,
silver and gold.   So he said, ' I'll sell everything
in this purse for one pound.   There are only a
few purses, and I am goin' to have a watch in every
purse.   I'll not say whether you'll have gold in
it or not, but ye see what I'm doin', I'll promise
the purse and the watch and some money.   How
much the money will be, I'll not say.'

"Well, do ye know, Doalty, I saw the money
go into the purse, I saw it with me own two eyes,
so I speculated a sovereign, got a purse and put it
in my pocket, because he told me to do so, and he
told everyone else who bought a purse to do the
same thing—to put their purse in their pocket and

not show the contents to anyone. And the reason for it all, he says, was because he was doin' this in penance for a sin that he had committed. The penance was put on him by the Pope. Well, he sold all his purses, and went away. After he had gone, we looked in our purses and there was nothing in mine but a watch and a chain and tuppence. So well! we weren't promised anything else, and we had our watches. After a bit one iv our own countrymen, second son of Shemus Wor iv Greenans, he was, that had been abroad, told us that the watches were not worth more than two shillings apiece. Now, listen to what happened, and that will show you what the old times were, Doalty!

" The fair of Ardagh came on a while after and the word came to us up the glen, that this man, this thimble-riggin' rogue, was seen going to the fair of Ardagh. We went, half a dozen iv us, from Glenmornan, and we found him there up on the cart, sellin' his watch and his purse. Ah! nothing could have stood against us then, and we— ah! what wouldn't we do! I can't tell ye what we did, but anyway, when that man was leavin' the fair of Ardagh he didn't leave it in the bare pelt because Father Dooney, the parish priest that then was, gave him a coat to hide his skin. But the old times—ah! the good old times! . . . Come across with me to Heel-Ball's and I'll stand ye a drink."

v

During the afternoon Doalty lost Dennys and could not find him. It was about eight o'clock in the evening now and most of the old people had gone home from the fair. The young country girls had come in, and Doalty had seen Sheila Dermod and her friend, Eileen Kelly, walking up and down the street for the past two hours. When Sheila passed him she looked at him with a bashful smile, but she did not speak to him. Men must open the conversation when they want to talk with the girls at the fair of Greenanore. Doalty would have spoken, if Drover Dennys had been with him, but Drover Dennys had disappeared.

It was when he was passing Quigley's public-house that he saw him again. Looking in from the street he saw a crowd of men, almost hidden in the smoke of their pipes, drinking at the bar. Drovers they were, most of them, and their talk was about the bargains of the day. Drover Dennys was there, leaning his back against a sack of meal, his face inflamed a little, his hat thrust well back and his curls, wet with sweat, hanging down over his eyes. His exclamations, innocent affectations, spoke of youth and the recklessness of youth. He looked such a splendid fellow that Doalty stopped for a moment to admire him.

Beside Dennys, Owen Briney was standing, his

swarthy face, prominent jaw and high cheek-bones, lit up with the light of a swinging paraffin lamp that was suspended from the roof. Between his lips he held his clay pipe, the bowl turned down and the ash falling from it whenever he moved his lips. In his eyes the furtive expression, which Doalty had noticed that morning, looked more pronounced, and Owen seemed to be taking stock of every man round him and hanging on every word that was spoken, as if for the purpose of using the talk to his own advantage. He loved gossip, was very secretive about his own affairs, but was eager to listen to any conversation. He had drunk quite a lot that day, but he was a man who could hold his share and keep his senses about him. It was hinted that he could drive his best bargains when drunk. He seldom stood treat and generally drank at the expense of others.

Behind Owen, sitting on the counter, with his hands palms downward under his thighs, was Micky Neddy, a red-haired, buck-toothed young-ster, chewing thick black tobacco and spitting on the floor. He had a great reputation in the glen, for he was a poacher of repute, who, in addition to poaching, was able to make potheen better than any other man in the four corners of the barony. As he sat there, his moustache fringed with porter foam, he swung his legs carelessly from one side to another and blinked at the lamp. He would have to be carried home that night, for he was very drunk, and was now trying to pick up a quarrel with old Oiney Leahy, who was seated on a bag of meal, near the door. Hot words were passing between the two men for the last half-hour. When sober they were the greatest friends possible.

It was at the moment when Doalty was peering in through the window, that Micky Neddy lost complete control of himself.

"Ye damned Cath-breac ye," he suddenly shouted, bounding off his seat and sticking his fist up under the old man's chin. "Ye were a fighter once, they say, ye Schol Gaelig ye! Ye ugly old Greedy Gut, ye Scrape-the-pot. Where's the glen turf, that go be night, I want to know? Where do they go and who does take them? Tell me that, I say."

Through the window Doalty could see the profile of the old man. Oiney kept chewing his lips, while his white beard moved up and down, as if in protest, and he looked Micky Neddy between the eyes without flinching.

Suddenly over the melée the voice of Dennys The Drover was heard.

"What the hell is all this tongue-banging about?" he yelled, stretching out a big hand and gripping the shoulder of Micky Neddy.

"I don't mean nothin' nothin' at all," stammered Micky, edging away towards the counter, but unable to free himself from the Drover's grip. "I'm not meanin' anything, Dennys The Drover."

"Then hold yer dirthy tongue between yer big buck-teeth!" said Dennys, releasing the man, and the scornful curl of his lips became very pronounced. Even as he spoke he looked through the window and saw Doalty. The Drover came outside.

" I was lookin' for ye, Doalty, he said. " Where have ye been hidin'?"

" I have been looking for you," said Doalty.

" Well, have ye seen any girls about?" asked Dennys.

" I have seen some of them about here a minute ago," said Doalty.   " The Stranameera girls."

" Then come with me now," said Dennys, " and we'll stand them a trate.   I was speakin' to a couple iv them a wee while back, and I was tellin' them that me and yerself was goin' to see them home."

" Who were you speaking to?" asked Doalty.

" Sheila Dermod and Eileen Kelly," said Drover Dennys.   " Amongst others," he added, as an afterthought.

" Eileen Kelly?" said Doalty, in a voice of feigned indifference, and all the time he was thinking of Sheila Dermod.

" Ye don't want to go with Eileen then," said Dennys.   " She's a warm girl I'm tellin' ye. Then try Sheila and ye'll find her not so far behind.   She is just as good as the other if she wasn't so proud."

" Shall we go along and meet them now?" asked Doalty.

" Now's the time," said Drover Dennys, with a laugh.

VI

The two men went down the street and encountered the two girls.

"We've been on the look-out for ye all the night," said Drover Dennys. "We thought that ye had gone home afore we could give ye a trate. . . ."

"It's drinking that ye were instead iv lookin' for us," said Eileen Kelly, with a shake of her head.

"Get away!" said Dennys. "We'll go into Micky Ryan's shop and get out of sight now. Come with us and have some fun."

"So ye were lookin' for us, the two iv ye!" Eileen Kelly persisted, sarcasm in her voice. "It looked like it, be the way ye were lanin' against that bag iv male in Heel-Ball's shop. Ye had no eyes for anybody."

"Hadn't I then?" said Drover Dennys, mock reproach in his eyes. "Listen, Eileen Kelly, and I'll tell ye. . . ."

He bent down towards the girl and whispered something in her ear, then the two of them walked down the street, leaving Doalty Gallagher alone with Sheila Dermod.

"Where are the two iv them goin' now?" asked Sheila, following Dennys and Eileen with a glance.

"Oh, they're going to have a talk about something," said Doalty, and he looked in Sheila's eyes. "We'll have a talk too."

"What have we to talk about?" asked the girl.

"Lots of things," said Doalty grimly. "Do you mind the other day when I met you? I said that you were very beautiful. And I meant that. I'm in love with you, Sheila."

"Are you?" she asked, with a little start of surprise, apparently due more to Doalty's avowal, than to the feeling that caused the young man to make it.

"Yes, I am," said Doalty. "I never have met a girl like you."

"Haven't ye now?" she asked, and a blush rose to her cheeks. "But how am I to know that ye're telling me the truth?" she enquired, knowing all the time that Doalty was in earnest.

"Now come on the two of ye!" said Drover Dennys, coming back again, with Eileen Kelly hanging on his arm. "We're goin' in for a trate."

The four of them made their way to a public-house opposite and went upstairs to a small narrow room, which had a fire alight in a grate, and half-a-dozen spitoons on the floor. A table stood in the centre of the apartment and the four sat round it. A servant girl came in, and took Dennys' orders. When she left again, after bringing the drinks, Dennys rose from his chair and closed the door, turning the key in the lock. Then he sat down again.

He was in a merry mood. When all had drunk he got to his feet and went to the door that opened into another compartment. Standing with his back to the door he beckoned to Doalty, and the young man went across to him.

" I'm goin' to take Eileen in here," he said, whispering in Doalty's ear. " Ye stop with Sheila. Me and Eileen has arranged it. When we're ready to come out again, I'll cough. Ye can turn the lamp out and tell her everything in the dark."

Going back to the table, they found the two girls holding a conversation in whispers.

" What plans are ye two makin' up between ye?" exclaimed Dennys, pushing the girls' heads apart with his hands. " Come with me, Eileen," he said. " We'll go into this room, next door, where I'll have something to tell ye."

Putting his arm round the girl's waist he took her towards the adjoining apartment, a bedroom. At the door Eileen turned round, looked at Sheila and laughed.

" Come on with ye," said Dennys, shoving the girl into the room in front of him. Following her, he closed the door.

Doalty looked at Sheila, but he did not turn the lamp down, as Drover Dennys had directed him. He was quite at his ease, though for a moment he did not know what to say. It was Sheila Dermod who first broke silence.

" Ye haven't much to speak about, Doalty Gallagher," she said, quavering a little.

" Well, I've said all that I had to say when we were out on the street," Doalty protested, getting to his feet and coming closer to the beautiful girl. Sheila's nostrils quivered slightly and a sudden look, which was almost a challenge to the young man, showed in her steady, blue eyes. The direct glance which she fixed on Doalty seemed to say, ' Though the two of us are alone you dare not touch me.'

" What did ye say when ye were out on the street, Doalty Gallagher?" she asked under her breath.

" Surely you haven't forgotten it already," said Doalty.

" But what's the good iv keepin' what ye said in mind?" Sheila asked in a serious voice. " People can say anything at a fair and forget it the next day."

" Have people ever told you before that they were in love with you?" Doalty asked.

" Maybe they have," said Sheila in a trembling voice. " But that's nothin'."

Doalty bent down and put his arms round the girl's waist. She got to her feet, but made no effort to resist his clumsy embrace. Instead she put her lips close to his ear and whispered : " What will they be doin' in there in that room now?" She pointed her finger at the bedroom door as she spoke.

Doalty's eyes followed her outstretched arm, his whole body filled with a vague seductive yearning as he pressed the soft, clinging form of the charming girl close to his body.

" Maybe they are doing just the same as we are doing," he stammered.

" D'ye think they are?" Sheila asked, with a confiding caress in her voice.

Doalty looked down at her, the pink face and red lips. Her broad brimmed hat restrained her curls from falling down over her eyes; a faint flush mantled her cheeks. . . . She snuggled close to his chest. . . . He put one hand behind her head, pressing it gently against the soft, silky hair and whispered : " Sheila !"

She looked up at him and he lowered his lips to hers and kissed her. . . .

Sheila, all at once, drew herself up to her full height, and stepping back a pace, she looked Doalty in the face. Her whole countenance had changed : in a flash it had become stern and threatening. He could see her eyes light with scorn, her bosom heave under her tight blouse. . . . Never had he seen her look so beautiful as she looked at that moment.

" Doalty Gallagher, I didn't think that iv ye," she said, in a voice outwardly calm. But it seemed as if she were restraining herself from bursting into tears.

" What's wrong with you, Sheila?" Doalty asked impatiently. Good heavens ! He had done nothing wrong to her, he thought.

For answer Sheila shrugged her shoulders, walked to the door of the bedroom and tapped on it with her fingers.

" It's time for us to be goin' home," she called. " Come away with me now, Eileen Kelly."

" But it's not time yet," said Eileen, poking her mischievous little face out through the door and puckering her three-cornered lips in protest.

" Goin' home now and it a fair day. Ye are a funny girl, Sheila Dermod."

" Goin' home now!" said Dennys The Drover, coming out and standing in front of Sheila. " Well, yees can go if yees like, but I'm not comin' home with either one or the other iv yees. . . . Ye're not much good when there's any fun goin', Sheila Dermod! And ye look as if ye were goin' to cry too. Well, run away with yees!"

Dennys came across to Doalty Gallagher. The two girls made their way down the stairs. Sheila never looked back once, but Eileen Kelly turned round as her head was just disappearing from sight and fixed a knowing look on Doalty. Then she winked at Drover Dennys.

" Don't forget what I was sayin' to ye, Drover," she laughed back and disappeared.

" What have ye been doin' to the girsa, Doalty?" Drover Dennys asked, fixing his eyes on his friend. " Having a wee game with her, I suppose."

" No, I wasnt' doing anything," said the discomfited Doalty.

" Catch ye not doin' anything and ye all alone with a girl," said Dennys with a laugh. " But it's no good, when it's the girl Sheila. She's as proud as the hills. I can't stand her."

" But I thought you were in love with her," said Doalty.

" Sometimes I have a notion iv her," said Drover Dennys. " But I can't always be foolin' about after her and no fun at all in her. . . . It's hands off if ye touch her at all."

G–K

"I'm goin' to see if all the men have gone home to Glenmornan yet," said Drover Dennys, when he and Doalty had made their way out to the street. "I know that Micky Neddy has not gone back, for he was as drunk as a lord when I left him in Heel-Ball's a while ago. I'll go in there now and try and take him home. Don't ye trouble to wait for me, Doalty, but go home be yerself. It takes a lot of handlin' to get Micky home."

So saying, Dennys went across the street towards Quigley's and left Doalty to himself. The young man wandered up and down the street for quite half an hour, his mind busy with many thoughts. Then he made his way up the glen road.

VII

The last to leave the fair were returning home now. A hundred yards out and under a dim street lamp, Doalty could see a crowd of men deep in a heated discussion. Violent laughter came from the men and fierce imprecations. One man, whom Doalty recognised by his voice, was Micky Neddy.

"If ever I want to do a thing I'll do it," Micky was bellowing. "I'm always ready—always ready, for that's the kind iv me. Mother iv God look sideways on me! if I'm not always ready."

The speaker burst into a violent fit of laughter, scraped the ground with his fingers, and lifting a stone, he flung it at the lamp overhead and smashed it. Then he fell to the ground. Drover Dennys, who was in the crowd, bent over the prostrate figure.

" Come home with me, Micky!" said Dennys with a laugh. " Ye've a good step in front iv ye yet, me boy."

"A good step!" repeated the man on the ground. "Aw right! I'm always ready. Amn't I, Drover Dennys? But I can get home when I like, can't I? I'm always ready; always ready!"

Dennys The Drover bent over the drunken man and tried to lift him to his feet.

" Lave me be," said Micky. " Can I not be here on me lone if I like? Where's Owen Briney?"

" He's at home hours since," Dennys informed him.

" Oh! the damned Yalla Behind The Lugs; he would be! . . . And the Stranameera girsas. Are they at home too?"

" Iv course they are," said Drover Dennys.

"Well, that's enough anyway," said Micky, snuggling in against the curbstone, as if going to sleep. " I don't want to know any more. Lave me be, and I'll come home be meself. 'Twould be another matter if I had the chance iv goin' back with Sheila Dermod or Eileen Kelly, or Norah Gallagher . . . but now . . . Lave me be and go home be yerselves."

Doalty continued his journey up the glen road with long strides and came to his own townland. A white mist rose from the river and settled on the meadows of the holm. It was here that Doalty heard the sound of voices talking through the mist. Oiney Leahy was speaking to a Meenawarawor man across the river and the talk was of the market.

" 'Twas no market at all," Oiney was saying, speaking very slowly, as was his habit when he had drunk unwisely. "Poor rannies iv cattle and sheep they were there this day, as far as I could see. Not a fair at all for the makin' iv money, or the spendin' iv it. I had a springin' cow down there meself, a good baste, and I sold it for eight pounds ten and half-a-crown luck's-money. Indeed and I gave the baste away."

"Who bought it?" asked the other man.

"Owen Briney," said Oiney. "He has grass for the baste, and it's more nor I have."

There was a moment's silence.

"That's true, Oiney," said the Meenawarawor man with the acquiescence which decency demanded, for Oiney really had enough grass for two cows, but he had to sell one because he wanted money. But pride, Glenmornan pride, would not permit the old man to avow his poverty.

"Did ye see Doalty Gallagher at the fair?" asked the man of Meenawarawor.

"I did," said Oiney. "Was near him when he bought that cow from Grania Coolin. He gave the woman what she asked for the baste, money down, and wouldn't have luck's-money. I don't understand it at all. His father was a sensible man, God rest him! and could make a good bargain. And his mother, dacent woman, is a thrifty soul. No one can get the betther iv her. But people change when they go abroad, and not always for the best."

"D'ye think that the boyo has much money, Oiney?"

"He doesn't dhress up to it if he has," said the old man. "But he's a good-hearted fellow, and not one to begrudge ye a dhrop iv dhrink, when ye go to his house."

VIII

Doalty thrust his hands down into the pockets of his trousers, and leaving the road, he took the path across the fields to his home. Now and again he paused and looked at the white houses under the hills and the little modest lights in their windows. There was no moon, but the sky, coldly clear, was lit with a thousand stars. It was a night to be alive, but somehow Doalty did not feel very happy. It was evident that the Meenawarawor man considered him a fool. But then, the man did not understand Doalty, and for the matter of that, Doalty did not understand the man from Meenawarawor. There is a wider gap between men of different temperaments than there is between men of different nationalities.

Doalty, passing Breed Dermod's door, saw old Breed leaning over the half door, listening to the people coming back from the fair. She was always listening to the talk from the road, and she

could hear the very grass growing. She was a
very inquisitive old woman and became, in some
way or another, acquainted with the most private
affairs of her neighbours; and secrets were never
safe in her keeping. She was a confessional with
ears and tongue. Nobody liked her, and at the
present moment she was not on speaking terms
with the Gallaghers. Doalty passed quietly by
and went into the boreen that led to his own home.

As he was nearing his house he heard the sound
of suppressed laughter in a meadow behind the
hedge. He looked quietly over, and saw two
figures seated in the grass. Instinctively he knew
that he was looking at Sheila Dermod and Eileen
Kelly. They were speaking to one another in a
low voice and, as far as he could judge, they were
not aware of his proximity.

"Has he much money d'ye think?" Sheila was
asking.

"I don't know," said Eileen. "But he's very
soft. . . . Ye can hear nothin' in Greenanore the
day, only about himself and old Grania Coolin.
. . . Just think of it! Givin' her seven-pound-
five for a cow, just what she asked, and if he was
cute, he could have the baste for a five pound note.
Grania didn't know whether she should take his
money or not. After he had left her, she showed
the money to the priest and he said that the money
was good enough."

"I suppose he'll be leavin' here soon," said
Sheila.

"Iv coorse he will," said Eileen. "Bein' so
long away he wouldn't stop here now. And he's

tryin' to be like one iv ourselves. . . . What
did he do to yerself the night? Ye didn't tell
me, ye know."

"Didn't I?" said Sheila, giggling. "So I
didn't. . . . Oh! but 'twas nothin'."

She laughed merrily.

"A person must do something when they're
alone with a one. Mustn't they now?" asked
Eileen. "But I can guess things." Doalty
could see Eileen nod knowingly.

"Was Dennys wantin' to come home wid ye?"
asked Sheila, not answering her friend's question.
"I let him come home with me the last fair and
the one before that, but I wouldn't let him come
home with me this time."

"And would that be yer only reason for not
lettin' him come home with ye?"

"Partly that, and also because he's often seen
hangin' round Maura The Rosses house up there,"
Sheila said. "If he manes to go about with one
girl why doesn't he stick to her? I wouldn't pick
up the leavin's iv Norah Gallagher."

"But who says that Dennys is always about the
Gallagher's?" asked Eileen.

"Who would it be, but Owen Briney," Sheila
replied. "Owen knows everything."

"I can't help noticin' but Owen's always about
yer house," said Eileen. "I suppose he'll be tryin' to put some sturks to grazin' on yer land."

"I don't pay any heed to what he's after," said
Sheila. "I don't like him."

"Nobody likes him much," said Eileen. "But
ye like none iv the young fellows, Sheila. That's

because they're all breakin' their hearts after ye?"

"Maybe that's it," said Sheila, with a laugh, getting to her feet. "What made us to come here and sit on the wet grass I don't know. Come, let the two iv us run down the lane and go into the house."

Laughing merrily, they caught one another's hands and rushed away towards their homes.

Feeling, for some unknown reason, very despondent, Doalty lit a cigarette and drawing only one whiff of smoke, flung it away. Then he went into his home.

CHAPTER VII

SHEILA DERMOD

Now, maidens, beware,
    For your youth doesn't stay,
But goes with the seeding,
    Like blooms on the brae—
As markets are changing
    Good prices don't keep,
And ware of the morning
    At noon-tide goes cheap—
And the glance of young eyes,
    Like the bloom on the brae,
Is always forgotten
    By Hallowmas Day.
        —*The Pretty Girl Milking Her Cow.*

I

NEXT morning, after his dip in the river, Doalty went across to Oiney Leahy's to borrow a spade. He was going to dig a drain in the field under the house, a job that should have been done earlier in the year. But there was not much help to hand on the farm and there was no time for the work.

The morning was one to be remembered. The meadows were wet with dew, the braes decked with blossom; the whins on the uplands in full bloom were covered with spiders' webs, on which the dewdrops glistened like diamonds. In the birches that rimmed spinkh and awlth the birds warbled merrily; a corncrake railed across the holms by the river; butterflies flitted from flower to flower, and the early bees were already out on their daily labour. The sun, rising over the hills, flung little broken rays of light through the sycamores growing outside the door of Maura The Rosses.

Oiney Leahy was putting on a fire when Doalty got to his house, and young Dennys The Drover was there, sitting by the table looking at a newspaper. He had not slept the night before, for when he got back from the fair, he went out with Oiney and the two men made their way to the hills on one of their mysterious errands. These errands were of common occurrence, and the police force of the village would give a lot to catch the two men when engaged on them.

" I was goin' down to the river to have a swim," Dennys remarked to Doalty as the latter came in. " But I was too heavy and sleepy to get up from the chair. Thanks be to heaven that there's not a fair every day."

" 'Twasn't much iv a fair yesterday anyway," said Oiney, placing a row of turf against the back of the fireplace. " I've never seen any as bad for a long while. . . . And that cow iv yours, Doalty," he said, looking at the visitor. " It's not a bad baste at all, and it'll be comin'* soon.

* Calving.

But ye gave a wee penny too much for it, I'm thinkin'. . . . But one never knows."

"It'll be worth the money when it calves," said Doalty carelessly.

"Oh! it may, then, and I hope it may," said Oiney, apparently endeavouring to give Doalty every possible credit for the bargain. "If the market improves, and if it calves well, ye'll maybe make somethin' by it." He spoke with the voice of a man who did not believe in the hopes which he held out.

"Here, look at this," said Drover Dennys, handing the paper to Oiney and yawning. "This picture. It's of a woman and she looks a funny card. Hasn't a rag to her back hardly."

Oiney took the paper, looked at it, and the expression on his face became invulnerably solemn. Doalty gazed over the old man's shoulder and saw the photo of an actress, attired in tights, who was then appearing on a London music hall. The paper had been used in wrapping up a second-hand coat which Oiney had bought at the fair.

"She's a shameless hussy true enough," said Oiney, with emphasis on the adjective, handing the paper back to Dennys. "Do the people often dress like that in London?" he asked, looking at Doalty.

"It's the custom sometimes," said Doalty, with a smile.

"There are strange customs every place," said Oiney, trying, as it seemed, to get this custom into line with some of his own fundamental views of life. "Now look up at the mountainy people and the ways they have," he said. "If they see the smoke iv a house, where there's a dead one underboard, they'll not do a hand's turn until the berryin' is done and finished. But down this arm iv the glen it's only the townland that leaves off work when one in it is dead. In Stranameera here, they carry a coffin on the shoulders to the grave-yard, and won't carry it any other way, out iv re-spect for them that's gone. But over in Meena-warawor they'll take the coffin in a cart and not mean any harm be it.

"Then look at the Night of the Dead," he went on. "Here in Glenmornan we go down on our knees in our own home, and say the Pather-an-Avve for the sufferin' souls in Purgatory, but down in the Rosses, they go to the graveyard that night at twelve, and say their prayers there.

"The Meenawarawor girsas go 'ut to the field and spread the dung on the ridges with their fin-gers, or go 'ut to the byre and clean it when it's the thing to do," he continued. "But catch the Stranameera girls doin' that, the proud heifers, and they not a bit better to look at than the girls iv Meenawarawor. So ye see it even here, Doalty," the old man concluded, with the tone of a preacher who has made his point manifest. "One barony or one townland is not the same as another and each of them has its own habits iv doin' things. And foreign parts will have their own ways, for that's the kind iv the world."

Drover Dennys, who was still looking at the actress, raised his head.

" Is this rale?" he asked, in a voice of unusual animation, " or is it only a picture?"

" Oh, it's real," said Doalty Gallagher. " I've seen that woman dressed like that at a music-hall."

" And ye paid to see it?" asked Oiney Leahy. " How much did it cost ye?"

" Oh, half-a-crown," said Doalty.

Oiney took the paper out of Dennys' hands again and looked at it with eyes of increased interest.

" As far as I can see she's bare to the pelt," he said. " Arms, legs, everything!"

" No, not the legs," said Doalty. " She has got tights on, a tight pair of drawers, which are made to look as if they were not on."

" And what would that be for now?" enquired the old man. " It must be a funny thing for a girl to come out before people as naked as a rush on a bog."

" She gets paid to do it," said Doalty. " She stands on the stage like that for fifteen minutes or so every night, and the money she gets for a week would buy your farm of land twice over."

" Well, it's money goin' to loss," said Oiney, shaking his head. " If a woman sib to me done that, the back iv me hand to her no matter what she'd make be it. Never would I let her get under me roof."

" But people abroad like it," said Doalty. " And that girl has more clothes on her than some girls here. See the Stranameera girls at the washing by the brookside, when they are tramping the clothes, with their skirts pulled up over their knees! If they were seen doing that in London, they would be put into prison."

"I suppose that bears out what I've said a minute gone," said Oiney. "Every townland has its own manners and that's all about it. Isn't it now?"

"I suppose it is; and again look at this, which happens here," said Doalty. "The young boys and girls go into the fair of Greenanore and boys treat the girls, taking them into a public-house and a bedroom to have a drink. It's the custom here, but abroad it would not be allowed."

"Foreign parts have their own ways iv goin'," said Oiney. "And it would be a sorry day here if a young fellow was not allowed to have fun with the girsas."

"Ah, but it's hard to know what fun like that might lead to," said Doalty.

II

"What would it be leadin' to?" said the old man, his voice a little severe, as if reproaching Doalty for thinking evil of local habits. "It ud be a poor day that a Glenmornan girl would come to harm with a Glenmornan man. A girl here, has more sense than that, and it doesn't take the law to take care iv them when they're out for the bit iv fun. . . . God forbid me seein' the day that a gasair here would play dirty with a girsa. Lave that for them abroad. . . .

"Once somethin' did take place here," the old

man went on, after a short silence. "One of the men from the butt end iv the barony did come home from abroad and he begin goin' after wee Eiveleen Murraghar, her that was, bad cess to her! blood relation iv me own. Well, this toe-rag iv a man went away from here, after he stayed for short on three months, but the harm was done when he left. Eiveleen became the mother iv a child that no man would lay claim to, and all because she wasn't as wise as a girsa should be. But them that's in the barony now have got sense and are as knowin' as any good girls can be."

The old man was quite correct in his estimate, and this Doalty knew. Though the sex instinct is as strong in Glenmornan as any part of the world, the peasants' purity of manners are a strong safeguard against any irregularities. Having fun with a girl at a fair means nothing more than a treat and a little flirtation in a private room of a public-house. A man and woman, not bound together by legal union, who enter a bedroom in a great city, are looked on with suspicious eyes, but in Greenanore, where almost every room in a house is a bedroom, a happening of this kind is viewed from a different standpoint. The young men and women of the Barony of Burrach, strict guardians of their virtue, seldom fall short in their observance of chaste morality. The discreet modesty of the peasant girls is strong enough to resist any wrong advances.

Drover Dennys had hold of the paper again. His face was wreathed in smiles.

"Here, listen to this that's in this paper," he

said. "'Catching hold of Doris with his two strong arms,' he read, 'Fred Reynolds pressed his lips against hers.' God! they're always kissin' the girls over in foreign parts," he remarked, putting his head to one side and quizzing at Doalty with his clear grey eyes. "It's a wonder that they don't get tired iv it. . . . There's not much kissin' done hereabouts."

"And that's as it should be," said Oiney. "A kiss is an invitation to do something that is not in keepin' with decency and good manners."

"But it's not wrong to kiss a girl," said Dennys The Drover.

"It's a sin," said Oiney gravely. "And if a girl would let a man kiss her it shows the poor purchase she holds on her soul. Did ye ever kiss a girl, Dennys?" he asked.

"I haven't yet, but I will one iv these fine days," said the young man, with an air of reckless decision.

"Ah! indeed and ye won't, me dacent boy," said Oiney, and there was reproof in his voice. "It might lead ye astray. It's the first step into the worst iv all sins, the sin iv the flesh."

The two young men laughed.

"Ye're a funny old shanahy, Oiney," said Drover Dennys. "Ye think that every sin is a bad one only the ones that ye are guilty iv yerself."

"If it's the drink that ye mane, I'll give way to ye and say that it's a sin against God and man," said Oiney. "But then, Dennys, me boy, men were made to sin. Badness is in the body iv every man."

"So you think that the sin of the flesh is the worst of all?" Doalty enquired.

"It is then," said Oiney. "The sin, and everything that gives rise to it, is bad. And givin' a kiss to a girl is not to be thought iv, if one wants to live a dacent and holy life. . . . They may kiss abroad, but it's not for Glenmornan people to follow a bad example. It's a sin to kiss anyone bar the dead here; but a mother is allowed to kiss her children until they come to the age iv seven. After that it's a mortal sin for her to kiss them. For meself I never kissed any woman, bar me wife, and that was before she was underboard. . . ."

He looked at the young men and stroked his beard.

"None iv ye have the drouth?" he asked. A sly look crept into his eyes, as he went over to the bed and brought out the black bottle. "Just somethin' to sweeten our discourse," he said, catching the cork with his teeth and drawing it.

"Has the fairies been havin' ye in their mind again?" asked Dennys, and he fixed a knowing look on Oiney. Both laughed, not so much at the joke, as the fact. that a secret between the two men was not known to Doalty Gallagher.

III

Leaving Oiney Leahy's with a spade across his shoulder, Doalty saw Sheila Dermod in front of him on her way to a neighbouring shop for provisions. She was walking through the wet grass, carrying eggs in a spotted handkerchief. Sheila had a shawl over her head and this fell down over her magnificent shoulders, with one fringe reaching her hips. She was barefooted and wearing a short baunagh-brockagh petticoat that reached a little lower than her knee. The hem of the petticoat kept rubbing backwards and forwards across the girl's shapely calves. At every step she raised a neat little foot high over the swaying heads of the ripple grasses and looked back with a swift, discreet glance at Doalty Gallagher. The young man was trying to pluck up sufficient courage to call to her.

"Sheila?" he said suddenly, in a hoarse whisper.

The girl turned the tail of her eye round, but did not answer. Probably she had not heard what he said. Doalty called to her again, and again she looked back, but said nothing. However, she shortened her steps and walked more leisurely, waiting for him to overtake her, and curious to hear what he had got to say.

Doalty overtook her.

"I'm sorry about what happened last night, Sheila," he said, with an awkward laugh. "I didn't think that you would get so angry with me."

The girl raised her eyes, looked upwards and nodded her head without speaking. In her look, Doalty fancied he saw reproach for his behaviour of the previous night.

" I don't want you to be very angry with me,"
he said nervously, and a moment's silence followed.   He could hear the girl's feet brushing
against the long grass.   She did not answer Doalty, but seemed to be waiting to hear him say something further.

" You know I did not intend to do you any
harm, Sheila," he said.

" Well, I don't see what harm ye'd be wantin'
to do to me, Doalty Gallagher," said the girl.
" Ye don't think that I'd let ye, do ye now?"

" I don't mean what you mean," said Doalty re-
proachfully.

" What d'ye mean then?" asked Sheila, with a
sidelong glance.   " I don't know what ye're
meanin' at all.   You're a funny boy, Doalty Gallagher."

" Am I?" he laughed, and felt that a more con-
fidential intimacy had suddenly sprung up between himself and the girl.

They came to the march ditch without another
word.   There they stopped, and Doalty asked,
" What time are you taking down the cows from
the hill to-night, Sheila?"

" The same time as every night," murmured the
girl with a look of wonder in her eyes.   " Just
when it's gettin' dark."

" You take them down through the awlth, don't
you?"

" I take them down that way," said Sheila.

" I'm going up there to cut an ash-plant when
it's growing dark to-night, so I'll look out for you,
Sheila," said the young man, in a husky voice.

" Don't forget that, Sheila, and don't go and hide when you see me."

" Hide! no fear," said the girl with a smile. " But mind, if ye come, ye are not to be the same as ye were last night. If ye are, I'll not ever speak one word to you again, Doalty Gallagher."

Walking sedately, the girl went down towards the road. On the way into his home Doalty encountered his mother, who was looking over the hedge, one eye on the doings of her neighbours and another on the stocking which she was knitting.

" Did ye get the spade from old Oiney?" she asked, and Doalty judged by her tone and the downward droop of the corner of her lips, that the question was a prelude to talk of a more serious nature. Doalty recollected that this tone and look of hers was assumed of old, when she held a birch in her hand, and when the children had been troublesome.

" I have got the spade," said the young man, as he put it on the ground.

" Was Dennys The Drover over there?" she asked.

" Yes, Dennys is over in Oiney's now."

" He was with Eileen Kelly in Ryan's last night they're saying," said the woman, meaning by " they" the people of the glen.

" Was he?" Doalty enquired.

" And ye know that he was, ye, yerself," said the mother, " for weren't ye with him there?"

" Who has been telling you this?" asked Doalty

in an angry voice, but feeling more discomfited than annoyed.

"Who, but everyone," said the mother, plying her needles rapidly, as if her very life depended on the job. "It's the talk iv the whole townland this day. It's bad enough to see ye spendin' yer money on that cow, but then to take and go about with Sheila Dermod and trate her when ye could get girls that's yer own equal who would be only too glad to have yer company."

Maura The Rosses compressed her lips and fixed her eyes on the hills that rose from the other side of the river. She still continued knitting and Doalty could see that she was dropping every second stitch.

"There's nothing wrong with Sheila Dermod," said Doalty gruffly. "I don't see any harm in speaking to the girl. Have you got some grudge against her?" he asked.

"Thinkin' that I'd stoop so low as to have a grudge against a one like Sheila Dermod!" said Maura The Rosses, disdain in her voice. "She's so proud, and so is her mother! Wait till ye see what will happen if ye keep runnin' about after her. She'll make ye the laughin' stock iv the whole glen."

With these words, Maura The Rosses left her son and passed into the house.

Doalty went out to the field and began digging a drain which was intended to divert the flood waters from the meadows in the rainy season. As he worked he thought of his mother's temper and laughed to himself. "The way she hates Sheila!" he muttered. "Why is there such bad feeling between some families? . . . Looking down on one another because of an extra cow's grass or an extra acre of spadeland. . . . But is it not the same all the world over? . . . Petty spite and jealousy. The same everywhere."

Doalty laboured obstinately for half an hour, without looking round. Then he straightened himself and gazed down the road to see Sheila coming back from the shop, a large parcel under her shawl. . . . He bent to his work again, and suddenly his fancy brought the girl to his side, her arms pressed tightly round his neck and her eyes looking down into his. He could see her soft, dark brown hair falling over her shoulders, her full white throat and her red seductive lips responding to his kisses. . . .

That evening, when darkness was falling, Doalty was in the awlth, waiting for her to bring in the cattle.

IV

It was very pleasant to sit there in the awlth, drinking in the night and gazing down on the glen between the hills. Doalty in his heart felt a greater love than ever for his native place, for the white houses with their snug coverings of thatch and their lights, already burning, gleaming modestly through the windows, for the clear

streams scooting down over the rocks and mean-
dering lazily through the calm meadows, for the
Owenawadda eeling its way seawards, and more
than anything else, for the kind-hearted people
who dwelt there, the honest people of Glenmornan.

Over Carnaween the new moon, a mere sickle,
was showing.   Under it the mountain stood still
and attentive, as if listening to the sounds of the
world that lay beneath it.   The awlth was full of
vague whisperings and rustlings and no wonder!
for it was here that the gentle people often held
their nightly revels.   A belated bee drummed
through the undergrowth on the search for its
home; a birch that grew by Doalty's side, bent
down towards him, moving its arms in a mysterious manner; a bat fluttered into air, circled round
and round for a moment, and disappeared.   From
where he sat Doalty could not see a soul, but all
manner of sounds floated up to him from the glen,
the happy laughter of merry children, the sharp
cries of the women driving the cattle into their
byres, and the loud shouting of men, calling to
their neighbours across the march-ditches.

"Ah! she'll soon be here," he said to himself,
his mind full of complex thoughts and emotions.
Although he had sat there for quite a long time,
he felt as breathless as if he had just rushed all the
way up from his home to the awlth on the brae-
face.

An old speckled cow came along on its way to
the byre.   It stopped when it saw Doalty, fixed a
pair of big, serious eyes on the young man, then

flicked its hind legs with its tail and soberly pursued its journey. Following the cow, a young heifer rattled into view, stopped dead when it saw the stranger, and gave a snort of surprise. For a moment it gazed dubiously at the man, then with a wild rush it careered by him, down the awlth, sending the stones flying against the bushes.

Sheila came into sight and saw the young man. Although expecting him her face flushed when he rose to meet her.

"This yerself, Doalty Gallagher?" she asked.

For answer Doalty reached and caught both her hands in his. She resisted a little and caught her breath, in what seemed to be a sob. Doalty pressed her fingers timidly, but Sheila did not raise her eyes to look at him.

"Let me be," she said in a whisper. "The cattle are near down at the house now, and who'll tie them?"

"Sheila, do you like me?" asked Doalty and tried to put his arms round her. She pulled herself away, but did not raise her eyes to his face.

"I like ye, Doalty Gallagher," she replied. "There's no reason for not likin' ye. Only, last night——" she stammered and stopped.

"But I only kissed you, Sheila. There was no harm in that, surely."

"But it's a sin," said the girl in a trembling voice. "Now let me go, won't ye, till I tie up the cattle."

"Well, let me kiss you, now," said Doalty coaxingly. "Just once, and then you can go away

down to the house. . . . It's not a sin· . . .
Everybody does it."

He hardly knew what he was talking about.

" Just once and then you can go," he repeated.

" Don't, Doalty Gallagher," Sheila faltered, in
a frightened voice, as she saw Doalty's face close
to hers.

" But you're not afraid of me, are you?"

" I am. . . ."

" But it's silly; it's———"

" Let me be, Doalty. Do now. I want to go
home. . . ."

Her voice was beseeching.

" I'm in love with you, Sheila Dermod," said
Doalty, drawing the girl close into his side. " I've
never loved anybody before."

" Did ye not?" she asked, still trying to free
her hands.

" Never till I met you, Sheila," said Doalty.
" You believe that, don't you?"

" How am I to know?"

Even as she spoke, she freed herself from Doalty's embrace with an agile movement and scram-
bled down the awlth, scattering the stones from
under her with her bare feet. Getting to a safe
distance, she looked back and laughed.

" Good night, Doalty Gallagher," she called in
a whisper and ran away.

The man felt annoyed, exasperated. What a
fool he was making of himself, he thought.

A few minutes later he could hear Sheila tying
up the cattle and scolding them.

" Come here, ye wee divil, ye !" he heard her

say. " Ye're standin' on me feet, ye rogue. . . .
Now! Now! Don't be tryin' to stick me in the
eye with yer horns."

" I believe she looks on me as some sort of natural curiosity," Doalty said to himself, as he lay
in his bed that night. A vague resentment rose
in his heart against the girl. " She's making a
fool of me," he whispered. " I amuse her and
. . . Well, it doesn't matter."

He wondered what the affair would lead to;
how it would end. Something would certainly happen. . . . Life surely had not the same monoto-
ny of a repeating decimal. Things would change.
If Sheila got married to somebody—not to himself, of course—he could see more clearly. Everything would then be simplified. But now, nothing was sure. Sheila obstructed his outlook.
She was real, and something he desired exceed-
ingly.

" I'll try and sleep!" he said with petulant
resignation.

But he lay awake for a long time, his head full
of thoughts of the girl. He slept heavily and
awoke early, as tired as when he went to bed.

CHAPTER VIII

BREED DERMOD

To the Hard Woman the back of your hand,
The Woman not liked in her own townland.
The road to her doorstep is snug and neat,
For it never is tramped by a beggar's feet.
The Man of the House is a quiet soul,
For a word from his lips she'll never thole;
And the woman's children know their place,
And they know the birch on the chimney-brace.
Tidy and thrifty she toils and spins
At the shut of day and when day begins,
And the dust she sweeps from the hearth and floor
Comes back in gold to the woman's door;
But people like her and ones of her get
Are never much loved wherever they're set,
And her neighbours say, "The back iv the hand
To a woman not liked in her own townland."
> —*The Hard Woman.*

I

MAURA The Rosses was a very civil woman with little to say. But she was very curious about the doings of her neighbours and the doings of Breed Dermod in particular. Seeing that there was bad blood between

187

herself and Breed, it was natural that she should be interested in the woman's doings. Maura kept surreptitious watch on the Dermods, although she tried to act as if she were not aware of their existence. If any untoward happening occurred on the Dermods' farm, if a cow broke loose from the fields, if a neighbour came to thatch their house, or if Oiney Leahy entered into a loud-voiced conversation with Breed across the ditch, Maura The Rosses set about washing the floor of her own house.

To do this, it was necessary to go out to the well for water, and from the well it was an easy job to keep an eye on the Dermods and see, or hear, whatever was taking place there. Maura often washed the stone floor and when doing so, she always went out for the water herself. So, who could blame her if she heard and saw things when engaged on her own honest work? Doalty often noticed these happenings, but now, when he had become interested in the why and wherefore of the feud, he did not dare to ask his mother any questions about the matter.

Not being able to ask his mother he asked his sister Norah.

"What's the quarrel between us and the Dermods?" he enquired.

"Why do ye want to know that?" Norah asked. She was sitting by the table with Kitty and both were looking at a boudoir cap which the latter had just completed. The convent school, in the village, was making great efforts to educate the young peasant girls, teaching them cookery and sewing. The young girls were ready and willing to be taught. "If we had the things that's wanted," the little ones often remarked, with a touching pathos in their voices, "we could make the nicest things that the glen ever seen." As it was, they acquired arts, but not the material to make those arts manifest.

"Well, it's a strange thing having a quarrel with the Dermods," said Doalty. "They don't seem to be doing any harm to us. When I was at home, long ago, they were great friends of ours."

"Is that all ye know?" said Norah, with a toss of her head. "The old woman was big enough with us as long as she was behoulden to us for anything. But when a brother iv hers, that is beyont the water, began to send her some money, she got as proud as the hills and wouldn't say a word at all to us after that. Before she got the money, it was Sheila, her that's so proud now, comin' in in the mornin' for a grater; in the middle iv the day for the len iv a scoop iv male, and be night for somethin' else. Now if it's passin' the door that she is, she looks to the other side iv the road. . . She's as distant as the town people and why it is, I don't know. For she's one iv the lowest iv the low."

"Now, what do you mean by the lowest of the low?" Doalty asked, with a smile.

"Ye're always laughin' at me," said the girl. "I don't know why, but I suppose it's because I'm not smart like the ones that's over beyont the water."

"I'm not laughing at you, Norah," said Doalty,

feeling a little awkward. "But you have a funny way of looking at things, Norah."

"Well, I suppose ye yerself was like me one time," said the girl. "But that ye went out into the world and saw things, ye now look down on us at home. I don't like people that bees like that."

"Bees like that," Kitty sniffed, for being a convent girl she was far above such local idioms.

"And ye yerself will grow up like Doalty, I suppose," said Norah to her superior sister.

"And ye'll be runnin' after Dennys The Drover," Kitty retorted.

Norah blushed. Doalty looked at her and laughed.

"So every girl in the place is after Dennys," he said.

Maura The Rosses came into the house at that moment, carrying a bucket of water. She was washing the floor although she had been engaged on the job only the day before. Emptying the water on the flags, she began scrubbing them with a besom. Presently she stopped, and looking at nobody in particular, she pointed her thumb over her shoulder in the direction of Breed Dermod's.

"The woman up there is goin' down the brae with her boots on," she said; "and I wonder where she'll be goin' to."

"She'll be goin' over to Ardagh," said Kitty, knowing that Breed Dermod, who generally went about barefooted, was going a good journey because she had put her boots on.

" I wonder what she'll be goin' there for now," said Maura The Rosses, trying to speak as if she had very little interest in the matter.

" I know," said Norah. " Owen Briney was speakin' about it the other day. She's goin' over there to see about gettin' her house slated."

" Slated!" exclaimed Maura The Rosses, making no effort to hide her surprise. " Goin' to get her house slated. And where will she get the money, I'd like to know? Owen Briney is often sayin' things that there's not much truth in."

By her manner of speaking, it was evident to Doalty that his mother hoped that there was no truth in Owen Briney's statement.

" There's not a lie in it, I think," said Norah. " Breed got a big lump in the last letter from America. Her brother, out there, has money and to spare."

" But to get her house slated!" said Maura The Rosses, contracting her brows, as if in an effort to discover why this could not be done. " Well, I don't know," she said after a moment's silence. " I don't know at all what to make iv it!"

She went out by the front door with the bucket in her hand, although previously she always made the journey to the well by way of the back door. But that would not give her a view of the glen road. When she came back she spoke about Breed Dermod again.

" She's away down the road now, as hard as she can pelt," she said. " And she's holdin' her head up too."

II

Maura The Rosses placed the bucket on the floor and looked at Doalty.

" This house iv ours would look very nice if it had the slates," she said. " If I had enough money I'd have slates on it long ago. But then, one can't do everything."

" A thatched house looks much nicer," said Doalty, who did not want to see a world of slates come into his picture of Glenmornan. It would not be in keeping with the memories of his youth. But people with slated houses were considered well to do, as it took money for the job, and when a peasant was able to afford the money he got his house slated.

" But everyone that can is gettin' the slates on now," said Maura The Rosses. " Over in Meena-warawor there are three houses with the slates on, and two more are just goin' to get them done. It's them that have their young abroad that are able to do it. Now, to get this house done it wouldn't take so much," she added; " but it is too much for me. If I had the money . . ."

Maura The Rosses continued scrubbing the floor, sweeping a flag that was already perfectly clean. After a moment she raised her head and looked at Norah.

" Run out," she said to her, " and see that the cows are not in the corn."

" But the cows were up on the top of the hill a minute ago," said Norah.

" Run out and do what ye're told," said the mother, " and take the basket with ye and dig some pratees for the supper. Ye go with her and gather them, Kitty."

The two went out, and at that moment Hughie Beag put his head through the door and fixed two big eyes on the nail over the fire. On this nail the birch for chastising unruly children was generally hung. Hughie had been out on the road rolling in the dust and his face, legs, arms and dress were covered with dirt. There was a long rent down the leg of the knickers which his mother had bought for him at the fair a few days previously. When his mother saw this! In a Glenmornan family of ten the birch is often used, and Doalty, as he looked at Hughie peeping round the door, remembered his own childhood and laughed.

Maura The Rosses looked at Hughie Beag.

" Run out and play yerself till tay-time!" she shouted. " And don't come in till then!"

Hughie scuttled back to the road again and the house was left to Maura The Rosses and her son. This was what the woman wanted.

" Have ye any money to spare, Doalty?" she asked him, and continued to scrub the same clean flag.

" I have a few pounds left," he said.

" Ye wouldn't miss as much as would slate the house I suppose?" she enquired timidly.

" Wouldn't I?" said Doalty. " It's far nicer

to have it thatched than slated," he went on. "It's warm enough here, without getting slates on the roof. Don't you think so yourself?"

Maura The Rosses did not think so. She wanted the house slated, not so much because it would be more comfortable, but because everybody in Glenmornan who thought anything of themselves, were getting done with the thatching and getting the slates on. And she did not want to be the last at the job, not now especially, as the "woman up there" was getting her house done.

"But I haven't practically a penny, mother," Doalty repeated. But the woman did not believe him, as he could see by the smile of unbelief that flickered across her face. He had money, and she knew that he had. Nothing would convince her to the contrary.

In Glenmornan children are looked upon as good investments. When they grow up, they are supposed to give all money they earn to their parents and the parents take it as their due. Maura The Rosses did not request a loan from her son, she simply wanted money that was hers by right. It is only when the young marry that the parents' claim to the wages ceases.

Seeing that Doalty would not fall in with her wishes, Maura The Rosses began temporising. She had a little laid by, only a few pounds, but, if Doalty would give her some, and if she could get two young heifers (they would be ready for the next harvest fair) and Grania Coolin's cow (she hoped it would calve well) off her hands, she might

be able to buy the slates.   There were also two
butts of butter, almost ready, . . . seven geese,
hanging with fat, . . . and maybe some heather
off the hill could be sold for bedding, . . . and
there was straw that would be good for the thatch
that other people needed, . . . and the pratee
crop looked promising, and down the glen, where
the fields suffered from the floods, the people
would need to buy pratees at the heel of the year,
. . . and the corn was heavy of ear, . . . and
there were twenty-five lambs ready come the next
market. Then maybe the childer away in America
would send a little money at Christmas.   In this
manner Maura The Rosses strove to win Doalty
over to her way of thinking, and all the time Doalty's thoughts were on Sheila Dermod, who was
now all alone in her house on the brae.   That
night her mother would be late in returning home,
for the journey to Ardagh was a long step. . . .
Doalty decided that he would go up and see Sheila when darkness fell. . . .

And now, won't ye do that?" he suddenly heard
his mother say.

"All right," he replied.   "I'll see that the
house gets slated."

"And ye'll pay for the slatin', will ye?" she
asked.

"I'll pay for it," said Doalty.

III

Oiney Leahy came into the house of Maura The
Rosses ten minutes later.   In one hand he carried
a strong ash-plant, in the other a bundle of ban-
nocks wrapped in a dotted handkerchief.

"Good morra t'ye, Oiney," said Maura The
Rosses.   "Is it goin' on a journey that ye are?"

"It is," said Oiney Leahy, placing his bundle
on the floor and sitting down on a chair, near the
fire.

"Then it's a good day that ye're havin' for the
same," said Maura The Rosses, making a brave
effort to restrain her curiosity.   She wanted to
know where Oiney was bound for, but Glenmornan is very loth to ask anybody about their business.

Oiney lit his little clay pipe; white and clean it
was, which showed that it had just been dug up
from the field behind the old man's house.   From
Oiney's expression it was evident that he was in a
very serious mood, and though relishing his
smoke, he was doing his best to hide his enjoy-
ment of a pleasant pipe.   He puffed soberly for
a moment, as if above such a performance, and
then, taking the pipe from his mouth, he held it
between finger and thumb and rubbed the stem
across his white beard.   Presently he spoke in
a voice of chastened humour.

"It is indeed a good day for a journey," he
said, "and a willin' foot will carry a man far on a

day like this, please God. Even old Breed, above there, has gone out the day."

"Where's *she* goin' the day?" asked Maura The Rosses.

"It's the slates that she's gettin'," said Oiney. "Once the harvest is by and in, she'll be gettin' them over her head. It'll be a snug home that she'll be lavin' behint her, for her girsha, when she goes."

Maura The Rosses, who was pouring a fistful of tea on the teapot which she had just placed on the fire, did not say anything. To evince curiosity in the doings of Breed Dermod was beneath her.

"It'll be a snug home for the girl and the man that has the luck to get her," said Oiney. "And there's some that would go far and not find as soncy a girl."

Maura The Rosses glanced covertly at Doalty, then back at the teapot again.

"So Breed is away to see about the slates," said Oiney, as if in agreement with some imaginary individual, who had just informed him of this fact. "And it's a grand day to be shakin' one's legs on the roads. For meself I have a much longer journey and now is the time for it, seein' that I have all the turf stacked, and all the pratees makin' a good show, and the grass gettin' ready for the scythe and not much to do at all on me wee bit iv land, bar the milkin' iv the cow and the puttin' out iv it to grass in the mornin', and the takin' in iv it at night, and the feedin' iv the dog and the cat. I'll be distant for a few days, so I'm gettin'

Sheila Dermod to milk the cow one mornin' and
one night, and Eileen Kelly will do the same another day and yer Norah, if ye'll allow it, Maura
The Rosses, will do the same on the third day.
Then, the morra, Dennys The Drover is goin' to
see me cow and young calf to the hill, and he's
goin' to take it in at night—a job that he'll not fail
to do, seein' that it's Sheila Dermod that will milk
the cow, when he takes it in."

A grateful look showed in the eyes that Maura
The Rosses fixed on Oiney.

"And on the day that Eileen Kelly is doin' the
milking I would like if Doalty would be as good
as to come over and see the cow in and out," said
Oiney. "Widye do that now, Doalty,"

"I'll be delighted to do it," said Doalty.

"And on the third day yer Norah and Owen
Briney will do the work for me, Maura The
Rosses."

"Iv course Norah will be glad to help ye as
much as she can," said Maura The Rosses, as she
lifted the teapot from the coals. "Now ye'll have
a wee drop iv the tay before ye go out on yer journey," she said.

"Not this tide, thank ye," said Oiney Leahy.
"It's to Lough Derg that I'm goin' and I'm takin'
me fast with me."

"Indeed, Oiney," said Maura The Rosses.

"It's true," said Oiney. "A person must once
in a time think iv God. When all's said and done
and one looks back on one's sins it's to be seen
that the flesh is weak, Maura The Rosses, and

there's sin in the marrow iv one's bones. . . . I
must repint because the faith says it."

"I wish that ye could take Doalty widye to
Lough Derg," said Maura The Rosses. "After
his long years in foreign parts he should go to
Lough Derg and get free from all his sins."

She spoke of Doalty as if the young man were
not in the room.

"I'd be only too glad if Doalty would make
the journey with me," said Oiney. "But he's a
good boy and not as much in sin as I am."

"So you don't think that I need forgiveness,
Oiney?" said Doalty. "My mother and that old
fool Devaney think different."

"It's the priest he means," said Maura The
Rosses to Oiney. "I don't know what's comin'
over the boy at all. He wasn't like this when he
was wee."

"Ah! but he'll come round to see things in the
right way one day," said Oiney hopefully. "Not
now, maybe, for he's young yet. But he has his
years before him."

"It's to Lough Derg that he should go, for he
needs it more than yerself, Oiney," said Maura
The Rosses. "I keep me eyes on him and I see
things. Since he came home here he hasn't been
in at the Paidreen* one night, at all. It's always
outside that he is, and lookin' at the lights comin'
out in the houses along the glen. He likes to look
at them, he says. And he's always lookin' at the
stars over Carnaween and listenin' to the winds

* Rosary.

blowin' down from the hills and he says that he's very near to God when he's foolin' about like that, the poor plaisham. . . . As if that will take him to heaven! Father Devaney was telling me that he was coming up to see Doalty one day, and I told Doalty. What did he say when he heard this but, ' If that old dog comes up here I'll pitch him into the duhal.' "

"But he goes to Mass every Sunday," said Oiney.

" He does, but d'ye know what he said the other day, Oiney?" asked Maura The Rosses, still speaking as if Doalty were not present. "He said that the priest was a funny old fellow. Think iv that. Callin' the holy priest a fellow! I'm afraid that Doalty is a Prodesan."

" No fear," said Oiney. If a man's born to the ould, ancient faith he'll never lose it. It's with us, no matter what we do. We may go away at times, committin' the worst iv sins, The Deadly Sins, there are seven iv them, The Sins That Cry to God For Vengeance, there are four iv them, The Sins Against The Holy Ghost, there are six iv them, and we may commit all these, and more, but in the end we come back again. So will yerself if ye have gone away, Doalty, though I don't think that ye have. Ye'll come back on yer dyin' day if not before. For once that ye're born in the faith, it is always yours. It may be like a silver coin with the rust all over it, but all ye have to do is to scrape the rust off and there ye find the coin as bright and white and shiny as ever. . . . Now

when I go over to Lough Derg, holdin' to me fast,
doin' the stations barefut and goin' to me duties,
I'll be as clean in my soul as the christened baby.
. . . I may fall again, but then, God is always
waitin'. . . ."

The old man got to his feet, put his pipe in his
mouth, raised his bundle and went out, sideways
through the door.

" Good luck t'yer journey, Oiney Leahy,"
Maura The Rosses called after him.

" Thank ye for the blessin'," said the old man
and full of a faith in God, much the more vigor-
ous because never disputed or analyzed, he went,
his fast with him, on the journey to Lough Derg.

" Does he often go there?" Doalty enquired
when the footsteps of the pilgrim died away.

" About once a year, good man," said Maura
The Rosses, fixing a look of stern disapproval on
Doalty and speaking of Oiney in a very respect-
ful voice.   From her tone, it was evident that
she considered Oiney had, by this simple act of
piety, risen far above the mundane world of Glenmornan.   " He needs to go, too," she added.
" He has been about all the turf-stacks in Stranameera since last Hall' Eve, for he hadn't a clod
saved at the end iv last harvest.   He'll be all
right the year that's comin', for he has all his bog
gathered now. . . . But will ye go to Lough
Derg, Doalty, as soon as the harvest is in?" Maura
The Rosses enquired.

" Well, I'll see," said Doalty.

IV

That night when the darkness had fallen, Doalty Gallagher went up to Breed Dermod's house. In front of the house lay a field, with the grass growing up to the very door. Sheila did not hear the young man coming, and when he went in he found her sitting on a chair, her red petticoat tucked up between her knees, washing her feet in a tin dish, filled with spring water. She sprang up when he entered, letting her dress fall down.

"Oh! ye've give me a fright!" she exclaimed, with a gasp, shy and indignant, fixing her eyes on Doalty. "I didn't hear ye comin' at all. Oh! I'm broke!"

"I've come up because I want to see you," said Doalty, looking at the girl. The lamp was not lit, but a dull fire showed on the hearth.

"Ye want to see me again!" said the girl, her lips twitching. "Why are ye always wantin' to see me?"

"You know quite well why I want to see you, Sheila," said the young man. "I love you, Sheila. You don't think. . . ."

"But ye're always tellin' me that," said the girl.

"But you believe me, don't you?" asked Doalty, and he reached out and clasped the girl's hand. He pulled the young girlish body towards him and pressed it with a mad passion. Sheila shrank back, frightened.

"Lave go iv me, Doalty Gallagher," she said.
"Anybody may come in now and ye doin' this."

"Let them come in if they like," said Doalty
recklessly, and bending down, he tried to kiss the
fresh warm lips of Sheila. But he was unsuccess-
ful. The girl bowed her head and he rested his
lips on her hair.

"Look up at me," he whispered in a hoarse
voice. "Look up at me, Sheila."

"Whisht!" said the girl in a whisper, pressing
her face against Doalty's chest and raising her
hand in an attitude of listening. "There's someone comin'. And I haven't got my boots on."

She pulled herself away with a violent movement, and rushing to a bed which stood in the corner of the kitchen, she groped under it and brought
out a pair of boots and stockings. At that moment Eileen Kelly entered the house, and seeing
Doalty Gallagher, she came to a dead stop and
looked at him.

"Is it ye that's here, Doalty Gallagher?" she
enquired, stretching out her hand to the young
man. "Ye're one iv the first in."

She pressed his hand firmly, relaxed her grip
for a moment, then squeezed his hand again, as if
complimenting him on some success which, in her
eyes, he had achieved. Doalty, agitated and confused, stared blankly at Eileen, but did not speak.
How he disliked her! Why had she not stopped
at home?

"Where are ye, Sheila?" Eileen called, peering
round the room, looking for her friend. "Ah!"
she exclaimed, noticing Sheila sitting by the bed,

pulling her stockings on; "I see ye. Ye're late gettin' ready. What has been keepin' ye?. . . . But it would be better to ask Doalty Gallagher that, I suppose. What tricks have ye been at, Doalty?" she enquired, fixing her eyes on the young man.

"Nothing," Doalty stammered. "I have only come in just now."

"Light the lamp for me, Eileen," Sheila called from the corner.

Eileen lit the oil-lamp that hung by a nail from the brace. Doalty sat down on a chair near the table. Sheila, her boots on, stirred up the fire and put a kettle of water on the crook. Eileen Kelly brought out a stocking from under her shawl, sat on a hassog by the fire and commenced knitting.

"It's a wonder that none iv the others are in yet," she said, looking at Sheila. "I saw Micky Neddy and Dennys The Drover down be the road talkin' to one another, just when I left the house."

"They're coming up of course?" Doalty enquired, dreading the answer to his question and at the same time trying to appear indifferent.

"Iv course they're comin'," said Eileen Kelly. "It's not often that Sheila has the house to herself."

"Then I suppose I'd better go," said Doalty carelessly, addressing the remark intended for Sheila Dermod's ears, to Eileen Kelly.

"What widye be wantin' to go 'way for, now?" asked Eileen. "The first time that ye've come here and wantin' to go 'way just as if ye didn't belong to the same glen as ourselves. Isn't he a silly card, Sheila?"

"He is . . . very silly," said Sheila emphatically. But she was not referring to Doalty's remark apparently, but to an event which had taken place some minutes before. For a while after speaking, she kept looking at the fire and the red tongues of flame shooting up against the soot.

At that moment Dennys The Drover, accompanied by Micky Neddy, the red-haired youngster with the fern-tickled face and buck teeth, entered.

v

"So ye're all here," said Dennys, fixing his gaze on the two girls. Then he looked at Doalty and a gleam of irony seemed to show for a moment in his eyes.

"So ye, yerself's here, Doalty," he said, with a laugh, as he sat down. "That's the way. When the hawk's in its nest the chickens can play tig."

"They can," said Doalty, who was lighting a cigarette. He handed the packet round.

Eileen Kelly took a cigarette, but when Sheila reached out her hand to the packet, Drover Dennys gripped hold of her wrist.

"Ye're not goin' to have one at all, till ye put the taypot on the fire for the tay," he said. "People comin' here to see ye and not gettin' a drop iv tay to drink!"

Still holding Sheila by the arm, Dennys got to his feet and led her towards the dresser.

"There's what ye want," he said, pointing at the delft teapot, "and the sugar is in the press and the tay is in a box somewhere. Ye get a move on ye, Sheila, and give us something to drink."

"Then I'm goin' to get a cigarette to smoke, amn't I?" asked the girl, with a laugh, as she tried to box Dennys' ears.

"Ye'll get one to smoke then," said Drover Dennys, coming back to his chair.

"There's no standin' ye, Drover Dennys," said Eileen Kelly. "Ye come in to a house, and ye gad about the same as if ye were under yer own roof."

"Now, will ye be quiet, Eileen," said Drover Dennys. "If ye're not I'll pull yer needles out."

"It'll need something better than yerself to spoil me knittin'," said Eileen Kelly, with a laugh, holding out her stocking and threatening him with it.

She held it close enough for him to grip a needle, which he pulled out.

"Give me back me needle," she said, giggling. For answer Dennys pulled another needle from her work.

"Well, that's too much," said the girl, making a face at the youth. "I don't like ye at all, Dennys The Drover. Ye should have more sense, and respect yerself, just like Doalty Gallagher or Micky Neddy."

Dennys got to his feet, lifted Eileen Kelly from

her hassock and sat down on it with the girl on his knees. She struggled a little, as if to free herself, from his grip, but to Doalty it was evident that she did not want to get away.

"Don't be holdin' me so tight now," said Eileen. "I can't move with yer big arms about me. Let me be, ye thick mountainy crathur!"

Dennys, however, pressed her tighter the more she struggled and now and again for a change he rubbed his chin against hers, "Just to give ye a bit iv beardy," he remarked.

All this time Sheila Dermod was preparing the tea by the fire, her face flushed a little as she bent over the red turf. Doalty Gallagher was stealing fugitive glances at her. Now and again, when she raised her eyes and met his, she bit her lips as if annoyed at the young man's persistent scrutiny.

"Don't be doin' this to me," Eileen Kelly suddenly exclaimed, pretending to free herself from Dennys' embrace, while trying to sink deeper into it. "Do this to Sheila Dermod and not to me. Ye're afeerd iv her, I'm thinkin'."

In this way the girl was trying to find what depth of feeling existed between The Drover and her friend. This Doalty Gallagher would also like to find out. He looked at Sheila.

"Afraid iv her, the wee cutty!" said Dennys. "Am I afeerd iv ye, Sheila?"

"Ah! ye're always blatherin', Dennys The Drover," said the girl, blowing the ashes from the teapot, and placing it on the table.

"Ye'll know somethin' different the morra,

then," said Dennys The Drover. "Wait till I get hold iv ye milkin' Oiney Leahy's cow. Then I'll be tellin' ye somethin' that ye'll never speak about at confession."

"If ye be carryin' on with tricks like that, Dennys The Drover, I'll run away and lave ye be yerself," said Sheila. "If ye say things ye'd be afraid to tell at confession it doesn't mane that I'll give ear to them."

"I don't know why the hell we've to tell everything at confession," said Micky Neddy, spitting on the floor. He had been chewing and spitting ever since he came in. "I don't believe in it. There's old Father Devaney and he has built that big house iv his at hundreds iv pounds. He said when he started it that it would be made for himself and the curates, but now, that it's built, there's nobody livin' there bar himself and his old sister. He won't let a curate get in there, for he's such a crusty old divil. And he'll go to the dances down the town and sit there till mornin' with the Quigleys and the others iv that kind, but if it comes to a dance up this way, he says that it's a sin. I wouldn't make me confession to such an old rascal." Micky spat on the floor. "I don't often go, but when I do it's never to him. It's one God for the people iv the town and another God for the people iv the glen, be the way that he looks at it. It's all humbug, I'm thinkin'. What d'ye think, Doalty Gallagher?"

"I think that you're quite right," said Doalty, who had his eyes fixed on Sheila Dermod.

"And so do I," said Eileen Kelly. "I suppose he thinks that all the people up the glen are fools."

"Eileen Kelly!" said Sheila Dermod reprovingly.

"So he does," said Eileen. "Micky Neddy is right about it."

"I didn't think that ye'd say that, Eileen Kelly," said Sheila, placing a large cake of homemade bread on the table. "It's not like ye to talk in that way about God and the holy priests."

At that moment Doalty saw something move outside the window. A cap rose up from the darkness and pressed against the lower pane, then a pair of eyes followed. These stared in for a second and disappeared. Eileen Kelly saw it also. She got to her feet and pulled the blind down on the window.

"Somebody was lookin' in," she said. "It was Owen Briney, I'm thinkin'."

"He's always nosin' about here," said Sheila.

"What will he be lookin' after?" asked Micky Neddy.

"He's wantin' to see what people's doin', I think," said Sheila Dermod. "But come, yees now, and sit down and ate somethin'."

The party sat down to the meal. They had a lot to talk about, the harvest that was coming, the slating of the glen houses and the fun of the hills, when Micky Neddy, Dennys The Drover and Oiney Leahy went out to make potheen. These three had several fights with the police, and by their talk Doalty inferred that the three men were equal to a dozen policemen when it came to a hand-

to-hand combat.   Oiney Leahy always went out
in the bare feet over the rocks and was never as
happy as when he had a ruction with the police.

When the meal came to an end Sheila hurried
the boys away.

" I don't want me mother to see ye here," she
said.   She may be in at any minit now, and if the
house is full iv yees what am I to say?"

" All right, we'll get out," said Dennys The
Drover.   " But mind the morra and don't be late
comin' over to Oiney Leahy's."

" I'll be there as soon as yerself, I'm sure," said
Sheila Dermod.

VI

The three men went out and made for their
homes.   It was only a step down the brae to
Maura The Rosses and when Doalty got there,
he stood outside the window for a moment and
peeped in.   He could see his mother on her knees
by the fire, giving out the Rosary, the children
making the responses.   Hughie Beag, already in
bed, with his two bright eyes peeping out from beneath the blankets, was waiting for his mother to
tell him the story of the bat and the cat and the
wee red hen.   Instead of going inside Doalty
turned back and went up the hill again, towards
Breed Dermod's house.

The road ran through the clump of hazel bushes,
in which he first met Sheila after his return from

abroad.   It was here he met her now.   She was
standing there, with Eileen Kelly, and the two
girls were apparently listening to hear if Breed
Dermod was coming back from the village of Ardagh.

"Oh! it's ye that's in it!" said Eileen Kelly,
when Doalty stumbled across the two girls.   By
her tone of voice it was evident that she was expecting somebody else; not Doalty, and presum-
ably not Breed Dermod.   "Are ye not goin' to
bed at all the night, Doalty Gallagher?" Eileen
enquired.

"It's far too early to go to bed yet," said Doalty.   "If I go to bed now, I can't sleep."

"That's a sign that there's something on yer
mind, if ye can't sleep," said Eileen.

"Maybe there is," Doalty replied.

"D'ye hear that?" said Eileen Kelly, turning
round to speak to her friend.   But Sheila had
stolen away and was already back in her house.

"Well, that's a funny thing, isn't it?" Eileen
appealed to Doalty.   "Goin' away without a
word and leavin' me here me lone."

"But you are not quite alone," said Doalty with
a laugh.   "Do you consider yourself alone when
you are here with me?"

"Well, Sheila's not with me," said Eileen.

"But still you're not alone," Doalty persisted,
looking closely into Eileen's face. He had never
been so close to Eileen before, and had never real-
ised what a charming girl she looked.   "You're
as safe here," he said, "just as safe as if you were
along with Sheila Dermod."

" But yerself would much rather that it was Sheila that was here instead iv me," said Eileen, coming closer to Doalty.

"What causes you to think that?" he asked.

" Me own two eyes are not blind," said the girl. "Who were ye lookin' at all this night?"

" Nobody in particular," Doalty replied, careless whether she believed him or not.

"But how was it that ye were up here before anyone, when ye found that Breed went away to Ardagh?"

" I did not know Breed had gone to Ardagh," said Doalty. " If I had known that Breed went, I wouldn't have come up here," he lied. " I would have gone down and seen yourself instead."

" I suppose ye've been wild after the girls away there?" enquired Eileen, with frank curiosity.

This question produced a singular effect on Doalty. A cloud seemed to rise round him, hiding the present and choking its desires, blotting out the future and its hopes. Sheila, for the moment, was forgotten, even the girl, standing by his side, was not in his world. Shadowgraph pictures of the past swept across the tablet of his mind with astounding speed. Lady Ronan, George Ronan, the deferential butler, the editor, all swept across his mental vision like figures born in the vapour of his mind. Suddenly the racing pictures stopped dead, as if a brake had been applied, and one stood out clearly, the picture of Myra Ronan in an English bedroom. The girl had been terrified by a footstep in the passage outside. . . . She clutched Doalty's sleeve. . . . He bent

down, put his arms round her and looked into the
eyes of Eileen Kelly. . . .

"Ye are all the same, every one iv ye," Eileen
said, pressing Doalty away from her. "I suppose
ye would say the same things to me that ye would
say to Sheila, if ye had the chance. . . . I know
it. There's no difference in any iv yees boys."

She stepped slowly back, then turned round
and ran into the house. Once there, she closed
the door behind her.

"What a fool I'm making of myself!" said
Doalty, turning hurriedly away and making his
way down the brae again. "And the two girls
are such strange creatures. . . . Am I in love
with one of them, both of them, or neither of them.
. . . I don't know. . . . But if Eileen
had not run away I'd have—— Does Sheila care
for me? . . . Eileen, I know, does not, but
she is in love with Dennys The Drover and Dennys is not in love with her. But is Dennys in love
with Sheila? . . . Is Sheila in love with
him? There is very little love in Glenmornan.
Marriages are affairs of convenience. . . .
Love has no romance here. . . . People get
mated. . . . Six cows' grass marries six cows'
grass. . . . If I married Sheila Dermod my
mother would be annoyed. . . . The lowest
of the low. . . . But I am in love with Sheila,
madly in love with her."

Doalty met Breed Dermod coming up the hill.
She was barefooted, having taken off her boots,
no doubt, because they hurt her feet. Or maybe
she thought that the roads wore them out too quick-

ly. Breed did not speak to him, but when he went past she stood for a long time, following him with her eyes. When she got into her home she looked at the bowl of sugar, the cake of bread and the box of tea.

" I'll be in no hurry leavin' the house under yer care again," she said to Sheila. "When ye get me out, ye have nothin' better to do than to feed the whole townland. Ye've a ready hand at givin' the bread away. One would think that all ye had to do was to go out and pull it from the ground like bockins* . . . but wait till the morrow!" said Breed Dermod harshly. " I'll go down to Maura The Rosses and tell her what I think iv her son, the dirty Prodesan turncoat!"

---

* Bockin—a mushroom.

CHAPTER IX

THE MOWING

A young man has ways with him of always letting on;
His feet they're supple at a dance but slow to shake at
dawn.
You'd think he owned the whole townland, he is so full
of airs,
And showing off he always is at dances and at fairs;
My man to be must be like that, a strapping boy and tall,
Or 'tisn't me to sleep with him at either stock or wall.
—A Kailyee Song.

I

ALTHOUGH he promised his mother that he would pay for the slating of the house, Doalty Gallagher had practically no money. When he left London he had some thirty pounds in his pocket, but he found, on arriving home, that Glenmornan sucked up money as a sponge soaks up water. One day Hughie Beag wanted a new coat, the next day Norah needed a new pair of boots, and again, Kitty being all in rags, could not go into the convent school, where all the quality ones were, until she got a new dress. When they informed Maura The Rosses of their needs the old woman's answer was invariably the same. "Tell Doalty about it," she would say. "He has money and to spare, and he'll not miss the wee penny that ye're wantin'."

Doalty gave the money while he possessed it, but now he had almost come to his last penny. Something had to be done, and being a journalist, Doalty's thoughts turned to his newspaper. George Ronan had advised him to send some "stories," and Doalty found that he had any amount of material to hand. Half a dozen good stories dealing with Glenmornan would be certain to sell, then these could be followed by others. . . . He took a table and a chair, a pen, ink, and a dozen sheets of paper out to the field in front of the house and sat down and wrote.

It was an easy enough job, jotting down impression after impression, incident after incident, portraying habits, customs and humours of the Glenmornan people. Oiney Leahy under another name, was described in detail; the fair of Greenanore formed a topic, but the girl, Sheila Dermod, was not spoken about. But even when writing Doalty's mind was seldom far removed from Sheila and his eyes followed her as she went over to Oiney Leahy's to keep house for the man who was away on the pilgrimage to Lough Derg.

Doalty stopped his work to watch the girl crossing the braes. Then when she entered Oiney's house, he lay back on his chair, lit a cigarette and thought of many things. A sort of inward calm had come to him and he did not want to work too hard; neither did he wish to talk to anybody. All that he wanted to do was to muse peacefully, surrounded by the unbroken peace of Glenmornan, and with which his own mood was in perfect accord.

He could see the river leaping over the ford beneath him, its spray rising as if to catch the glitter and sheen of the hot sun. Memories of his youth came over him, and with these memories came a certain sadness. But why he was sad he did not pause to analyze. All that he wanted to do was to laze and let his thoughts run whither they wist.

"Hang it all!" he suddenly exclaimed, getting to his feet. " I'm not going to write another line. To-morrow will do. I'm feeling tired, happily tired, just the same as if I had done a long day's work. But I have done nothing. I wonder why these people can sustain their energy in such an enervating climate."

As he spoke he looked across at Meenawarawor, where the natives of that townland were out on the hills, stacking peat for the winter's fire. Seen from where he stood the workers looked mere pigmies moving very slowly over the broken moor. But they were in reality working hard, sweating as they toiled. Little fires burned on the spreadfield. The white smoke curled up into the heavens. There was peace there, but the peace was such a lazy one. Nothing seemed to be getting done. To-morrow and to-morrow the same labour would be performed, the same energy would be expended, and for all the strain and stress of their toil, the people would be as poor at the end of the year as at the beginning. But they were happy enough. Petty cares and worries filled their day, and their years, and their lives. . . . But are not all cares petty? Is not Life itself, for Glenmornan and for the world at large, a poor and petty business?

"Good day t'ye, Doalty Gallagher."

The young man turned round with a start to find Breed Dermod behind him.

"Good day, Breed," said Doalty, and he wondered whether he should hold out his hand to the woman or not. But the threatening look in her sunken eyes, and the hard line of her tightly closed and sunken lips forbade such familiarity. Breed Dermod looked as if she were angry with Doalty. For a moment she stood without speaking another word, one hand hidden in her shawl and the other—how big and red it looked—hanging down by her side, against her bauna brockagh petticoat.

"So ye've nothin' to say for yerself, Doalty Gallagher," said the woman, glowering at the young man.

"Nothing at all," Doalty stammered.

"Nothin' at all!" repeated the woman, catching up the words as they fell from the young man's lips. "Nothin' at all is it that ye have to say, and ye runnin' round about our house up there all night, last night. The boys about the roads, here now, are bad enough, but when it comes to them that comes home from abroad, they should know better than run about the way that yerself was doin' last night. I went out and left Sheila to mind the house and then I comes back and find ye comin' down the braes, and when I goes into the house what do I find? The place has been scringed from top to bottom and everything ate. To think that Maura The Rosses hasn't enough money laid by to fill yer hungry gut when ye come back !. . ." She raised her voice so that Maura The Rosses would hear her.

" Breed Dermod," said Doalty, in as calm a voice as he could muster, though he felt confused and foolish. " I don't know what you are speaking about."

" Don't know what I'm speakin' about !" shrieked the woman, glaring at him. " Don't know what I'm speakin' about, Oily Tongue ! Talkin' there the same as if butter wouldn't melt in yer mouth ! Ye're a greedy gut, and if yer mother was the woman she sets herself to be, she wouldn't own up to a son like yerself, Doalty Gallagher."

" I wish ye wouldn't come down here with yer tongue-bangin'," said Maura The Rosses, coming into the field and standing in front of Breed Dermod. " If Doalty went up to yer house it wasn't my wish. If I had me way with him he'd keep out iv arm's reach iv you and yours."

Breed Dermod folded her arms across her breast, let her shawl drop back from her shoulders, and scanned Maura The Rosses deliberately.

" Ye must be proud iv yer family, Maura The Rosses," she said, in a calm voice, which the pallor of her cheeks and the agitation of her shoulders utterly belied. " Ye've been often talkin' about them and the way they get on so well when they go abroad. Iv course nobody knows what they do when they are away, but we can see the kind iv beauties they are when they come back again. They're a scandal to the townland and the glen, and it's down to the priest that I'll go the morrow and see what he can do to get this gulpin from comin' round about our house up there. I'll see about it . . . I'll see, Maura The Rosses."

Now that the two women were face to face, Breed Dermod seemed to take a greater delight in giving expression to her wrath. All the people of the glen, within ear-shot, were out listening.

" I'll see the priest about this," said Breed Dermod. " I'll get that fine boy iv yours, Maura The Rosses, read from the altar. Runnin' about me house when I'm out iv it. . . . Scringin' all over the place and makin' a huddle iv everything. . . . The boys about the road are wild enough at times, but they're not like him. He thinks that he can do what he likes when he comes back from across the water. . . . Thinks that we're all fools here. And the priest knows what he's like, for I've heard him meself, say that Doalty is a disgrace to the parish and to the country."

"All the glen's out listenin' t' ye, Breed Dermod," said Maura The Rosses, who was in reality a very quiet woman and preferred nursing a hate in secret, to airing it within hearing of her neighbours.

" Listenin' to me ! And as if I cared the turn iv a straw whether they are or not," said Breed Dermod, shouting at the topmost pitch of her voice. " There's nothin' that I am afraid iv. There's nothin' in me or mine that needs to be hid. . . . But it's not in yerself to say the same, Maura The Rosses, ye that's the mother iv a Prodesan turncoat!"

"All right, say what ye like," Doalty's mother replied. "I'm goin' into me home and ye can keep speakin' on here as long as ye like."

So saying, Maura The Rosses went into her home and Doalty followed her. Breed Dermod kept up her harangue for the best part of an hour. Three generations of the Gallaghers, dead and living, came in for the censure of the angry woman. Even Doalty's great-grandfather, accused of stealing sheep, double-branding them, and cutting their ribigs, was held up to scorn. Doalty, and all sib to him, were lashed with Breed Dermod's tongue. It was only when her voice failed her that Breed went back to her home.

"It's hard to get the better iv that woman in an argument," said Maura The Rosses, when the voice outside became silent. "She just came down here to let her spite out on me and ye have been the cause iv it, Doalty. She was just wantin' an excuse, and I'm sorry that ye gave her that excuse, Doalty. But I wouldn't give her the nose to say a word back to her. I wouldn't sink meself. But I wish that ye wouldn't go gaddin' about after Sheila, and her so much below ye. . . . After comin' back from beyont the water, too, where people should learn to know their own worth."

Maura The Rosses did not say anything further. The incident had upset her. The thought that a woman like Breed Dermod had cause to complain

of one of her children was as much as Maura The
Rosses could bear.

That night Doalty stopped in for the Rosary
and did not go out to see Sheila Dermod.

II

Bringing pencil and paper with him, Doalty
Gallagher went across to Oiney Leahy's the next
morning.   When he had put out the cow and calf
to the hill he sat down in Oiney's kitchen and completed two stories of the set of six which he had
started the day before.   In the evening, when
darkness was falling, he went up to the hill and
brought the cow and calf back to the byre.   Eileen
Kelly was there, waiting for him.

" You're here early enough," said Doalty, as
he tied the cow to its stake in the warm byre.

" I had nothin' to do at all," Eileen replied; " so
I thought I'd just come over and be in time.   I
may as well be here as anywhere else."

" That's true," said Doalty, looking at the girl.
She was a gracefully built creature who moved her
shoulders nervously when speaking.   The lines
of her face, clear cut and a little severe, softened
when she smiled, and there was something winning
and coaxing in the sidelong glance she fixed on
Doalty when she spoke to him.

" What roguery is hiding behind those black
eyes of hers?" Doalty asked himself, as she sat
down on the stool to milk the cow.   " All the time

she seems to be trying to resist some mad impulse.
. . . I wonder why I am taking such notice of
her. I almost feel in the same mood as I felt the
other night when I was in her company. . . .
It's youth I suppose," he mumbled, in a reckless
whisper, fixing an earnest gaze on her red three-
cornered lips, where a faint smile hovered. "A
mood like this remains for a day or two, and then
goes, never to return."

"Ye're talking to yerself, aren't ye, Doalty Gallagher?" Eileen asked, her clear voice rising above
the sound of the milk falling into the pail held between her knees. "Do ye often be talking to
yerself?"

"Not often, Eileen," said Doalty.

"It's what the old men bees often doin', talkin'
to themselves," said the girl. "Oiney Leahy is
always talking to himself when he's out in the
gubby, diggin' up the pipes."

"He's a good old man, Oiney, isn't he?" asked
Doalty.

"Oh, he's not such a bad old shanahy," said
Eileen. . . . "But God help him! poor man,
for he has his own troubles and nobody with him
at all, to help him in this wee house. It's a poor
thing when one is left alone when they get very
old. . . . Aisy now, wee cow, and don't be
wipin' me face with yer tail!"

"Why did you run away and leave me the
other night?" Doalty enquired, looking at Eileen.
"You turned away all at once and left me alone."

"But ye didn't want me to stay with ye, did ye
now?" asked the girl.

"Of course I wanted you to stay," said Doalty.

"Then why didn't ye say so?"

"You did not give me time."

"But ye'd plenty of time, Doalty Gallagher," said Eileen. "If ye had it in yer mind for me to stay, ye would say so before ye let me go away. . . . But I knew what it was. Ye were only wantin' me, seein' that ye had no one else to speak to. Ye're like all the other boys."

"Which boys?"

"The boys about the road," said the girl. "Now ye wee divil ye! ye're waggin' yer tail about me face again."

The milking finished, Eileen got to her feet.

"Take the stool into the house widye, Doalty Gallagher," she said, as she went out. "I'll make a drop iv tay ready for ye if I can find the sugar at all."

"It was dark inside when Doalty got there and the turf fire, burning red on the hearth, did little to light up the house. Eileen Kelly was standing by the dresser, straining the milk into a big crock, the dog was nosing about her feet, looking for something to eat.

"Light the lamp, if ye can," she said. "Put some oil into it first and trim the wick. Ye'll find the bottle iv oil under the bed. Ye'd better pit yer nose to the bottle when ye find it and see what it is," she added with a laugh. "Oiney has miny's a strange bottle under his bed."

Doalty found a bottle, smelt it.

"This is oil," he said, and going to a corner of

the wall, near the window, he brought down the lamp, filled it with oil, trimmed the wick and lit it.

"That's better be far now," said the girl, smiling at Doalty, who was rubbing his soiled fingers against the leg of his trousers.

He sat down and watched her at her work. Eileen was dressed in a striped blouse and a neat serge skirt pulled in a little at the ankles. Stranameera girls were imitating the Greenanore fashions and Greenanore was now making a brave display of hobble skirts. Eileen also had her boots on, though earlier in the day when Doalty saw her going to the neighbours' houses she was barefooted. But her reasons for wearing boots now could be easily understood. She wanted to show Doalty that she could dress just as well as the people abroad. The Glenmornan girls are as vain as women generally are supposed to be.

Eileen put the kettle on the crook, stirred up the fire and sat down.

"Ye've been in here all the day, haven't ye?" she enquired shyly. Although bashful, she was very eager to talk.

"I have been writing all day."

"And what would ye be writing about now?" she enquired. "I suppose it will be to some girl that ye've been spakin' to over there."

"It's not to any girl."

"Ye haven't one?"

"No."

"And ye think that the people about here are goin' to believe that?" she asked, with an incredulous quiver of her lips. She spoke rapidly, as if she was going to say quite a number of things in a short time. "Ye'll be back here for a wee while I know, and then ye'll leave us again," she said.

"I'm never going away from here again," Doalty told her.

"Catch ye stayin' here, Doalty Gallagher, where there's not a decent girl at all to be seen," said Eileen. "Ye'll be soon tired iv us all, even iv Sheila Dermod that ye're mad after."

"She's a strange girl," said Doalty without contradicting Eileen's assertion. "A number of the glen fellows are in love with her, are they not?"

"Some are, maybe," said Eileen petulantly, "but one can never tell what's in the mind iv a boy, can they?"

"Did you hear Breed Dermod down at our house yesterday?" asked Doalty.

"That's the way that she has with her, poor woman," said Eileen. "She's very thran and throughother, but no one takes much heed iv her at all, once they get to know her. . . . She doesn't like the young people to have their wee bit iv fun and that's what's wrong with her. . . . But are ye in earnest, Doalty Gallagher, when ye say that ye're never goin' away from here?" she asked.

"Yes, I'm in earnest."

"Cross on yer neck, then."

Doalty made a cross on his neck with his thumb as a proof of the truth of his words.

"Then ye'll marry and settle down here, won't ye?"

"I may," said Doalty, with a laugh.

"Well, nobody here thinks that," Eileen confessed. They think that ye'll go away with the tourists when the wet and cold weather comes."

The girl, as she spoke these words, got to her feet and made the tea. Then the two of them sat at the table and had their meal together.

When it was finished Eileen reached out and caught Doalty's bowl and looked at the tea-leaves at the bottom of it.

"I can read the bowl," she said, bending her head down over it and scrutinizing the tea-leaves.

Then as if reading from a book she said:

"There's a parcel comin' for ye, and ye're goin' to have a quarrel with a dark woman, and ye're goin' to cross deep water, and ye'll have a lot iv trouble, and then ye'll be happy."

"But how do you know all this?" asked Doalty.

"The bowl says so," was Eileen's simple answer. "Can yerself read a bowl?"

"I'm afraid not."

"Can ye read the hands?"

"Not even the hands," said Doalty.

"Show me yer hand then and I'll read it for ye," said Eileen, and with a complete absence of shyness or self-consciousness she caught Doalty's hand and read his fortune from the palm. The second reading differed from the first and when Doalty remarked on this, the girl looked at him, and it seemed to the man that she pressed his hand with a warmer grip as she spoke.

"It may not be the same this time," she agreed. "But one of them must be right and whither it's the palm of the hand or the bottom of the bowl I cannot say."

That night Doalty was late in returning home, and when he got there he found that his mother was out.

"She's away up to Breed Dermod's," said Norah. "Breed, poor woman, has got the sickness and she's lying very low. So our mother has gone up to see her, and Owen Briney has gone as hard as he can for the priest."

III

Oiney Leahy came back from Lough Derg next day and the evening had fallen when he arrived in Glenmornan. On his way home across the braes, he called at Maura The Rosses' house. Maura was out, having gone to see Breed Dermod, who was still poorly. Now that sickness had come the neighbour's feud was forgotten. Doalty was at home; Norah and Kitty were also there, and Hughie Beag was sitting by the fire, his heels in the ashes, and a book in his hand. Hughie, who had never been at school, was imitating his elder brothers and sisters, reading an imaginary lesson in a sing-song voice, halting now and again for a moment, as if puzzling over a word, and at times putting a local incident into the lesson.

"This was how the lesson proceeded.

"Jack has a cart. He can—draw sand and—clay. Micky—Neddy has no cart. . . . He has a—buck tooth. . . . Paddy Heela has a—crook-ed leg. Breed—Dermod has the—sickness. . . . Doalty is a—Pod-isin, etc."

Oiney Leahy came in, his hat well to the back of his head, his pipe in his mouth, the bowl turned down and resting on his white beard. As he came in, he staggered a little and put out his hand against the air as if to steady himself.

" Bejara! it's the corns," he said in a slow voice. " Bejara! I can hardly walk with them at all. . . . Slow and stiddy goes far in a day and an old dog—an old dog for the—for the hard road, but a pup for the level. . . . It's the corns, Maura The Rosses, the corns."

Oiney Leahy leant against the wall by the door and looked round the room.

" It's the corns," he said. Can't shake a leg with them !"

" Now sit down, Oiney," said Doalty, catching the old man by the arm and conducting him to a chair. " Sit down here and rest yourself."

Oiney sat down and puffed at his pipe.

" Gi'mme a light," he said. " It's gone out."

Norah Gallagher lit a fir spale and handed it to Oiney. Hughie Gallagher turned to his lessons again.

" Jack has a cart," he read. " He can draw sand and clay. Oiney—is—drunk. He was—at—Lough—Derg. He is back now. He has the—corns—he is drunk."

The little boy put down the book, looked slyly at Oiney and laughed. Then as if overcome with shame at his own boldness, he rushed up to the

little room and hid himself.   He was in no hurry
to come back, but now and again, he could be seen
peeping round the corner of the door, his bright
eyes twinkling roguishly.

"I'm not the worse iv the drink," said the old
man.   "It's the corns.   They are not good for
a journey."

He looked at Doalty.

"Where's Maura The Rosses?" he enquired.

"She's out," said Norah Gallagher.

"Out at this hour," said Oiney.   Where will
she be now?"

"She's away over to the shop to get some male,"
said Norah, for the girl did not want Oiney, who
was hardly in a fit condition for a sick visit, to go
up to Breed Dermod's that night.

"Well, I don't know what the glen girls are
comin' to," said the old man.   "Lettin' their
mothers run out to the shop at—at this hour of the
night!   Did ye go over an' milk me bit—bit iv
a cow, Norah Gallagher, when I was away?" he
asked.

"Iv course I went over.   But I didn't think
that ye'd come back this way," said Norah, in
tones of mock severity.   She had never seen
Oiney Leahy come back sober from Lough Derg.

"It's the corns, first and foremost," said the old
man.   "I'll grant ye that I had a drop when I got
my duties done and past, but—but there's nothin'
wrong in that.   I'm not a man to take the pledge
as long as I can carry a wee drop aisy.   What's the
good iv a pledge to me anyway?   What I can't be,
be nature, I'm not goin' to be, be obligation.

That's me in a word, a man of eighty if a day, too. If it wasn't for the corns I could shake a ready foot on the floor under me this very minit."

"I've no doubt of that, Oiney," said Doalty.

"And in the old times I was a great singer," said Oiney. "Come now, I've a bit iv a voice."

"Won't ye sing a bit iv a song for us now?" asked Norah.

"I won't be troublin' Doalty d'ye think?" said Oiney, looking at Norah, and taking no notice of Doalty.

"Iv course Doalty will be glad to hear ye at the singin', Oiney," said the girl. "So let's hear ye at the song."

Oiney sat back in his chair, pressed out his chest, pulled his chin and stomach in, thrust his hat to the back of his white head, buttoned the lower button of his coat, put his little clay pipe in his pocket and began his song:

" Old Ann Eamon Dubh went to market one day,
    Went up to the standin's and this she did say :
    ' I've money to bargain and money to spare,
    And I'll give ye a crown for yer crockery ware.' "

Oiney put his head to one side, shut his eyes, waved his hand over his hat and went on with increasing energy :

" She came home in the dark, with the crocks in her
    shawl
    And her daughter did not expect her at all
    And the girsha was sittin' with a man in a chair
    When her mother came in with the crockery ware."

Oiney, his beard quivering, and his feet marking time on the floor, turned to Norah and winked at her.

" That's the way that love was made in the ould times," he said. " It was then that the people knew how to do things. When the hawk was in it's nest the chickens played tig in the streets."

Oiney winked again, but this time at Doalty Gallagher. Then he caught the young man's hand and went on with the song :

" The man he was Shemus, The Rachary Wor,—
When the woman came in he ran out be the door
And Anne in her fright, then she tripped on a chair
And she broke every bit iv the crockery ware."

The song was quite a long one, but Oiney knew every verse of it. It told how Ann Eamon Dubh was very angry, how she claimed seven-pounds-ten, for the damage to the crockery, and how Shemus, The Rachary Wor, being a good, decent man and beholden to none, paid every penny of the money, rather than go to the law about it. Then Shemus married the daughter of Ann Eamon Dubh, and a finer wedding was never seen before or after in the seven corners of the country.

"A good man Shemus must have been," said Oiney, when the song came to an end. " It was wise iv him not to go to the law too, for the lawyers are able to catch the best fish in troubled waters. So Shemus must have been a cute one, not to get into their hands."

At that moment Owen Briney came in. He had never been in the house of Maura The Rosses since Doalty came home. Norah shook hands with the man and whispered something in his ear. No doubt she was advising him not to let Oiney know that Breed Dermod was not keeping well. Without a word to anybody else, Owen went out again and Norah followed him.

"Well that's a funny caper," said Oiney, when the man and woman had left the house. "I never thought that Norah Gallagher would be so big with Owen Briney as to go out in the dark with him. What is there between the two iv them?"

"Nothing that I know of," said Doalty.

"Well there shouldn't be," said the old man. "What could there be between a fellow iv that get and a decent, respectable girl like Norah? Ah! I don't know what this glen is comin' to at all. . . . I'm goin' home across the braes now. Doalty."

"I'll go over with you as far as your home," said Doalty.

The old man stood up and looked sternly at Doalty.

"I'll go home be meself," he said gruffly. "I don't want to be taken home like a man that's drunk, with nothin' wrong with me, only me corns that are bad. Good night t'ye all."

He went out sideways through the door, his pipe in his mouth, the bowl, turned down, resting on his beard. Presently he poked his head in again.

"Isn't it time that ye were startin' on the hay, Doalty?" he said.

"I'll start mowing to-morrow, I think," Doalty replied.

"That's the way," said Oiney. "It's best to get it in han'cocks before the corn is drop-ripe, and the weather is good for the job. I'll come over the morra and give ye hand, for I'm owin' it to ye since ye've helped me with the turf. Every one in the glen will be at the hay the morra."

"When will you be here in the morning?" Doalty enquired.

"At the first light, me boyo, the first light," said the old man. "Good night t'ye again and to all in the house."

As Oiney staggered off, Norah Gallagher came in again.

"Breed Dermod is very low," she said. "Our ma is goin' to stay and look over her all the night."

"So the quarrel is settled," said Doalty.

"Well, who would be havin' a quarrel with a sick person?" asked Norah Gallagher. "What kind iv people d'ye think are in the glen nowadays? . . . Hughie Beag, come down and let us see ye be the fire," she called, shaking her fist at the touseld head which stuck through the door of the little room. "Ye've got to get into bed at once."

Doalty went out and took down the scythe from the rafters of the byre, and put it into the spring well. The cold water would tighten sned and handles and the implement would be fit for its labour by dawn.

IV

It was not yet light next morning, when Doalty got up from his bed and took down the sharping-stone from a shelf of the dresser. Going out, he lifted the scythe from the well in which he had placed it the previous night. He found it a bit rusty, for it had not seen service since last harvest. The sned, home-made, was rather a clumsy one, and its handles fashioned from seasoned ash had lost some of the polished finish which the strong hand of Connel Gallagher had given them the season before.

"It will take some work to get this into order," Doalty mused, as he slung it over his shoulder. Hanging unused in the dry byre for the preceding Winter, the scythe had been falling to pieces. "It wants a good clean edge," Doalty reasoned. "But how fine! how grand! . . . Mowing again."

He went into the field under the house, the dog following at his heels. The sun was not yet up, but the birds were. They chattered in the trees and hedgerows. A breeze swept across the braes, whitening the leaves of the birch trees as it passed through them. Up from the bottom lands a thin, white mist was rising, and the river under the shadow of the hazel bushes was still dark. A fog circled lazily round the hills, and many colours showed in the sky behind Carnaween. As Doalty went down the brae towards the holm the grasses brushed against his knees, wetting his trousers. The dog, in a sportive mood, careered madly through the field, rolling over and over through the wet ripple-grass in mad abandon. A corncrake railed near the river. . . . Up by Oiney Leahy's a cock was crowing.

The holm was ready for the scythe, though up on the braes the grass was as yet sparse and thin. In the bottom land, between road and river, the luxurious and sappy hay had fallen level with the ground and the meadow was one big carpet of green that had dropped flat under its own richness. This lazy grass, over-fat, hard to cut and dry, had to be saved as quickly as possible, for the river in flood had a tendency to rise over banks flush with the holms. It happened many a time that the results of a hard week's mowing were washed away by floods that only took a couple of hours to rise.

Doalty began to sharpen his scythe. He placed the end of the sned on the ground, the thick butt of the blade under his oxter, allowing the left arm to rest on its back, the hand over the tip. With a firm movement he rubbed the stone backwards and forwards along the top, raising his left thumb at intervals, to allow the stone to pass.

The sharpening of the main blade-edge was more difficult. To do this, Doalty bent on his left knee, the sned placed diagonally across his leg, the top of the handle and the tip of the blade on the ground. He brought the stone down one side of the blade, then down the other, in long sweeping movements, swinging it free on each occasion, when it almost touched the ground. This movement was repeated many times, for the temper of an old blade, grown rusty with disuse, is hard to pacify. When Doalty finished he felt the blade with his thumb and hit it sharply with his nail. The blade tinkled musically.

" It rings true," he said with a boyish smile. " Now I'll begin. . . . And there . . . the sun. And old Oiney's afoot with smoke in his house. All the glen people are getting up, but none are as early as me though. . . . But why should I chuckle?" he asked himself. " I have got up like this just once in a while and it's their daily life."

He unloosened his braces, tied them round his waist, thrust up his shirt sleeves and bent to the work. Round the corners of the field, where the grass was short and dry, it could be cut in long swathes. It was here that Doalty commenced his work. Swinging his scythe with energy he tested its temper. The blade, a good one, cut like a razor.

" My hand has not forgotten its cunning," he said with a laugh. " This is heavenly! . . . I'm swinging it too wide though. If I'm not careful it will tire me out before breakfast. . . ."

He cut a swathe some fifteen paces in length, then bending down he lifted a wisp of hay, rubbed his scythe, put it on his shoulder and retraced his

steps.   As he walked the scythe got dry.   At the
original starting point he sharpened it again and
commenced a second sward.   Before he came to
the end he felt tired.   His breath came in short
gasps and beads of sweat stood out on his forehead.   The sward was too wide and took too
much out of the mower.   But he would not stop.
All the glen were watching him, he knew.   A rich
man home from foreign parts and mowing hay,
just like one of themselves, would evoke no end
of interest and comment.   "They'll say that I'll
not be able to keep it up for very long," Doalty
muttered, and the thought braced him up.   De-
termined not to be beaten, he finished the sward,
sharpened his scythe, spat on his hands and commenced another.

The sun got up over Carnaween, and every
house in the glen was smoking.   The cows, already milked, were now out grazing.   Norah, her
hair plaited down her back, brought out the Gallagher's cows, putting them into the park behind the
house.   The girl was barefooted, her face half
hidden by a big blue-spotted handkerchief.   From
where Doalty was at work it seemed as if the handkerchief was wholly white.

Unconscious of the passage of time, the mower
swung round his scythe in great semi-circles, rib-
bing the field with long, heavy swathes.   As the
blade cut through it, the grass toppled slowly
down, carrying with it nodding plumes and delicate and graceful flowers.   The holm was a world
of colour and bloom, and to Doalty, the work was
full of delight and pleasure and healthy weariness.

Towards the end of each sward he felt as if he were going to drop from exhaustion, but he was none the less eager to start on the next round of work. The sweat stood out from every pore. It trickled down his brow into his eyes, paining him not a little; into his mouth and he could taste its salty savour.

He did not see Oiney coming, and was only aware of the old man's presence when he crossed the ditch and laid down his scythe on the ground.

"God bless the work," said Oiney. "It's up and at it early that ye are."

"The morning was such a good one that I could not lie in bed," said Doalty.

"Of course ye couldn't, man," Oiney made answer. "Ye're just like me when I was yer years long ago. Then I was afoot, late and early. . . . But you're not a bad hand with the scythe, Doalty, and ye're able to make a good fist iv the job. Just as good as one iv ourselves ye'd be, if 'twasn't that ye bear too much on yer hand, and stoop a bit too low on the sned. But ye'll get over that when ye get yer hand in."

As he spoke, he pulled his old battered hat well down over his head, felt in a pocket for his pipe, and put it in his mouth.

"But I was bad with the corns last night," he said, shaking his head.

"Yes, you were, Oiney," Doalty assented.

"I never had them so bad."

"But that was on account of the long journey, and maybe your boots were too tight," said Doalty, who saw that the old man was sorry for the drink which he had taken the day before.

"That was it," said Oiney, a smile of relief showing on his face. "The boots were bad for the journey. Far too tight across the uppers they were. . . . But this is a good bit iv land that ye have here," he continued. "Grass second to none in the townland. And see how low it lies, and doesn't want to show itself off. The best grass keeps lowest to the ground, and the thin famine grass that rises on the braes, sticks its head up as if it owned the whole field. It's the same with people just."

Norah Gallagher came out in front of the house, put her handkerchief on a holly bush that grew there.

"That's the sign for breakfast, Oiney," said Doalty, pointing at the holly bush. "We'll go in and have a bite."

Maura The Rosses was in the house when they got there. She had been up all night, attending to the sick woman. Breed Dermod was in a sore way, and in the early morning she had been playing with the blankets. This was a sure sign of death, Maura The Rosses said. "And Breed was such a good woman too," she added, already speaking of Breed as if she no longer remained on this world.

V

The two men went out to the field again when they had taken their meal. Oiney led the sward and Doalty followed. The old man worked easily, cutting the grass without any apparent energy. Now and again when Doalty pressed close on his heels he would turn round, rub his hand over his wrinkled brow and say, " Slow and stiddy goes a fair pace, me boyo, and the day's young yet."

At noon Oiney was mowing with the same untroubled serenity and he had no longer to turn round and advise Doalty to go easy. By this time the younger man was unable to force the pace; to keep up with Oiney required all the energy that he possessed. Once or twice he tried to draw Oiney into a conversation, and the old man spoke as easily when mowing as when standing still.

" What will happen to Sheila Dermod if her mother dies?" Doalty once asked when in the middle of a sward.

" What will happen to the girsha?" said Oiney, without losing the swing of his scythe. " Ah! that's easy enough seen. She'll get a young gassair to take her in charge and he'll be a lucky boy too, for when Sheila gets all thoughts. iv fun out iv her head and settles down to work, she'll be as steady a woman as is in the whole barony. . . . Ah, ye rogue, ye almost got cut in two!"

As Oiney said this, he bent and lifted a frog

which had narrowly escaped the scythe, placed it out of harm's way on a swathe of lying grass and gazed sternly at it.

" Now hop off widye, ye limb!" he admonished it, "and don't be runnin' in the way iv me edge or ye"ll maybe get a cut across the belly."

He shook a warning finger at the little animal, already hopping away, and resumed his mowing. Coming to the end of the sward he looked back on the stretch which Doalty had cut.

" There's one thing that ye should always bear in mind, Doalty," he said, " and that is this. Never sharpen yer scythe in patches as ye've been doin'.   Try and have a keen edge all the way along and ye'll not leave the shiffins standin'. The blunt bits iv the scythe are slippin' over the hay and that will never do, ye know.   Ye can always tell the worth of a mowster be the field behind him."

" The scythe was in a bad state when I got it," said Doalty deferentially.

" It shouldn't be, seein' that yer father, God rest him! had the last handling iv it," said Oiney. " None bar meself, maybe, could get a better edge than him."

The two were half way down the next sward when Oiney stopped to look up the brae.   Doalty followed Oiney's gaze and saw Maura The Rosses coming down from Breed Dermod's, making the sign of the cross over her brow, chin and breast as she hurried down to her own home.

" Breed Dermod's gone," said Oiney, blessing himself and making a silent prayer.   When he finished he lifted his scythe over his shoulder and made his way to the road. Doalty followed. The work of the farm was at an end for the day. Not a hand's turn would be done by the people of Stranameera now, until Breed Dermod was buried.

CHAPTER X

THE WAKE

Now in our own townland they say,
" To every man alive, his day
To dig and delve and set and sow
And labour as the seasons go,
To let a rope or make a creel,
To sing a song and foot a reel,
To keep a trust and never budge
From what is right, and bear no grudge
Against his neighbours, near and far,
No matter who or what they are. . . .
The man who lives like this will find
He gets respect from kith and kind,
And good strong backs will bear the load
When he gets carried down the road,
Shoulder-high, at close of day,
A tenant to a house of clay."
                              —*Across the March Ditch.*

I

ALL Stranameera was early in attendance at the wake that night. Being near, and having no work to do, the neighbours might as well be there as anywhere else. When Doalty Gallagher, who had been busy writing all through the afternoon, went up, the house was crowded and more were coming in. The Meena-warawor people, not having to forsake their work, because they belonged to another townland, were late in arriving. The weather being good for the hay, the reapers kept to the fields till darkness fell.

The kitchen was crowded. A big turf fire blazed on the hearth, and hanging from a crook above it, was a large three-legged pot filled with water. Three lamps were lit. One, hanging from the rigging by a long string, waved backwards and forwards over the table, placed in the centre of the room, another nailed to the wall, near the door, flared fitfully as if lacking oil, and the third, the globe of which was blackened with soot, was attached to the brace over the fireplace. Grania Coolin, barefooted, with her gosling-grey handkerchief over her head, was sitting on a stool by the fire, beside Maura The Rosses. Both women were speaking in whispers and nodding their heads from time to time. The hot room was filled with the odour of tobacco smoke and perspiring bodies.

In a corner of the room, furthest away from the door, the dead woman lay in a bed by the wall, her white face showing above the blankets. Seen from the doorway by Doalty, as he entered, those who sat or knelt there were mingled together in a strange blur. The young man made his way to the bed, went down on his knees to pray. As he knelt there he could hear Oiney Leahy speaking, and his talk was of death.

" I'm not afeard of death," said the old man. " It's a thing that'll only happen once and I'll go

easy when it comes to me own time.   It's not in
me to be sorry when God sees fit to take me.   The
goin' away iv any one iv us will not intherfere with
the gatherin' iv the turf, or the cuttin' iv the corn.
. . .   We'll all go one day and it's all one to
the grave-digger who dies first. . . .   If a
man goes after the kibbin', someone will be left
to dig the pratees.   And for all iv us, the time
that we live is well worth the money that we pay
for it."

Doalty got to his feet and took a seat beside
Oiney.

"Good night t'ye, Doalty," said Oiney, shaking the young man by the hand.   "Feelin' tired
after the mornin's work?"

"Not in the least, Oiney," said Doalty.

"Doesn't Breed, God be merciful to her, make
a good corpse," said the old man, looking on the
dead with the eye of a connoisseur. He had helped
to dress many a dead man in his time.   "It's hard
to think that she was with us this morning. . . .
And now she's gone.   But she was a good woman
and never had an evil word for anyone. . .
And to think that she would have gone away the
day," Oiney continued.   "This day is the day iv
all days, the master day.   It passes judgment on
all the years iv one's life and acquits us iv all
bonds."

"That's true," said Doalty.

"But ye're not havin' a smoke at all," said Oiney, getting to his feet and taking out a bundle
of white clay pipes and a lump of thick black tobacco from a recess in the wall, near the fireplace.

"I don't smoke a pipe," said Doalty.

"There's nothin' like a pipe," said the old man with an air that brooked no contradiction. He went round the room, giving pipes to the company, and Doalty looked for Sheila, to find her coming towards him.

"Good night to ye,' Doalty Gallagher," said the girl, and they shook hands.

"Good night, Sheila," Doalty replied. "I'm sorry that your poor mother has died. May she rest in peace."

A tear showed in Sheila's eyes and Doalty felt at a loss what to say. A strange constraint had seized hold of him. He still held her hand, pressing it warmly while thoughts, tumultuous and incoherent, surged through his mind. He felt no sorrow for the dead, and strange to say, very little sympathy for the girl. Every emotion seemed scattered. A sense of suffocation filled his being, and he had the illusion that both of them were alone. He spoke, saying the first thing that came into his mind, words without significance or meaning. But when he released the girl's hand, sat down and looked round, he saw that nobody was taking any notice of him. He was glad and tried to recall what he had said to the girl. But he could not remember.

Owen Briney was sitting near the fire, his coat and shirt open at the neck, his head bare. His hair, turning white at the temples, hung so low on the narrow forehead, that only the eyebrows were visible. Owen had, from the moment of

Breed Dermod's death, placed himself at Sheila's disposal and ran twice to the village on errands. He bought the tobacco and tea and carried a bag of loaves up to Stranameera on his back, running most of the way on his journey home. Never had such whole-hearted zeal been shown by any man. Now he was sitting by the fire silent as a fish; his face beaded with sweat, his eyes continually following Sheila, as the girl moved through the room. If she wanted anything done, he was ready to help her.

Doalty's eyes also followed the girl, watching her every motion and movement. She kept very busy, sorting the chairs, welcoming the new-comers, giving directions to those who were help-ing her in the house. At times she would sit down by the bed, rub her temple with her finger as if trying to steady her mind to thought. But the next moment she was on her feet again, per-forming some duty which she had forgotten. Her whole bearing was calculated to attract attention. Her every feature showed a touch of self-reliance that in no way detracted from the delicacy and grace of her movements. Her blue eyes, a little red with weeping, looked soft and appealing when she fixed them on Doalty. Now and again she smiled and her sad face was then enlivened as with a ray of sunshine.

Oiney, continually going the round of the house with pipes, tobacco and snuff, stopped opposite Doalty on one occasion and whispered in his ear.

"See the way that Owen Briney, the toe-rag, is havin' his eyes on Sheila."

"He has been helping her all day, I believe," said Doalty.

"Catch him doin' anything for nothing," snorted the old man. "He has his own pot on the fire."

"In what way?" asked Doalty.

"He thinks that he'll get her to marry him, maybe," said Oiney. "He's a sly, cute fox, Owen Briney."

Doalty tried to appear amused and laughed awkwardly. But the thought of a man like Owen marrying Sheila turned him sick with disgust.

"He won't have much of a chance with Sheila," he said.

"Iv course not," said Oiney. "She'll never let the march ditch be made level for Owen Briney to cross it. . . . . Ye're not goin' to try a pipe this time, are ye?"

When Oiney had gone the round of the wake, he came back and sat by the side of Doalty.

"Dennys The Drover hasn't come back from the fair iv Reemora yet," said the old man. "He took half a dozen young sturks there the day. But the moment he comes home he'll be up here to the wake. Then Owen Briney will sit low. Sheila has a notion iv Dennys, ye know."

"Is that so?" Doalty enquired lightly, as lightly as he could.

"That's so," said the old man. "And a brave couple they'll make, the two iv them, when both settle down and get into the way iv workin'. Dennys doesn't care much for the work iv the

fields as yet. But he'll soon put that past him.
I was the same meself, when I was a youngster.
.' . . . Ah, young fellows!" he added. "It's
them that has the time! They're always on the
rampage and roamin' and cannot stand still. The
only way that Dennys can rest is by rollin' about,
just like a child in a cradle. A boy with no control over himself, he has folly in his feet. He's
ready to go in for anything, but he's not willing
to stick it. . . . But yerself, Doalty, is a very
quiet boy for yer years."

"Do you think so?" asked the young man in
an absent voice.

Oiney pinched Doalty's thigh with a strong finger and thumb.

"Well ye look quiet anyway, but that is nothin'
to go by," he said. "There is Owen Briney and
he's quiet enough. And he's after Sheila Dermod! Oh! the old plaisham. And what d'ye
think iv Sheila, yerself, Doalty?"

"I'm afraid I haven't given her a thought,"
said Doalty.

"Get away widye, Doalty," said the old man,
pressing Doalty's thigh again. He had not wholly relaxed the grip at any time. "D'ye think an
old fellow like me never sees anything at all?
What about the night at the fair when ye went into
Heel-ball's with her? Eh, now!"

"Who has been telling you this?" enquired
Doalty gruffly.

"Who, but Dennys The Drover," said the old
man. "He had a great laugh over it. He saw
that ye had a notion iv Sheila, so he let ye get on

the talk with her; and himself, he went into the next room with Eileen Kelly."

" Dennys has a notion of Eileen," said Doalty, in a voice of apparent indifference. He was really trying to get as much information from Oiney as possible.

"A notion iv Eileen!" laughed Oiney. " Ne'er a fear. He just went with her for a bit iv fun and in a fair one may as well go with one girsha as with another. They're all out for the fun."

"Was Sheila out for fun too?"

"She was that day," said the old man; " but after the berryin' she'll be out for somethin' else, and she'll not be long lookin' for what she wants. Nobody would have taken the girl from her mother, God rest her, when she was alive. Breed was a hard woman to get on with, but now, as the girl has her bit iv land, and no man to work it, she'll be glad to take someone to dig the fields for her."

" And do you think that Dennys The Drover will ask her to marry him?" asked Doalty.

" He could do worse," said Oiney. "Worse and far worse."

So saying, he got to his feet again, and made the rounds of the house with the pipes.

II

By this time the young people were playing a game called " The Silly Old Man." A number of boys and girls were standing in a circle on the middle of the floor; boy and girl about, catching one another's hands.   Young Micky Neddy, who stood in the centre of the circle, was the Silly Old Man for the time being.   He had to choose a woman from the circle for his wife.   As he looked at the young faces the boys and girls sang at the top of their voices :

> " He's a silly old man that lies alone,
>   That lies alone,
>   In bed alone—
>   A silly old man that lies alone,
>   Wantin' a wife but can't get one."

Micky Neddy chose a wife from the ring, and his wife was Eileen Kelly.   He put his arm round her and drew her into his side.   Oiney Leahy, his hat well back on his head, paused for a moment, in the midst of his pipe distribution, to look at the fun.   The boys and girls, with their eyes on Micky Neddy and Eileen Kelly, burst into song again :

> " Now young couple ye're married together,
>   Married together,
>   And bedded together.
>   From this day on ye must love one another—
>   Obey yer father as well as yer mother,
>   And live in peace like sister and brother."

" That's the way to do it," Oiney laughed, stroking his white beard in towards his throat. " It's just like the old times."

This game went on for quite half an hour, and at the end of that time Micky Neddy had chosen three different wives and got married to each of them. Even old Oiney, not to be outdone when fun was going on, got married twice, once to Norah Gallagher and again to a girl from Meenawarawor by the name of Nancy Parra Wor a Crick (Nancy the daughter of Big Patrick of the Hill).

One game followed another. The next was "The Priest of the Parish," with Oiney Leahy as the priest. He sat on the floor and placed the young men in a row on either side of him. When all had settled down, Oiney pointed his finger at Micky Neddy and said: "Ye're my man, Jack." Then looking at the other players he said: "Choose yer caps."

"I'm Black Cap," said one.

"And yer cap?" asked Oiney, looking at another.

"White Cap," was the answer.

"And yer cap?"

"Green Cap."

Oiney coughed, when all the men had chosen their caps. Then he spoke:

"The Priest of the Parish has lost his considerin' cap; some say this, and some say that, but I say my man, Jack."

Micky Neddy, quick after Oiney's words, shouted:

"Is it me, sir?"

"Yes, you, sir."

"Ye lie, sir."

"Who then, sir?"

" Black Cap."

" Is it me, sir?" Black Cap, who happened to be
Owen Briney, enquired, and the same series of
answers and questions went their round between
the two men.   The game required a supple
tongue, for the man who was unable to answer to
a cap before the priest named him was made to
stand up and take punishment.   He stood with
his hand, palm inwards, on his hip, and the priest
hit him across the knuckles with a stick.   After
such a castigation the dilatory man became the
Priest of the Parish.   Before the game was at an
end all the knuckles in the party were bleeding.
Meenawarawor was very severe on the knuckles
of Stranameera, but when it came to Stranameera's
turn Meenawarawor got its due meed of punishment.

The fun of the wake was in full swing now.
Oiney Leahy, his priesthood at an end, was sitting
in a corner with pipe aflare, telling a story of the
old times, of the years far back, when there was
no burial ground in Greenanore, and when the
dead had to be put under earth ten miles from
where Oiney was now sitting and twenty miles
from Meenaroody, a townland at the butt-end of
the parish.   One snowy mid-winter, a Meenaroody man died, and he had to be carried over
hill and holm, twenty miles, to the graveyard.
The coffin left Meenaroody at night; Oiney Leahy
was one of the bearers.   It was a raw journey in
the snow, and when the coffin came to Meenawarawor the men left it on the roadside and went to
Hudagh Reedagh's house for a drink of potheen.

Hudagh (dead, twenty years, come Candlemas next) had a still going on the hills day and night. The men went there and got well tight. Meantime the coffin lay on the roadside, with the snow falling all over it, for the night was a wild one entirely. It was when the men were drunk, and when everyone was full of his own worth, that somebody remarked that no one had the courage to go alone and have a look at the coffin. Oiney said that he would go, for he was not afraid of anything. The other men of the party laughed at him, but Oiney got hold of an ash-plant from behind the rafter of Hudagh Reedagh's home, and went to visit the coffin, all on his lone. "If the divil from hell's there I don't care," Oiney said, making his way out into the darkness.

When he came to the coffin, there was something there waiting for him, something white as a ghost, that tried to hit Oiney with its horns. As the strange thing rushed at him, Oiney stepped back a pace, to get the swing of his arm behind the blow and hit the ghost right between the eyes with the ash-plant. Then he turned and ran back to his friends. "And in the mornin'," Oiney concluded, "there was a dead ram lyin' across the coffin."

Near the door a Meenawarawor man, rugous and big-boned, was playing hard knuckles with Micky Neddy, whose fern-tickled face was beaded with sweat, and whose hair stood out in wisps under his cap. The two were hitting one another's knuckles turn about, their fists all covered with blood. The last man to hit would be the man to win, and one

townland was loth to give in to the other townland.
The onlookers were betting on the result of the
contest, while the two men, looking very sorry for
themselves, continued the brutal game.

Sheila Dermod, weary after many nights' watching over her sick mother, was now asleep, sitting
on the stool by the bed, her head back against the
blankets, her full throat and lovely face showing. Doalty, looking at her, suddenly detected
in her face a striking resemblance to her dead
mother. In what the likeness consisted, Doalty
could not determine. How could there be any
similarity between the two faces? They were so
different. He recollected Breed Dermod's expression when she came down to see him a few
days earlier; the sunken eyes and mouth, the
wrinkles raying out from the corners of her eyes
like a fan, the skin drawn tightly in across the
cheek-bones. . . . But how could there be
any similarity between faces so essentially different, between the blue-eyed, soft-complexioned
Sheila and the hard-featured, scowling mother?
But despite all that Doalty could urge to the contrary, there was an inexplicable likeness, an un-
mistakable family look.

" It cannot be," Doalty thought, speaking to
himself in disjointed words. " It does not matter
how many years. . . . There's not a scowl in
the big blue eyes . . . steady and clear, but
not menacing."

Another man looked on Sheila at intervals, and
from Sheila, his eyes would turn to Doalty Gallagher. And Doalty noticed the expression on

this man's face. There was a look of greed all over it. A similar expression showed on the face of the man when he was trying to make a bargain with Grania Coolin at the fair of Greenanore. The man was Owen Briney.

Oiney Leahy looked at the sleeping girl, then round at the asembled company. " Many a man would marry that girl for her face alone," he said.

III

It was now time to say the Rosary. Oiney Leahy knelt on the floor, first taking care to put his old battered hat under his knees.

" Now boys, on yer knees for the Paidreen," he said. The household knelt down in a body. Micky Neddy and the Meenawarawor man stopped their game of hard knuckles, glad of the respite. Sheila Dermod woke up. Maura The Rosses and Grania Coolin, kneeling by the fire, kept their eyes fixed on the pot of tea. Supper would be served when the Rosary came to an end.

Oiney gave out the prayers in Irish. Responses were made in that language by the old and in English by the young people of twenty or thereabouts. The children from the school answered in Irish, now a compulsory language in its own country.

Fifteen decades of the Rosary were given out and then prayers were said for all who were dead. Oiney gave a short introduction to this prayer, speaking in a low voice that was deep and tender, while all the household listened in silence.

"One Pater and Ave for the suffering souls in Purgatory," said the old man. "Especially for fathers, mothers, brothers, sisters, neighbours, near and far, friends and enemies and all who have gone away from the world, that they may be released from their torments and taken to God, their Father in Heaven. Amen."

After prayers and before supper was served to the crowd, Doalty rose and went out, with the intention of going home. Sheila Dermod followed him and overtook him in the park that stretched down the brae from the door.

"Ye're not goin' home now, Doalty, are ye?" she asked.

"Oh! I think I'll go, Sheila," he replied, looking at the girl. "There are plenty inside to keep watch all night."

"But ye should stay, Doalty," she said in a voice that was almost supplicating. She looked up at Doalty and in the darkness the young man fancied that he could see a tender beseeching look in her blue eyes. With an involuntary movement he stretched out his hand and caught hers.

"I'm very sorry for you, Sheila," he said. "Being left all by yourself, up here on the brae. Death is very sad."

"Ah! well, it had to be," said the girl in a voice of resignation. "Everyone has to die when it comes to their time."

She pressed his hand warmly as she spoke, and

looked at the ground, but did not release her hold.

Presently she spoke again.

"Ye're comin' in to have somethin' to ate anyway, aren't ye?" she asked. "Ye're not goin' away, without havin' a bite and ye've not ate anything now since six o'clock this evenin', maybe."

"But Sheila, you have trouble enough in the house not to bother about me," said Doalty. "I did not think that you would care for my company after what has passed between us. You remember . . . and you were so angry with me. . . ."

"Who said that I was angry?" Sheila enquired, separating Doalty's fingers, one from another, with her hand.

"Nobody; but I thought you were," Doalty replied. "And you weren't angry?" he enquired, drawing the young girl towards him.

"I wasn't angry," said the girl. "But ye were so strange and not like other boys that ye made me afeeard."

She spoke in a whisper and the hand that held Doalty's quivered like a leaf.

"But now, you're not afraid, Sheila!" said Doalty in a passionate voice. "If I asked you now . . . you would . . . wouldn't you, Sheila?"

"Doalty Gallagher!"

"All right, Sheila. . . . I'm sorry. . . . Is the supper ready yet?"

The two went into the house together, passing Owen Briney, who had come out to the door to see if the weather showed any signs of breaking.

There were heavy clouds on Sliav a Tuagh that afternoon, a bad sign. So Owen informed Sheila, but all through the evening, up till now, he had not shown the least interest in the weather.

Doalty Gallagher did not leave the house of the wake till the next morning. All Stranameera stopped till dawn, knowing that it could sleep all day. But Meenwarawor went home after supper, for with good weather and no wakes, they could make a speedy finish to their harvest.

IV

The weather continued dry and warm and the workers on the far side of the glen made great progress with their hay. Stranameera, held up by Breed Dermod's death, was pleased when the burying day came round. Six deep, under her coffin, the men carried her down the glen road on their shoulders, sweating as they walked. Breed, big of bone and build, was not an easy burden on the hottest day that Glenmornan ever knew. Oiney Leahy, front bearer on the right of the coffin, with his coat and hat off and his pipe in his pocket, grunted wearily as he walked. Other men took turns at the bearing, but Oiney would not allow any man into his place. Seeing it was the last journey of Breed Dermod, God rest her! down the glen road, he was going to carry her all the way. This generous thought did not prevent him, however, from saying when the churchyard was sighted : " Thanks be to God that we're near there, now !"

They buried Breed in the grave where her husband, who also died on a harvest-day, was laid to rest. Father Devaney, a well-preserved priest, despite his years, with shiny, bald head and oily face, read the offices over the dead woman and counted the offerings after the burial. The glen people had paid well and a sum of nine pounds, eighteen and sixpence was collected. The priest counted the offerings, put the money in a large cloth bag and handed it to Micky Neddy.

" Run away with this, Micky," he said, " and put it in the car be the gate for me." A jaunting car stood by the entrance of the churchyard, waiting to take the priest back to his residence.

On his way out, Father Devaney overtook Doalty Gallagher, who had been one of the bearers at the funeral.

" Good day, Doalty Gallagher," said the priest, with an air of jollity, stretching out his hand towards the young man. " I haven't been speakin' to ye since ye've come home at all. And ye've grown big since ye went away !"

" Well, I've had plenty of time to grow," said Doalty, taking no notice of the outstretched hand.

" Ye have grown in more ways than one," said Father Devaney, dropping his hand to his side as he noticed the acrid and savage disdain of the young man's voice. " Ye've grown to learn things abroad, Doalty—things that are not good for ye. A lot of the young fellows who go away, come

back just like yerself, but they'll learn better as
they grow older."

"If people grow older in the way that I'm growing old they'd damned soon get rid of gross,
self-satisfied creatures like you, Devaney," said
Doalty in a voice hoarse with anger. He spoke,
almost, as if he had been rehearsing for the scene,
as indeed he had, for often, when abroad, he
thought of Father Devaney and had a certain grim
satisfaction in an imaginary condemnation of the
man. "As people get more educated it will be
found that men like you will be the means of driving Catholicity from the country."

"Quiet now, Doalty Gallagher," said Father
Devaney, with an authoritative wave of his hand,
speaking with the air of a man, sure of his power,
who was unwilling to enter into argument in de-
fence of his own behaviour. "Quiet now, me
boy, and don't be speakin' things that ye'll be
sorry for afterwards."

Doalty knew that words were futile against the
smug, self-possessed priest. He was an over-fed,
blatant tyrant whom the people obeyed like sheep!
Poor people, poor, silly, stupid people!

At that moment Doalty saw Maura The Rosses
coming, and without another word he gave the
priest one look of killing scorn, turned on his heel
and left him. All that he had said seemed to
Doalty to have been flat and hateful. This feeling increased as the distance between himself and
the priest lengthened. He was annoyed with
himself, bit his lips and cursed at the awkwardness
with which he had dealt with Devaney. He

should have knocked the man down, he reasoned. Even his years should not have saved him from chastisement.

" He's afraid of his mother, anyway, and that's a good sign," thought the priest as Doalty walked away.

Maura The Rosses came up and bowed almost to the ground in front of the clergyman. The priest did not return the salute. Instead he fixed a stern eye on the woman.

" Maura The Rosses, I've been talkin' to that boy iv yours," he said in a severe voice. " I'm afraid that he has forgot the teachin' that was given to him, when he was a youngster in the glen. . . . He spoke to me just the same as if I wasn't his parish priest."

" But he's been so long abroad, father, that he has maybe lost mind iv a lot of things," said the woman in an endeavour to placate the man. " If he stays here for a while he'll just be like any iv the others in the glen. Don't fault him, father, for he's only a young gasair yet."

" I'm sorry to say it, Maura The Rosses, but from the look iv things I think . . . no, I don't think it, but I'm sure iv it, that your boy has wandered away from the old faith. And ye know what that manes !" he said in a stern voice.

" Don't say that, father," Maura The Rosses entreated. " He may be like that at times, but he'll soon grow past it. Maybe if ye spoke to him yerself, father, he would take heed iv what ye'd tell him. . . . I can't do much for him, bar say a prayer for him be night and put some holy water under his pillow before he goes to bed."

" Oh, that's no good for the like iv him, Maura The Rosses," said the priest. " It would be the best thing for the parish if he was sent back to where he came from. Then he couldn't give scandal to yerself and to the young iv the glen."

" But maybe if he goes to yerself, father," faltered Maura The Rosses, whose dread of the priest was much stronger than her desire for Doalty's salvation.

" No, no," said the priest. " I'll have nothin' to do with him. Let him go his own way. He's young and headstrong, but one day . . ."—the priest shook his head—" and it may be too late then," he added.

With these words he got up on the car and looked in the well of the vehicle to see if the bag of money was safe. This was done, more through force of habit than from fear that anyone would be so rash as to lay hands on the offerings over the dead. Money was not in the priest's mind at that moment, all the old man's thoughts were on Doalty Gallagher, and he was forming schemes of revenge against the youth.

Devaney was a covetous and crafty man, holding unlimited control of his flock. Though the peasantry did not love him, they feared him and he played on that fear. The poor were his legitimate prey, and not a soul in the parish dared gainsay his wishes or disobey his commands. He kept the parish under his thumb.

For all that, he was afraid of Doalty Gallagher and of any man who might speak to him as Doalty had spoken. And he had reason, for it happened once that a young man, named Reelan, who had been abroad, returned to Greenanore and opened a grocer's shop in the village. Reelan's mother was a very poor woman, and when the priest was building his new house this woman was unable to pay all the dues. Devaney remarked on this event several times from the altar, holding the woman up to ridicule and contempt. When young Reelan came home and heard of this, he was very angry and went and saw Devaney about the matter. During the interview he lost his temper and knocked the priest down. For this Devaney had his revenge. He spoke about the affair from the altar, pointing out the evil of which the young man, who had struck his own priest, was guilty. Needless to say, the peasantry were indignant; the villagers would not speak to the young man afterwards and the women of the parish would not buy at his shop. In the end Reelan had to close up his business and leave the parish. "I'll treat Doalty Gallagher the same as I have treated Reelan," muttered the priest, as he made his way homewards. "I'll show him what it is to speak back to his priest. But it's better not to anger him as yet, maybe," he added as he recalled the incident in which Reelan had figured some years previously.

When Devaney came off the car and entered his home he forget to take his money bag with him. The jarvey who had driven the priest to all the funerals in the parish for years had never known Devaney to forget the offerings before.

" I suppose it's because he is growin' old that he's forgettin' things," said the jarvey, as he followed the priest into the house with the bag in his hand.

CHAPTER XI

THE FLOOD

It's poor washing for a woman when there isn't a shirt in the tub.—A Glenmornan Proverb.

I

DAY after day passed by and the weather kept up. Never had Glenmornan known such heat, and never had the hay dried so quickly. On all the spread of bottom-land, bounding the Owenawadda, the tramp-cocks were rising brown over the after-grass. The peasantry worked hard, busy at their toil day and night, the odour of drying hay in their nostrils, the rustle of waving corn in their ears. In the clear moonlight, when dews fell thickly and mists rose from the pores of the land, the swish of the reaper's scythes could be heard between dusk and dawn. In the morning the fields were ribbed with straight new swards. In the hot sun the grass dried quickly; the hay had merely to be cut and it was saved.

Doalty and his brother Teague worked at the

mowing, making great headway. The neighbours marvelled at the young man who could
keep at his work so steadily and now they were
of opinion that Doalty was really going to remain at home, and work on the farm for the rest
of his life. On realizing this, they shook their
heads in a knowing way. "There's something
in it," they told one another. "A boy comin'
home here and workin' just like one of ourselves,
when he has the learnin', and can make money
and to spare abroad, is . . . well, there's
more in it than meets the eye." The shopboy,
who put on airs they disliked, Doalty, who was
humility itself, they distrusted.

"And ye're never goin' away at all any
more?" Eileen Kelly asked him one day as
she met him on the road.

"Well, it doesn't look like it, does it?" was
Doalty's reply.

Eileen shrugged her shoulders and curled her
three cornered lips in a pert grimace.

"Stayin' here, when ye could be away out
in the world," she said deprecatingly. "Ye've
never set eyes on a place as backwardlike as
this, I'll go bail."

"It's a most lovely place, Eileen," Doalty
replied. "The hills, and the meadows, and the
streams, and the people. You like the hills,
Eileen, don't you?" he asked her.

"I hate them," the girl replied. "Always
the same and never any change! They are so
ugly! I suppose yerself thinks that they are
very nice because ye've been away and seen

other places. But I've always been at home here, and I've never seen anywhere else. . . . Maybe if I was away I would like this place to come back to, if it was only for a holiday."

Doalty continued writing the articles on Glenmornan in his spare time. The editor of the London paper was quite pleased with them and used a series. Then other papers published further contributions and Doalty got rid of his stuff easily. He gave the money sent from London to his mother, but she showed no signs of slating her house now. Doalty spoke to her about the matter.

"Well, the thatch will do for a couple iv years more," she said, "so I'll put the few ha'pence by."

This really meant that since her next door neighbours were not slating their houses, she had no need to slate hers. Maura was now a great friend of Sheila Dermod, and called on the young girl daily, helping her at her work. All the neighbours took a kind interest in the girls' welfare; the boys of the townland helped her at the hay-making and turf-saving, and Owen Briney was not last in lending her a hand. At this time an aunt of hers, Anna Ruagh of Meenaroodagh, whose husband was away abroad at the harvesting, came to live with Sheila and help her to keep house. The girl also engaged a servant boy, named Murtagh Roonagh, blood relation, but far out, of Oiney Leahy, and Oiney saw that this boy did fair and honest labour for his wages.

One thing however was certain and that was this. Sheila would have to get married presently. A man was needed to run the bit of land, and as the girl was left all alone, it would not be a sin on her part to get married as soon as possible, after her mother's death. There were plenty of young fellows going about, who would be glad to bespeak the girl's hand. They were all mad after her, and now that Breed was dead, the lucky young man would have Sheila's farm to go into on the day of his marriage to the beautiful girl.

Doalty spoke to Sheila several times. When coming in from the mowing in the evening, he would call to her across the ditch.

"Good evening, Sheila," he would say. "Still working away."

"Always workin'," she would answer in a quiet voice, as if she had resigned herself to a future which showed clear in front of her. Now and again, when Doalty spoke to her, an expression of embarrassment would flit across her features. She would smile awkwardly, apparently not at anything which the young man had said, but at some thought which his remark brought up in her mind. Her big blue eyes never looked straight at Doalty now when she spoke to him. Instead her eyelids would sink down, as if the girl were abashed and shamed of something which was only known to herself. Doalty, for some reason, felt very sorry for the girl and with the sorrow came a sense of isolation. As day and day passed, he felt further and further removed from the girl. Some great barrier seemed to be rising up between the two of them, but what the barrier was the young man could not determine.

II

One afternoon Doalty had a conversation with her. She was sitting by the River Owenawadda at a point where the Dermod Farm jutted out, into the stream. The day was very warm, but a cold breath rose from the river and fanned the young man's face as he sat on the bank beside the girl. The water beneath them was still and clear. Under the shadow of the bank a big trout, facing the run of the stream, was waving its fins lazily. Doalty looked at Sheila's reflection in the water and he could see her form as distinctly as if she were looking into a glass. The girl was leaning forward, her hair falling over her shoulders, her feet touching the water. As the ripples, raised by the water-spiders, swept across the girl's reflection, her hair waved outwards, as if caught by a gentle breeze. For a long while Doalty gazed at the likeness in the water without speaking.

"What are ye thinkin' about, Doalty Gallagher?" asked Sheila suddenly, fixing her eyes on the young man.

"Thinking about!" said Doalty, as if considering the question. He knew what the true

answer would be, if he had the courage to speak
it. "Thinking about, Sheila? . . . . It's
about you, always about you."

"About me, Doalty Gallagher?" asked the
girl, with an earnest look as if she had never
heard him make such a confession before.

"Yes, about you, Sheila. I think of you the
first thing in the morning when I get up and the
last thing at night. You remember the time I
kissed you, do you not, Sheila?"

"Ye're always thinkin' about that," said the
girl. "Do you ever think about the other girls
that ye've kissed when I didn't see ye."

She laughed as she spoke, and plucking a
flower from the grass by her side, she threw it
into the water.

"A throut will maybe rise to that," she said.
"Do ye think that one will, Doalty?"

"Be sensible, Sheila," he said impatiently.
"When I want to speak of one thing, you always turn to something else."

"But have ye ever been kissin' the girls
abroad?" Sheila enquired mischievously.

"No, no," Doalty hastened to assure her.
"But why do you enquire?"

"I'm just only askin'," said the girl. "But
ye are tellin' me the truth, aren't ye now?"

"It's quite true, Sheila."

"Cross on yer neck then," said the girl in a
voice of mock-command.

Doalty made the sign of the cross with his
forefinger.

"Now," he said, nodding his head and looking at her under his brows. His word seemed to challenge her to further remarks.

" Well, it's time to be gettin' on with the hay now, I think," said Sheila rising to her feet and walking backwards. She kept her eyes fixed on Doalty, as she edged away from him.

" But not yet, Sheila," he entreated, also getting up. " Don't run away like that. Just a minute. . . . I have something to say to you."

" Ye've always somethin' to say," said the girl in a hesitating voice. " But ye never say anything. . . . I must get to the hay anyway, for it's ready for the hancocks."

With these words, she turned round, and ran off towards the road.

Doalty went back to the holm where the hay was scattered broadcast over the ground. In case of floods coming, it would be well to heap it up now that it was almost dry. But his thoughts were not on the hay as he walked. He was thinking of Sheila.

" How empty and dull everything seems," he muttered to himself. " I have been in Glenmornan now for quite a long time and what have I done? I have fallen in love, and I say meaningless things to that girl. She doesn't understand them, and no doubt she thinks that I am a fool. What silly things I've been saying to her and then she tells me that I never say anything. One hour after another passes and nothing is done. But what can be done? . . . Suppose I went and asked her to marry me what would she say? I would marry her to-morrow if she took me. . . . But maybe she'd refuse. . . ."

He looked at the girl working in the hay-field, her whole attention concentrated on her labour. She wore a red-speckled handkerchief on her head, and her long tresses hung down over her shoulders, almost reaching her waist. She lifted the hay in her arms piling it on the han'cocks, and never once looked towards Doalty.

"She doesn't care," he said sadly. "She doesn't know what love is. Her heart is not for me and not, as far as I can see, for any other person. She's a strange girl."

III

The weather broke two days later, at noon. All morning the mists lay thickly on Carnaween, but it remained close and dry down in Glenmornan and no rain had fallen by the turn of the day.

"It will be rainin' here in a wee minute," said Maura The Rosses to Doalty, at noon. Both were standing behind the hedge, Doalty wedging a rake-head on to its haft, Maura The Rosses knitting a stocking. The mid-day meal had just come to an end. "It's too meltin' warm to stay like this for long," the woman continued, "but I hope when it comes it's not too hard on the hay. . . . And there's old

Oiney down be the river pullin' the han'cocks back from the brough. . . . And he has a new flannel shirt on, too. Now, when did he get it at all? . . . There's Sheila Dermod goin' out with her cow and calk to the grazin'. An ould ranny iv an animal, it, and no good for the milkin'. . . . It's a wonder that Dennys The Drover is not gettin' married to Sheila. She's a good, hard worker, when all's said and done, and it's not a bad match, for the two farms are just about the same size and rent. There's the rain now and it will be heavens hard as far as I can see."

Even as she spoke, a violent storm broke and the rain came in torrents. The streams from the uplands becoming swollen, rushed down with violence and burst their bounds. Reeling over the rocks, with a noise like thunder, they set all the echoes going on the hills, and dragging out the bushes from the ravines, they flung them broadcast over the brae-faces. The river could be seen rising, rising.

"Doalty, come into the house widye!" shouted Maura The Rosses, who was already inside.

Doalty went in, to find his mother with her boots off, her red petticoat tucked up to her knees, and the sleeves of her blouse thrust up to her shoulders. In one hand she held a bottle of holy water. As Doalty crossed the doorstep she flung the holy water over him, then over herself.

"May God save us from this flood!" she said,

"and protect the hay . . . and ye, Hughie Beag, get into bed there and don't show yer nose past the door till the draggin's done!"

"Must go down the river," said Hughie, clutching hold of his mother's petticoat.

"Get to bed and do what ye're told!" said Maura The Rosses, giving the boy a skelp with the flat of her hand.

Catching hold of a rope that hung from the rigging-beam, Doalty Gallagher, followed by his mother and Teague, rushed out and made his way to the holm. The Owenawadda was now flush with its highest bank, and where the banks lay low the river was sweeping over them, on to the meadows. The glen people were all rushing down the braes to the holms; a few were already dragging the hay back from the flood. Three tramp-cocks, on Oiney Leahy's Gubbin, were surrounded by water. Up behind the Dermod's house the stream was breaking free from the awlth and tramping down the fields of ripening corn. Sheila Dermod already down by the river, was pulling the hay back from the rising waters. Where Maura The Rosses' holm touched the river, the water was now ankle deep.

"The ones in most danger first the ones be the brough!" said Maura in a stern voice of authority, pointing at the hand-cocks surrounded by water. She was carrying a wooden pole, a hand-spaik it was called, in her hand and Teague carried another. Bending down beside a hay lump she raised one side of it and Teague shoved his pole under it. A second hand-spaik was placed under the cock, parallel with the first, and with the aid of these, the mother and son lifted the hay and carried it out of harm's way. In the meantime, Doalty put his rope round a hand-cock, slung the end of the rope over his shoulder, leant forward on it and dragged the hay up to higher reaches of the holm.

Norah Gallagher, who had been to the village on an errand, came into the field now.

"What kept ye slouchin' along the road, when ye saw the flood," said Maura The Rosses to Norah. "Ye should have been back an hour ago. Don't stand gapin' there and the flood almost over the glen."

"Well, what'll I do?" asked Norah help-lessly. "I have nobody to help me and I can't work like Doalty."

"G'over and help Sheila, if ye can't see any-thing to do here," said Maura The Rosses, who never stopped work for a moment while shouting.

Doalty kept hard at it, doing the work of two men. One hand-cock followed another, and all were piled in an ungainly huddle up near the road. Here the hay would be comparatively safe for if the flood rose to the knoll on which it was heaped, a thing which it seldom did, the water would not have the strength to drag it into the river.

But the water continued rising. The glen was a lake and in many places the houses near the road were surrounded by the flood. On the braes the streams were washing the potato patches from the rocks, and the hills were slipping down to the bottom-lands.

A round, dirty, white object, washed up by the river, rested against a hand-cock which Maura The Rosses was just raising on the handspaiks.

She looked at it for a second.

"One iv Dennys The Drover's sheep," she said. "I know the brand on the horns. I hope he doesn't lose many iv the crathurs."

She was waist-deep in the water, and when she stooped the red petticoat spread out over the water like a flat mushroom. But all the time nothing escaped her attention, she had an eye for everything even the doings of her neighbours.

"Now, Doalty, there's a han'-cock behint ye and it'll soon be goin'," she said. "Put the rope round it and pull it out! . . . Teague, get hold iv that spaik and don't be gapin' like a scaldy* . . . There's Owen Briney comin' down from the brae to help Sheila Dermod with her hay. It's about time too! There's Hughie Beag out and at the road! He'll get drowned! I'll give him such a skelpin' when I get in to him the night! And look, Doalty! There is one iv poor Oiney's trampcocks on the way to the river. God help him!"

It was quite true. Oiney had three trampcocks built together on his holm, small, stumpy ones they were, containing about half a ton of hay each. One of these, caught by the volume

* Nestling.

of the flood was going riverwards. Oiney, impotent, in the face of this calamity, was watching it, as it drifted away. Only the hat, face and shoulders of the old man was visible; the water was almost reaching his chin.

Maura The Rosses, as she went through the water with a burden, kept her eye fixed on the trampcock floating towards the river. Suddenly she disappeared in the flood. Doalty, who was following, threw down his rope and rushed to where the bubbles were rising near the handcock, which the woman had just been carrying.

"She's done for! Drownded!" shouted Teague.

But Maura The Rosses re-appeared again, spluttering and choking, the water running down over her hair, which unloosened, straggled out across the water. Doalty never knew that his mother had such long hair. It would have reached her waist, and even yet, it was not turning white.

He reached down, caught her by the arms and pulled her up on the holm. She had fallen into a drain.

Maura The Rosses shook her head, caught her hair between her hands and wrung it. Then, not having a hairpin, she allowed it to fall down her back. Coughing and spluttering, she bent down and proceeded with her work.

"You can go back home now, mother," said Doalty. "There is only another half hour's work and then all will be finished. Teague and myself can do the rest now."

" I'll help for just a wee while longer," said the mother. "Then I'll leave it to yerself and Teague to finish. . . . There! Oiney's trampcock is in the river now."

The trampcock was indeed in the river and nothing was visible, but the solitary horn of the goat spinning round like a top. Other tramp-cocks followed as if trying a race . . . . Another sheep was washed in on the holm at Doalty's feet.

"What's the brand on the horn?" Maura The Rosses called.

"Drover Dennys again," shouted Doalty in answer.

At the end of another half hour when all the hay was placed in safety the rain ceased, a breeze blew from the hills and the sky cleared. Maura The Rosses went back home and Doalty made his way across the fields to see Oiney Leahy. On the way he encountered Owen Briney.

"Did ye see Oiney's trampcock?" Owen enquired, smiling, with the corners of his lips down.

"I saw it go into the river," said Doalty.

"And it was the best cock iv the three," said Owen. Previous to now Owen had often re-marked that one cock was the spit of another and neither of them were worth looking at.

Doalty spoke to Oiney across the ditch, both men deep in the water, with only their heads and shoulders showing.

"I'm sorry, Oiney, that your trampcock has gone away," said Doalty to the old man.

"Ah! well it was to be, I suppose," said Oiney, stroking his chin-whiskers. "It was the lightest one that went, and that in itself is some comfort. . . . The floods will come and when they do, there's nothing more to be said. If the big rock that caps the water, down at the town was blown up, the river would have a freer run and the floods wouldn't rise so high."

Doalty recalled that once, when he was a little fellow, the blowing up of this rock was proposed. The rock, which stood in the river bed, down by the village, checked the flow of water in flood-time.

"But why don't they get it out of the way now?" said Doalty. "If that was done and the trees rooted out from either bank, the floods wouldn't rise so high. If all the men in the glen, whose farms touch the river, spent a week at the work they could get it done quite easily."

"'Twas spoken about iv old, but what's the good iv talk," said Oiney. "The people below the rock say that if it was taken out iv the river they'd get flooded out iv house and home. The river was good enough for the people that went before us, they say, and why is it not good enough for us? Then, below us here, there's Grania Coolin's holm that sticks out across the river and it's almost touching Micky Neddy's holm on the other side. There are bushes growing on both lips iv land, and between them the river has no flow at all. But will Grania or Micky let anybody widen it? No fear! They make a penny or two, be sellin' the sally rods that grow there, and they're not goin' to lose the few ha'pence that can be made this way, in order to save the hay iv them that's further up the glen than themselves. And I don't blame them, for they wouldn't get much thanks after they had done it.''

'' It looks as if it's going to dry up, now,'' said Doalty as he clambered up on top of a ditch that stood beside him. '' We'll maybe have some good weather again.''

'' Iv coorse we'll have lashin's and lavin's iv it,'' said Oiney. '' I'll bet the morrow will be good. The wind is comin' from the east, a dry quarter, and God is good! And we'll need it, if it keeps up, for the corn is settin' ripe on the braes, and be the look iv it, the crop is goin' to be a good one for the grain is heavy iv head. Never saw it as good for miny's a year. And the pratees are grand too. God is still watchin' over us and if he takes away from us in one way he sends us back seven-fold in another.''

IV

That evening, when darkness had all but fallen, Sheila Dermod came down through the awlth, her cattle in front of her, the animals sliddering and stumbling over the stones which the torrents had washed from the hills earlier in the day. The flood on the braes had fallen rapidly when the rain ceased, but a dark sheet

of water still lay on the holms and the river could
be heard roaring, as it made its way to the sea.
A strong breeze was blowing from the east and
the bushes verging the awlth were already dry.
The hazel-nuts which ripen with the corn, hung
in clusters on the branches, and Sheila, who had
pulled a number kept cracking them between her
white teeth and spitting the kernels into the
brook, as she followed her cows to the byre.

Suddenly she saw Doalty Gallagher, sitting
astride an ash, which projected over the stream
and cutting a young sapling with a clasp-knife.
He did not look round as the girl approached.

"And it's here ye are, Doalty Gallagher!"
she said, looking up at him and spitting the nut,
which she held between her teeth, into the rivu-
let. "Ye're everywhere."

Doalty glanced at the girl, a look of feigned
surprise in his face. He had been watching her
through the bushes for the last five minutes.

"I've just come up to cut an ash-plant for
the next fair," he said. "I did not think I'd
meet you here, Sheila."

"Then who did ye think ye'd meet here?"
she asked, with a laugh, enquiry in her big blue
eyes.

"Well, to tell you the truth, Sheila, I expected to meet you," he confessed, "I've come
up to see you."

There was a moment's silence. Sheila looked
down at a cluster of nuts which she held in her
hand. Selecting one, she leant back a little as
if going to fling it up to Doalty.

" Now, catch it if ye can! " she called. " I'm goin' to throw it up! "

" Just one minute! " said the young man. "Wait till I get a better hold! "

He twined his legs round the branch, which he gripped with his left hand. Then leaning outwards, he held his right hand open, fingers outstretched, and waited expectantly.

" Throw! " he called.

She flung the nut up. Doalty made one wild effort to catch it, missed, and almost toppled off his perch.

" Ye almost were comin' down! " laughed the girl.

" Throw another one," said Doalty.

" No fear," said Sheila. " I don't want yer death to be on me head."

" Then I'm coming down, Sheila," said Doalty, scrambling out to the end of the branch, which bent with him until his feet touched the ground. Then he released his hold and the branch shot up again. He turned to Sheila.

" I've come up to see you," he said, reaching out and clasping her hands.

" But ye said that 'twas to cut a stick for the fair that ye came up," said the girl diffidently. " Ye're the one for lettin' on."

She drew her hands away from Doalty as she spoke, and stepped backwards into the stream. The muddy water covered her bare feet and played about her ankles. She looked down at the ground.

"I've come up to see you, Sheila," Doalty repeated. "I cannot live without you. My eyes follow you all day and I'm thinking of you all night."

"And I suppose I'm not the first that ye've told the same story to," said the girl, the slightest note of railery in her voice. "What about the girls that ye have been talkin' to, beyont the wather?"

"Who has been telling you stories?" Doalty enquired and he caught the girl's hand again.

"I was just told," said Sheila.

"Who told you?"

"Oh! I just heard."

"Well, if anyone told you things like that, it was all a lie," said Doalty, as he seized her in his arms and pressed her to his breast. He hardly knew what he was doing; all ideas left him and it seemed as if he were going to fall. He could feel her bosom press against him, her tresses brushing his lips. She leant back her head and looked up at him and he could see the sparkle of her eyes. Her lips moved, as if she were going to speak but no words came. Doalty trembled; he felt his heartstrings quiver, his will weaken. The fresh night, the moist odour of the damp soil, the penetrating fragrance of the autumn, the soft, yielding young girl in his arms, excited an ecstacy of passion in Doalty's heart. Almost without knowing it he pressed his hand on Sheila's bosom. She shuddered but clung more closely to him. He bent down and pressed his lips against hers.

"It's a sin, that, what ye're doin'," she faltered.

"Sin," Doalty stammered. "It's no sin; it's . . ."

He kissed her again, then released her from his arms.

"Your feet are all wet, Sheila," he said. "Come up on the bank."

She obeyed meekly and stood beside him.

"And where will the cows be now?" she enquired. "They'll be all over the glen."

"Well, what does it matter?" said the young man. "You'll have plenty of time to trouble about the cattle to-morrow, and the day afterwards. But at present we'll talk of something else."

"And what widye be wantin' to talk about now?" she enquired, edging away from him.

"About love," said Doalty. "I've told you often that I am in love with you and I want you to marry me if you will. Will you, Sheila?"

"Are you in fun about it?" she asked, taking a step backwards.

"I never was more in earnest in all my life," said Doalty.

"Cross on yer neck, then."

Doalty made the sign of the cross with his finger and fixed a pair of serious eyes on the girl.

"Tell me, now," he enquired. "Will you marry me?"

"Well, I'll tell ye . . . sometime," said the girl. Now that she was free from his embrace she had more confidence in herself.

"Maybe I'll tell ye the morra and maybe next week. . . . I must have time to think. . . . I'll see ye at Mass the morra and then I'll tell ye . . . maybe."

As she spoke she blushed crimson, but still kept edging away. Doalty fixed a steady look on her and she suddenly winced, turned round and ran off. His eyes followed her until she disappeared through the bushes, but she did not turn round once.

The young man stopped where he was, for a long time, and listened to the cows going into the byre. But he did not hear Sheila speak. From the distance he could hear the sound of a fiddle playing "The Moving Bogs of Allen," and he knew that Oiney Leahy was seeking solace from the fiddle for his lost trampcock.

CHAPTER XII

READ FROM THE ALTAR

His gnarled fingers against his hips,
A wee black dudheen between his lips;
Bearded and wrinkled. . . . The mart is full
Of the herdsman's sheep and the mountain wool-
Woollen wrapper and woollen socks—
Bawnagh-brockagh. Keeper of flocks,
Branded and ribbiged wethers and ewes;
A man of substance whom everyone knows,
See him stand in the market town,
Paying in guineas, money down.
Ready to bargain and ready to spend,
Or stand a drink to a drouthy friend—
A man that his neighbours speak about
As they sit at the bar and drink their stout,
And they wish, to the Man Of Flocks, increase,
Who has not his heart in the penny piece.

—The Mountainy Man.

I

DOALTY, early on the road the next morning, was one of the first to enter the chapel of Greenanore. The morning being very hot he took a seat near the

288

door, where a breeze blew in from the fields.
Sitting there he watched the congregation file
in. Those who had furthest to come, were the
first to enter. The big-boned and hairy mountainy men tramped in, their sticks under their
arms; their barefooted women followed, their
perspiring feet leaving impressions of toe and
heel on the dry floor of the church. One of the
first of the men was big Hudagh Murnagh, a
man with a beard like a besom, full of money,
and not a word of learning in his head. But
for all that he was very astute and dealt largely
in sheep. The mountains were white with his
wool. He came up the aisle of the church, took
a seat opposite Doalty and looked round, his
shrewd eyes taking in everything. Then, spitting on the floor, he knelt down and said his
prayers.

Next to come was Grania Coolin, her gosling-
grey handkerchief wrapped tightly round her
head and her white wisps of hair hanging down
over her yellow and wrinkled forehead. When
she came opposite Hudagh Murnagh she knelt
on the floor, looked at the altar, and made the
triple sign of the cross. Getting to her feet
again, she coughed with the hollow cough of
age, and went in and sat beside Hudagh.

Eileen Kelly and Sheila Dermod came up the
church together. Eileen gave Doalty a sidelong
glance as she passed him, and a little roguish
smile played round her three-cornered lips.
Sheila, with her eyes fixed on the altar, did not

bestow a glance on the young man. She seemed
to be saying her prayers as she walked.

Heel-ball took a seat in front of Doalty. His
bald head, rimmed by a red weal made by the
hat, rose to a point and shone as if polished.
From it a light vapour was rising, as if Quigley's
very sins were evaporating from him at sight of
the altar. When he knelt down, he blessed
himself in a slow, calm, authoritative manner,
pressing his white flabby hand against brow,
shoulder and chest, with an air of decision.
When he had blest himself, he looked round at
the congregation as much as to say: "I've made
the sign of the cross in the correct and proper
manner, and you all see that." The poor of the
congregation knew this look and had often seen
it on the man's face when he robbed them of
their hard-earned pence. But he was always
within his rights and nothing could be said, for
as gombeen man, behind the counter, or wor-
shipper in the village church, he did everything
in the correct and proper manner. All his ac-
tions being fair and above board, he was a man
removed from reproach, an honest business man
and a credit to his church and congregation.

His three daughters came in, just in time for
the prayers before Mass, Gwendoline leading,
her broad-brimmed hat well down over her face
and only a little bit of the chin showing. Her
bosom and hips were padded, and she wore a
hobble skirt, then fashionable with the quality
of Greenanore, but a thing of the past in larger
towns. Gwendoline had a nickname which

Rabelais, were he a Glenmornan man, would have used as copy in his book. This nickname was given to Gwendoline, when she first padded her hips and used too much material in the process. The girl's other two sisters were named Stephanette and Winifred. They dressed well, used rouge for their cheeks, but their clothes and paint did not make up for their lack of beauty. " It doesn't matter what they put on, they'll never be but what God made them," Greenanore often remarked, when referring to Heel-ball's daughters. "A worm in a rose is always a worm."

Then there was Miss Mooney, the doctor's daughter, the two Miss Rooneys, children of the village draper, and Miss Boyle, stumpy and low-set, like a winter trampcock, who was a school-mistress at the convent school.

These, being part and parcel of the quality, made the whole rounds of the church before sitting down. While looking for comfortable seats, as it seemed, they were in reality, showing off their finery to the congregation. On seeing these women, one would form a very high opinion of the wealth of Greenanore, but nobody would believe that old Hudagh Murnagh, the man, with the beard like a besom, who was spitting on the floor, was, with the exception of two or three others, the wealthiest man in the building.

Father Devaney officiated, and when he looked round during the service his face had the same stubborn look that Doalty had noticed there on the day that Breed Dermod was buried. But the look was not peculiar to any occasion. It was the habitual look of the man. He seemed to be always ready to pounce on everybody whom he saw. His look was the look ecclesiastic as made manifest in the face of the gombeen priest.

When the first gospel was read a collection was made. The priest sat down by the side of the altar and waited until his dues were lifted. Doalty noticed Grania Coolin put a halfpenny in the plate. She put it down slily amidst the copper coins, looking round as she did so. The old woman did not want her neighbours to see her poor contribution. Heel-ball placed a pound-note in the plate. He pulled it out of his pocket with surreptitious fingers and kept the collector waiting for a moment. The congregation looked at Heel-ball, who, knowing that all eyes were on him, concealed the note in his hand, allowing only one end to show. Placing it on the plate with quiet assurance, he covered it up with pence so that it would not be blown away as the collector made the rounds of the church. When the plate passed to the next man there was only one end of the note, peeping out from beneath Grania Coolin's halfpenny, to be seen. But that was sufficient.

When the collection was taken, the priest got up on the altar steps again and read the Epistle and Gospel of the day. Then he gave a sermon. Never before had the priest a congregation so attentive, so subdued. The worshippers listened in breathless silence. Not a soul coughed, not a foot stirred. Hudagh Murnagh ceased spit-

ting on the floor.   A feather might be heard
dropping in a crock of milk.

II

" My dear children," the priest began, in a low,
quiet voice of studied calmness, which the threatening eyes, that seemed fixed on every soul in the
congregation, utterly belied; " I'm goin' to speak
this day on a matter that I would rather not have
to talk about here in the holy Church iv Greenanore to the good men and women, the good boys
and girls, iv the parish.   Here, to-day, I have in
front iv me a congregation iv good Catholics, as
religious and God-fearing as any ye can find in all
Ireland.   And when that's said, what more can
I say? From the earliest days the Catholic Church
has found its strongest supporters in the Irish
people.   The Irish people and the Catholic
Church are one and the same.   The Danes came
to Ireland iv old and tried to over-run the country, but priest and people stood together and de-
feated the Dane and drove him into the sea.
Then the Sassenach came and put the country to
the sword.   A price was offered for the head iv
a priest in the penal days, but even then, when
hunger was at every door and a sword at every
throat, did the people iv Ireland ever sell their
priest to the Saxon?   No fear!   They stood by
him in thick and thin, and he stood by them,
tended the dyin' and celebrated Mass on the lone

hills, covered with snow, in the darkest hours iv stress and danger. But that was in the old times."

The priest's voice sank as he said this, and those in the back seats had to strain their ears to catch his utterance.

"But, my dear children, it is not the same to-day," Devaney continued, his voice rising in a grand burst of passion. "The priest of Ireland and the people of Ireland are in danger now, and the danger does not come from abroad. It is not the Saxon who is to blame now. The danger is within, like a worm in an apple. The danger is here, in the parish, aye, and here in this very chapel, where all iv ye, good people, come to say yer prayers and make yer peace with God. The devil has sent his minion here."

The priest paused and the beads of sweat stood out on his pink forehead. Doalty Gallagher felt that all eyes were fixed on himself.

"I'm not goin' to mention any names," said the priest. "I'm just goin' to tell ye what has come to me notice. A young man, a young Irishman, and God forgive me for callin' him an Irishman! came back from abroad, where he has been at work writin' for the papers. That, in itself, is bad enough, for all papers away abroad, have, for their first aim and object, the destruction iv the holy Roman Catholic religion. But worse was to follow, for this young man came back here and began to work on his mother's farm. As if he wanted to help her! Ah! my dearly beloved brethren, Satan has cunning in his ways and no one can do enough to keep clear from him. This young man who pretended to work on his mother's farm came to Greenanore with another purpose. He came here to make all ye people the laughing stock iv the whole, wide world. He listened to what ye said, he saw what ye did at wake, fair and funeral, and he wrote about it and what he wrote came to light in papers in London. I read it all in black and white yesterday, for as a priest I must read the papers, a thing that none iv ye must do, bear in mind, for ye have not been educated up to it and ye might fall into sin if ye do things that yer priest forbids ye to do. Well, this young man wrote about the people iv the parish and held them up to ridicule. He told how one iv them, an old man, went to Lough Derg to do penance for his sins, and this man returned drunk. He doesn't give the man's name at all, not even the name iv the parish, but it's easy seen by readin' between the lines that Greenanore is the place that he manes. And the lies that he tells about it! Think iv one iv ye, me dear brethren, goin' to Lough Derg and comin' back again, drunk! Ah! no, this parish is far above things like that!"

The priest paused, and as he did so, Doalty Gallagher got to his feet and walked out into the middle of the church. For a moment he stood, facing the altar; then he turned on his heel and went out.

III

Maura The Rosses, who was in chapel, heard
Devaney's sermon. She was one of the last to
leave her seat when the service came to an end.
She had no eyes for anybody at the gate and came
up the glen road alone, her thoughts on her own
moral excellence and the iniquities of Doalty her
son. " To be read out from the altar!" she said
to herself, speaking half aloud. " And everyone
in the place listenin'! As if I wasn't a good
mother to him, and kept him at school, and got
him to learn the cathechiz, and made him go to
Mass every Sunday, and to his duties at laste
three times a year, and made him say his prayers
every morn, noon and night. But now, and before everyone, he has brought shame on me house
and home. And it's known to everyone!" Maura
The Rosses said. " To everyone from the mountains to the sea!" In Glenmornan, as in many
other parts of the world, the sin made public is
much worse than the sin concealed.

When she got home she found Doalty there,
sitting on a chair by the fire, telling stories to
Hughie Beag, who was sitting on the flagged floor,
with his heels in the ashes. Maura The Rosses
looked at Doalty steadily for a moment, as if trying to make certain that he was still in existence.
Anything might happen to a man who has been
read from the altar. He might wither away, go
mad, cut his own throat. If he did any of these
things the woman would not be surprised. But

to find Doalty sitting there, smoking a cigarette, and telling a story as if nothing had happened, was more than she expected.

"And ye're here?" she enquired in a voice of wonderment.

"Of course I'm here," Doalty replied. "Where did you expect me to be?"

"Askin' me that!" said Maura The Rosses, taking off her shawl and hanging it on a nail behind the half-open door. Then, shaking her head, she sat down on a stool as if recognising her inability to find words suitable for the occasion. Doalty glanced at his mother. Hughie rubbed his tousled head with a grubby hand, and gazed in turn at Doalty and his mother.

"The old priest was very angry to-day," Doalty commented coolly. "One would think that he, himself, was the only person in the congregation free from sin. I suppose he meant me in his sermon."

"And to think that it was yerself that was read out from the altar, Doalty," said Maura The Rosses, speaking as if she had not heard his remark. "Yerself, iv all the boys in the glen, that has the edication and the good upbringin'. As if I didn't do all I could for ye when ye were wee, and not the height iv two turf. And now ye come home and this is the way that ye behave in the eyes iv the glen. Ye should be ashamed iv yerself!"

"But I'm not," said Doalty, with the red blood of anger rising in his cheeks. "By God! if I hear anything more about this matter I'll go down and pull the damned priest, old man though he is, out of his house and trounce him on the street. To think that all the people about here are such fools, as to suffer a tyrant like that to rule over them! . . . Poor unhappy Ireland! If it's not the landlord who is the tyrant, it's the gombeen man, and if it's not the gombeen man it's the priest. . . . If they were only educated, if they only read books, papers, anything."

"That's what has put yerself wrong," said Maura The Rosses, with an air of finality. "It was the readin' and the books. I did me best to keep ye from the readin' but ye wouldn't take heed to what I said. . . . Even if ye stopped away from Glenmornan and done as ye're doin' now, it would be bad and bad enough; but to come home and make yerself the laughin' stock iv the whole glen. But ye'll go away now. . . ."

"No fear!" Doalty replied. "Do you think that I'm going to leave here because that old fool spoke about me to-day?"

Maura The Rosses looked at Hughie, who was now sitting on the kitchen bed, looking at his toes and listening to the conversation.

"Run out, Hughie," she said to him, "and see if the cows are up on the hill and don't come in until I call ye."

When Hughie disappeared Maura The Rosses turned to Doalty.

"Ye've got to go," she said with a decided nod of her head, "back to where ye've been for the last five years, and I'll not mind if ye never put yer foot inside this door again.'

As she spoke she fastened a button of her blouse

with studied care, rose to her feet, and went out, leaving Doalty alone in the house.

The blood beat like a hammer in his head and his heart got chill as a stone.   He gazed at the fire, at the dying turf embers and the little red flames licking up against the soot.   The kettle hanging from the crook was bubbling merrily. The ashes littered the hearth, and by the hob where Hughie had been sitting Doalty could see the impressions of the youngster's heels.   .   .   . But everything was shattered, finished.   His whole little world was torn up by the roots, leaving nothing to cling to. Sheila Dermod, Oiney Leahy, Dennys The Drover,   .   .   .   all the inhabitants of the glen and parish would treat him with de- rision and contempt.   The simple-minded peasantry would look on him as a turncoat, a Cath breac, a renegade.   A man at variance with their ideals, the people would no longer endure him. To the children, growing up, he would be spoken of in the same breath as Judas Iscariot and Luther. As Doalty thought of Luther, he remembered how he had been taught to hate the memory of the re- former when at school.   " Luther went straight to hell when he died," the schoolmaster used to say.   " Even when he was dying the devil was standing over his bed so that everybody could see him."   And Doalty believed it then, and hated Luther.

" I'll not mind if ye never put yer foot inside this door again," Doalty repeated, with a bitter laugh.   A momentary rage rose like a whirlwind in his heart.   " That hideous priest !" he repeated. "How he hates me, and how he'll chuckle with glee when he finds that he has chased me out of the place! How my mother fears him! . . . And what a strange eloquence his hatred towards me, gave to his sermon to-day! . . . Just a few words from the altar is sufficient and I will have to clear out of the glen. The people, the poor, silly people, will boycott me now. They'll shun me on the roads, pass me by in silence at the fairs, cast me out. . . . But what's to be done?" he asked himself. "Will I go and see her?"—he meant Sheila Dermod—"or will I see about getting a car to take me to the station to-morrow morning?"

He got to his feet, lit a cigarette and peeped out through the door. His mother was up on the brae and Hughie was with her. She was to all appearances looking after the cattle, but Doalty had never before seen her show such interest in the cattle on a Sunday afternoon.

"What am I to do?" he asked himself again, hardly knowing what he was saying. "I must see Sheila. That is certain. I yearn for the girl and I cannot live without her. If she consents to marry me I'll stay here, it doesn't matter what happens. If anybody dares to say anything, I'll——" He clenched his fists in desperation, but did not finish the sentence.

"But does she love me?" flashed through his mind. "She must! She does! If she did not, her hand would not press mine so tightly last night. . . . And what was she going to tell me to-day?"

His cigarette had gone out.   He lit another, puffed at it for a few moments, then flung it in the fire.

" I'll go up and see Sheila to-night," he said, after a few moments' silence.   He spoke in tones of obstinate decision.   " It doesn't matter what happens I'll go and see her.   And for once I'll be firm.   I'll make her answer me."

He went out and made his way to the river, which had fallen very low during the night.   The hollows in the holms were rapidly drying.   From the hay, which had been dragged the day before, a thin vapour was rising into the air.   Oiney Leahy's two trampcocks drooped abjectly towards one another, as if in sorrow for the one which had gone away.   On the way to the river Doalty met Oiney, who was on his way to a near shop for provisions. The old man looked at him in passing.

" Good day, Oiney," said Doalty in a constrained voice.

But Oiney did not reply.   He raised one shoulder, the one next Doalty, higher than the other, held his head up, so that his white beard stuck out almost straight, and passed by in silence.

IV

In the evening when darkness had fallen Doalty Gallagher went up the brae to see Sheila Dermod.   The girl was all alone in the house; her aunt Anna Ruagh had gone to Kelly's house to borrow a wash-board for the morrow's washing. There were only two wash-boards in the townland and these used in turn by the families of Strana-meera.

Sheila was baking scones on the pan, that hung from the crook over the fire, when Doalty entered. She turned round with a start when she heard his foot on the doorstep.

"Good evening, Sheila," said Doalty, going up to where she was standing at the fire and stretching out his hand to the girl. But apparently she did not notice the outstretched hand. If she did, she did not touch it. Her face was flushed and crimson, due, no doubt, to bending over the hot fire. The lamp, lit on the brace, showed up her girlish features; and her blue eyes, fixed on Doalty, seemed to have in them a look of anger, not un-mixed with fear.

For a moment Doalty stood silent and looked at his hand.

"You're not angry with me, Sheila, are you?" he asked, letting his arm drop to his side.

"Well, what are you wantin' here when I'm all alone?" said Sheila, drawing a deep breath as she spoke.

Doalty looked at the girl, and recalled the emp-ty days that he had passed before he came to know her. His former life seemed so fatuous and lacking in purpose, and now, if he went back to London, the same dull, empty and useless routine would again assert its sway and eat up the mean-ingless and foolish hours of his future life.

"You know very well what I'm wanting," he

replied. "Last night I did not go to sleep from thinking of you. . . . I love you, Sheila, and I want you to be my wife. I want you to marry me, Sheila. Tell me that you care for me."

The girl edged back against the wall and fixed a frightened look on Doalty. Her cheeks grew very white, her lips trembled. Her fingers fumbled nervously with her petticoat. Doalty was seized with a mad, exquisite passion, acute and terrible in its strength. He could catch her in his arms and squeeze her, crush her in one mad ecstacy of love! He would grip her white, full throat with his hands, squeeze it until she yelled with pain. She was the thing which he desired, which his whole body yearned for. She was his, his!

"Leave me be, Doalty Gallagher," he heard her say in a faltering voice. "I don't know what ye're talkin' about. I don't want to be yer wife, not after what was said about ye be the priest the day. Go 'way, Doalty Gallagher, and leave me be meself," she pleaded, almost on the point of tears.

Then she suddenly seemed to pluck up courage and an angry light showed in her eyes.

"Comin' here when I'm all alone!" she exclaimed, her voice rising a little. "If ye had decent thoughts in yer head ye wouldn't come here and talk about me marryin' ye, when ye are the talk iv the parish, because ye're makin' fun iv everybody about the place. Ye're not everybody to do as ye like here, Doalty Gallagher!"

As she said this her eyebrows contracted firmly,

her lips met in a hard straight line.　Only once
had Doalty seen a similar look, and that was on
Breed Dermod's face, when the old woman came
down to Maura The Rosses' house a few months
before.　The dead woman was now looking out
through Sheila Dermod's eyes.

"That's it, Sheila Dermod!　Show the dhirty
turncoat what ye think iv him!"

Doalty turned with a start to find Owen Briney
behind him.　The man, who seemed to be always
hanging round the door, had slunk into the house
when Doalty was speaking to Sheila.

Doalty, filled with a consciousness of his own
superiority, fixed a look of scorn on Owen.

"So you are guardian of the morals of the
young women of Glenmornan, Owen?" he enquired in a deliberate and ironical voice.　The
young man's voice was low and almost apologetic
and he smiled as he spoke.　But behind all this
a fire was burning, ready to break forth at any
moment.

"Clear out, ye dirty scapegoat!" Owen shouted.
"Out iv the door with ye, and out iv the country
as well, ye turncoat."

As Owen spoke he raised his fist and rushed at
Doalty, only to find himself lying on the ground
the next moment.　He got to his feet again and
tried to close with the young man.　But the effort
was futile.　Doalty seized Owen's right arm by
the wrist, twisted it outwards and pressed the elbow inwards.　Owen uttered a shriek and dropped
to the floor again.

"Come in!" he yelled.　"He's killin' me!"

As if waiting for this call, half a dozen men appeared at the door.   All had their caps drawn down over their eyes, and a few carried ash-plants. Doalty loosened his grip on Owen, turned round and faced them, scornfully indifferent to their numbers. He was just in time to dodge a blow aimed at him by Micky Neddy.   A mad scramble followed and Doalty, getting pressed back against the wall, saw big, strong hands rising and hitting him on shoulder and chest.   But somehow the blows caused him no pain.   He was shoved back against the wall, and kicked on the shins by the attackers.   He could not raise his arms.   .   .   .

" That's the way, Micky Neddy!" said a voice from the doorway.   " Go for him and tear him to pieces.   He's only one agin six iv ye and ye have every chance."

All, including Doalty, looked towards the door, to find Dennys The Drover standing there, one hand in his coat pocket as if searching for a match, the scornful smile on his lips more pronounced than ever.

" Go for him, and tear him to pieces," Drover Dennys repeated, and stepping towards Micky Neddy, he caught him by the scruff of the neck, swung him round with a mighty sweep, and shoved him bodily through the door.   Two others went out in a similar fashion and the remainder hurried away like whipped dogs.   The last to leave was Owen Briney and Dennys helped him out with the iron toe-plate of his boot.

" Well, that's settled, anyway!" said Dennys The Drover in a most casual voice, speaking, as if the incident in which he had just taken part was one of every-day occurrence. "I didn't think Micky Neddy would be party to a thing like that. . . . And Sheila?" he enquired, turning to the girl, who was still standing as Doalty had left her, "how are ye keepin'?"

"Don't ask me," said the girl in a petulant voice, "after all this happenin' in me house!"

"But what else can ye expect?" Dennys enquired, sitting down on a chair and fixing a sly glance on Sheila, "seein' that ye're the beauty iv Glenmornan, ye must expect us all to be fightin' after ye."

"Get away with ye," said the girl, and her eyelids dropped.

"Isn't that the truth, Doalty?" asked Dennys, turning round to the other man. But Doalty had gone.

"Where did he go to?" asked Dennys.

"He's just gone out," said the girl.

"He did it very quiet," said the Drover. "Well, tell me now, how all the row started?" he asked.

"'Twas like this," said Sheila. "I was bakin' the bread . . . it's all burned now . . . when Doalty Gallagher came in. He began to speak silly about all sorts iv funny things, and him after bein' read from the altar. He wanted to . . . I don't know what he didn't want to do, but just then Owen Briney came in."

"But what was Doalty wantin' to do?" Dennys enquired, waving the account of Owen's entry aside as a matter of no import.

" How am I to know what he was manin' to do?" said the girl with a blush.   " But anyway Owen came in and said the sharp word to Doalty Gallagher, and Doalty, without showin' the colour iv temper, gets hold iv Owen and Owen falls to the ground.   It must be the black art that he has, to make a man fall without hardly touchin' him at all."

" It's what he learned abroad," said Dennys, with an air of authority.   " He was showin' me them tricks.   It's rasslin', the kind that's done in Japan.   .   .   .   But I would have give a lot to see Owen Briney go to the floor on his back, the dirty ranny !"

" But I don't know why everybody's down on poor Owen," said the girl.   " He's very good to me and he's always ready to help me when there's any work that's needin' doin'."

" Then he must have somethin' in his mind," said Dennys.   " Catch him doin' anything for nothin' !   If he'd give ye the sweepin's iv his fireplace he'd want it back in gold.   .   .   .   But ye haven't told me yet what Doalty wanted to do, Sheila !   Was it that he wanted to put his arms round ye?"

" As if I'd let him," said the girl, and a tremor played round her lips.

" Ye'll never let anybody play with ye, Sheila," said Dennys.   " Ye're far and away too proud. If the lamp was out I wouldn't be sittin' here, lookin' at ye, when I could be doin' somethin' else, I'm tellin' ye."

" What would ye be doin', then ?"

"I'd be havin' me arms about ye and tellin' ye things," said Dennys.

"If ye'd dare," said Sheila with a laugh.

"I'd dare more than that," said Dennys.

"Yes, ye would," said Sheila, lifting the pan from the crook and placing it on the floor. The little scones were charred and blackened. "But it will be with Norah Gallagher that ye'll dare it, Dennys The Drover."

"But I haven't a notion iv Norah Gallagher."

"But ye have no notion iv anybody," said the girl in a laughing voice. "Ye think that everyone is dirt under yer feet be the way ye carry on. Run away home widye, Dennys The Drover," she commanded, speaking in hurried tones with her hand over her ear. "There's Anna Ruagh comin' back with the washin' board."

Dennys got to his feet, went up to Sheila and chucked her under the chin with a playful finger.

"I'm goin' away," he said.

"Well, it's time anyway," was the girl's reply as she looked at him. "Ye're always about everywhere."

"Ye've splendid eyes, Sheila," said Dennys, looking tenderly at the girl. "I've never seen eyes as nice as yers. . . . But that doesn't matter, for I'm goin' away."

He put his arms around her as he spoke, and pressed her head in against his shoulder.

"It's a funny way that iv goin' away," said the girl, making no effort to free herself.

"Yes, I'm goin'," Dennys repeated in a firm

voice as if he had been contradicted. "Away out iv the country altogether."

"Glory me!" Sheila exclaimed, looking up at him.

"Yes, out iv the country," the young man continued, pressing the girl with a strong arm. "I can't live here where there's nothin'. If I stay here what will it all end in? I'll have me bit iv land and I'll maybe marry and get old and never have seen anything. That is not the life for a young man. See Doalty Gallagher! He has been away and he came back, and he's not afraid iv anyone. Some may laugh at him, but what does he care? He has the laugh iv them all the time. He doesn't care for anybody, not even for the priest. We're all afraid iv the priest who is nothin' more or less than an old rascal. But Doalty! See the way he put Owen Briney on his back the night, and that was because he learned how to do things like that when abroad. And he's goin' abroad again; maybe the morra morn. If he goes I'll be with him."

"And leave us all here and forget all about us," said Sheila with an angry toss of her chin. She moved away from Drover Dennys as she spoke.

"Oh! I'll come back again," said Dennys. "Next year maybe. But to stay here! It's only men like Owen Briney that stay here, where everything is always the same and no change. . . . . Maybe I'll not see ye again," he added, holding out his hand to the girl. "So I'll say good-bye t'ye."

She gave him her hand and as he pressed it very tightly she drew it away again.

" I suppose ye'll be up here the morrow night just the same; that's if ye're not down seein' Norah Gallagher."

v

Dennys went to the door, stood there for a moment and looked back. Then, shrugging his shoulders, he went out into the night.

Ten minutes later he called at the house of Maura The Rosses to find Doalty busy at work packing all his belongings into a trunk. The old woman was washing the supper dishes. She had been washing them for the last half hour, though on ordinary occasions the job was completed in a space of five minutes. Her thoughts were not on her work now. She was thinking of Doalty, who had been read from the altar, and who was going away with the first train in the morning. Maura The Rosses, in great distress, was finding relief from her feelings in work.

Norah was helping Doalty at the packing, Kitty was learning her lessons for the school in the morning, Hughie Beag was in bed, still awake, but waiting for his story. Teague had gone to Greenanore to order a car to take Doalty to the station at dawn.

" Good night t'ye, Maura The Rosses," said Dennys The Drover, when he entered. (Glen-

mornan people know no afternoon.   Evening
with them starts at noon and finishes at dusk.)

"Good night, Dennys The Drover," said Maura The Rosses with a sigh.

Hughie Beag looked from under the bedclothes
and fixed his bright eyes on the visitor.

"Dover Denny!" he called.

"What are ye sayin', ye vagabone?" said the
Drover, going up to the bed.

"Bought a bull de day?" Hughie asked.

"I did," said the Drover.   "A big bull with
six horns and I've left it outside.   If ye don't
go to sleep at once the bull will come in and take
ye away on its horns."

"Will de bull take Doalty 'way?"

"It will."

"And Teague?"

"It will."

"Can't take Teague 'way," said Hughie with
a chuckle.   "Teague 'way down de town for car
for Doalty.   Priest read Doalty from altar de
day and Doalty's goin' 'way."

"Now get off to sleep," said Dennys The Drover.   "If you don't the bogey man will come
down the chimney for ye."

"Me don't care for bogey man," said the little
boy.   "Bogey man will take oo; not me, cos I
say me prayers.   Doalty not say prayers."

"Hughie, get a sleep on ye," said Maura The
Rosses.   "Ye're always talkin'."

Teague came in at that moment.

"What time will the car be here in the morning?" Doalty enquired.

These were the first words he had spoken since Dennys The Drover came in. Teague stammered, blushed, and looked confused.

"I couldn't get a car," he said. "Micky Ronan's horses are mostly all lame, and the other cars in Greenanore are wanted be other people."

"So I can't get a car on account of what the priest said this morning," said Doalty bitterly. "But it doesn't matter. I'll carry my box on my shoulder and I'll walk down to the station."

"I'll help ye," said Dennys The Drover. "I'm goin' to the station meself."

"Don't trouble to come on my account," said Doalty. "Teague will help me down."

"But I'm goin' away," said Dennys The Drover, fumbling nervously with his pocket. "I'm leavin' this place for I'm sick iv it. I can't stand it, for it's so backward like. All that people do here is to grow old and die. It's only a place for sick people and old people. . . . Not the place at all for us young fellows. I should have been out of it ages ago."

"But yer mother and yer sister, Dennys The Drover," said Maura The Rosses, glad of a topic that would make her forget her own troubles. "What will they do, not havin' anyone to help them with the farm?"

"It's not much help that I give them, except in the money that I bring them," said Dennys The Drover. "Whether I'm here or away they'll just work the same, for they can't help it. But I'm goin' out into the world to see what it's like. I'll be a sailor, maybe. . . . Anyway I'll go to

London town with Doalty and then I'll have a look round me. Ye don't mind if I go with ye?" asked the young man, turning to Doalty, who was tying up his trunk.

"I'll be delighted," said Doalty.

CHAPTER XIII

A LETTER FROM HOME

The winds come soft of an evening o'er the fields
       of golden grain,
And good sharp scythes will cut the corn ere we
       come back again—
The village girls will tend the grain and mill
       the Autumn yield,
While we are out on other work upon another field.
              —*Soldier Songs.*

I

DENNYS The Drover's sister, Rose Darroch, was a big-boned, dark-haired girl, of terrific vitality. Glenmornan nicknamed her Rosha Dhu (Black Rose). Being strong and energetic, the girl was a grand hand at hard work, but she was nothing to notice at a dance. In fact, Rosha was not at all goodlooking and no Glenmornan boy ever accompanied her home from an airnall. She was one of those simple souls who lack all claims to personality. When a man met her, he was in a hurry to get away from her; when he left her company he forgot her. There are many people like Rosha in the world, women for whom no man would yearn, for whom no man would sin, and against whom, no member of their own sex would entertain any feelings of envy.

When in Ireland Doalty Gallagher met her several times; and when he left the country he forgot her, an easy matter.

But he became conscious of her existence again, two years after the events described in the last chapter. It was in the early summer of 1915 that an orderly handed a letter and a newspaper to Lieutenant Gallagher, D.S.O., who was sitting in a dug-out in the Flanders firing-line. The newspaper came from Lady Ronan and contained an account of her daughter's marriage to the editor under which Doalty served his first years of journalism. The letter was from Rosha, the sister of Drover Dennys. Sitting on the firestep, where the light was good, Doalty read it. It ran:

II

" Stranameera,
" Greenanore,
" Co. Donegal.

" Dear Mr. Doalty Gallagher,
" A line to let you know we are well, hopin' yourself the same. I must say that you are a very nice gentleman not to forget us. My mother would write to you only she hasn't the learning, for she was never at the school. The two of us is broken-hearted since the War Office wrot to us and said that poor Dennys was killed, and mother says that nobody knows what black war is as much as people

that is left alone with nobody to help them and
them that used to help them killed and ded.　I
can't help thinkin when I'm be myself that if
Sheila Dermod had taken Dennys he would be
here with us still, though for myself I dont like
Sheila Dermod.　She is almost one of the lowest
of the low and I would be ashamed off my life if
our Dennys had married her and him such a
handsome boy that could have any of the girls in
the place.　Even the town girls were lookin at
him when he went in there on a fair day.

" My mother dose not know what was the reason
Dennys went away to the black war when he had
his farm at home and nobody to say a word against
him, but she thinks that he must have a terrible
pain when he was dying, and I suppose there was
no priest to look at him and give him forgiveness
for his sins.　I can hardly live at home without
him and he was so good to me, and he always
bought me pink and green ribons from the fair
when he came home at night.　It's an awful thing
to die at the war with not one days sickness so
that you can prepare for deth.　To go away just
like a leaf from a tree in a big wind is a afful thing.
My mother is hart-broke over poor beloved Dennys,
but she trusts in God that his soul is in heaven,
and this life is very short and full of trouble.　I
have to console her.　If I did not she would die off
greef.　She is always saying that she has nothing
more to live for in this dark world, and that it can
do nothing more to her than it has done alredy.
I hope you are keepon alright, but I have no doubt
that you are for you always have the greatest luck
and was able to get on so well in the world.　We
have got very hard work to do on the farm now,
and we must do the best we can.　We did not
think once that we would be lef here alone, but
people don't know what the have to come thru in
this world.　I hope that after the war you will come

back to the glen again. Poor Dennys thought a
lot of you and he was always saying that you were
the nicest man that ever came back to the glen from
forrin parts, for you were just as simple-minded as
one of ourselves and never put on airs like a shop-
boy that has nothin' on him but a white collar and
wouldn't take off his coat to do a hand's turn on
his own people's farm.

"Things are much the same as when you left
here but a lot of men and women died. God rest
Grania Coolin for she is ded and her wake was a
poor one, and at the grave the offerin's was only
a bit over three pound ten. Old Mister Quigley
is dead to, and he left the bulk of his mony to the
church for he was full of gold. His people wanted
the money and they had a lawsoot with the church,
and it's not settled yet. I think for myself that
people sib to a ded man should be give the money
and not the preests. All the young people think
the same, but the old people think that nobody
should go to law with the church. . . . . Father
Devaney is ded, and a good job too, for nobody
cared very much for the man. You should hear
the countrey boys talking about him and saying
that he was not worthy of his coat. He met his
deth in a strange way. He was at a dance in the
town, and this was a dance give by the quality and
all the peeple with money was at it as well as the
priest, him that wouldnt allow the countrey boys
to have dances in their own house. But when the
quality were having a dance it didnt matter. None
of the countrey boys were allowed into the dance,
but it was such a grand dance that the preest himself went with his sister. Well, it was a night of
big snow and the countrey boys went down to the
town and the would not be allowed in, but had to
stand outside and freez, so the picked up snoballs
and flung them thru the window of the market hall
where the dance was. Then the priest came out

with his stick and chased them away with a stick.
So the ran off. He followed them for a bit and
the somehow got angry and turned on him
and began to throw snoballs at him. The
knocked his hat off, thru the snow down his
back and sent him running back. As he was going
into the hall again he fell and the boys covered
him up with snow. When he got in he was white
with fright for he thought that the were going to
kill him. Next day he had a bad cold and he died
from it. The war is doing a lot of good for the
glen one way and another, and them that has beasts
bringing up now are getting no end of money.

" Your mother is well and she has three cows
coming come Bonfires night next. Sheila Dermod
is marrid now to Owen Briney and the to farms
are made into one. The have to servant boys and
the make them to work for Sheila is very like her
mother that's ded god rest her, and always tries to
have a white shilling for her sixpence. Also Eileen
Kelly is married to Micky Neddy.

" Oiney Leahy is still living but he has the
notions now and is more fond of the drink than
ever he was. He is always forgetin things, and
he can be seen every morning out in the park under
the house lookin for the pipes that he put under
the ground. . . . .

" Your obeedin servant,
" MISS ROSIE DARROCH.

" Send me a line when you get this at the war
and you'll find the address at the top of the leter.
May, 1915."